Rivalry Unmasked

Iris Frost

Published by Iris Frost, 2024.

This is a work of fiction. Similarities to real people, places, or events are entirely coincidental.

RIVALRY UNMASKED

First edition. October 31, 2024.

Copyright © 2024 Iris Frost.

ISBN: 979-8224036288

Written by Iris Frost.

Chapter 1: A Fractured Beginning

The sunlight slants through the tall windows of my office in Manhattan, casting shadows over the sleek lines of my desk. My mind buzzes with thoughts of the charity gala I'm planning—a pivotal event that could not only bolster my reputation but also help me forget the emotional wreckage of my last relationship. I can already picture the exquisite floral arrangements, the clinking of glasses filled with crisp champagne, and the glitter of elegant dresses sweeping across the polished floor. It's everything I need to rise from the ashes of my career. Just as I gather my notes, preparing to fine-tune every detail, the door swings open, and in strides Nathan Blackwood, the man I've vowed to detest.

 He is the very embodiment of effortless charm, his sharp jawline and perfectly tousled hair exuding an air of casual confidence. I can practically hear my resolve crumbling beneath the weight of his presence. "I didn't realize this was a party," he says, his tone dripping with playful sarcasm as he leans against the doorframe, arms crossed. The audacity of that grin makes my stomach churn, but it's his arrogance that truly ignites the flames of my irritation. We're both vying for the same clients, and his smug smile is a constant reminder that he thrives on competition, a quality I both admire and loathe in equal measure.

 "Perhaps you should take a cue from your own office decorum," I retort, not bothering to mask the sharp edge of my voice. My heart races; I'm not here to indulge in his games. "This isn't your playground, Nathan."

 He saunters in, unfazed, and takes a seat across from me without waiting for an invitation. The familiar tension crackles in the air, thick enough to cut with a knife. "I just thought I'd check in on my biggest competition. You know, the charity gala—the one you're trying to make a comeback with? It sounds... ambitious." He smirks, and I swear I can feel my cheeks flush in a mix of embarrassment and anger.

"Ambitious is my middle name," I snap back, raising an eyebrow. "Unlike some, I actually believe in the causes I support. Not everything is a game for me, Nathan."

He leans forward, resting his chin on his hand, his expression transforming from playful to something more intense, a flicker of seriousness in those dark, penetrating eyes. "You think I don't care about the causes I work for?"

I scoff, unable to hide my disdain. "I think you care about the limelight, Nathan. The events, the clients—they're all just another way for you to stay relevant in this ruthless industry."

His brow arches, and for a brief moment, I catch a glimpse of vulnerability. "Relevance has nothing to do with it. It's about impact, Chloe. I've seen firsthand the difference a gala can make for those in need."

His words hang in the air, and for an instant, the rivalry feels like a distant memory. I see the genuine passion behind his facade, a reminder that perhaps there's more to him than the smug exterior he wears like armor. I shake my head, trying to clear the fog of confusion. "If you're here to play mind games, I don't have time for it," I reply, my tone steely as I gather my notes, determined to cut through the tension like a knife.

"Mind games? You wound me." He leans back in his chair, feigning an air of innocence that I know he doesn't possess. "I came to offer you a proposal, but if you're too busy fuming, I'll take my brilliant ideas elsewhere."

I pause, the challenge piquing my interest despite myself. "A proposal? You're serious?"

"Very," he replies, and the cockiness in his voice is undeniable. "Why don't we combine forces for the gala? Think about it—your vision, my connections. We could create something spectacular."

For a moment, I'm taken aback, caught off guard by the unexpectedness of his suggestion. "Team up with you? Have you lost your mind?" The very thought feels like a betrayal to my independence, to my very core. "What's in it for you, Nathan? What kind of game are you playing?"

His expression shifts, a flicker of sincerity breaking through his playful demeanor. "You're good, Chloe. You're great at what you do, but this event could benefit from both of our strengths. We can elevate it together."

My mind races. The idea of collaborating with Nathan Blackwood, of all people, sends a thrill of unease through me. I know better than to trust him, yet the prospect of success tantalizes me, taunting the cautious part of my brain that screams to say no. "And what do you expect in return? A share of the glory? You think I'm going to let you take credit for my hard work?"

"I want no credit," he replies, his tone earnest, as if my skepticism stings more than he lets on. "I just want to create something that matters. You're not just a competitor to me; you're someone I respect. And yes, I could use the boost myself."

The tension in the air shifts again, and for a moment, the competitive spirit feels almost collaborative, the lines of rivalry blurring in an enticing haze of possibility. Yet, I know better than to let my guard down completely. Nathan Blackwood is a slippery slope, and I can't shake the nagging feeling that there's a trap somewhere within his carefully crafted words.

"What's it going to be, Chloe?" he asks, the challenge lacing his voice pulling me closer. "We can either fight each other until one of us collapses, or we can make this gala a night to remember."

As I meet his gaze, I realize the choice isn't just about the gala. It's about confronting my fears, embracing the unknown, and perhaps—just perhaps—trusting the man I've been determined to despise. The stakes are high, and with a deep breath, I lean back in my chair, a spark of defiance igniting within me.

The air in my office hums with the tension of unspoken words, as if the very walls are eavesdropping on our standoff. Nathan leans back, his casual posture contrasting sharply with the storm brewing in my mind. I can feel his gaze piercing through the uncertainty, assessing me with the precision of a hawk eyeing its prey. "Look, Chloe," he begins, breaking the silence. "This isn't just about us. It's about the people we can help. The more we raise, the more lives we change. Isn't that worth the hassle of working together?"

The sincerity in his voice is a refreshing surprise, yet it doesn't wash away my instinct to resist. "You really expect me to believe that your motivations are purely altruistic?" I quip, crossing my arms in defiance. "This sounds more like an excuse to make a grand entrance at the gala and steal the spotlight."

"Who says I can't do both?" He grins, unabashed, as if he thrives on my ire. "Imagine the headlines: 'Dynamic Duo Saves the Day' or 'Chloe and Nathan: A Match Made in Philanthropy.' It has a nice ring to it, don't you think?"

I roll my eyes, but a reluctant smile creeps onto my face. "Is that the best you can come up with? You might want to hire a better marketing team."

His laughter fills the room, rich and infectious. "Point taken. But think about it, really. We could attract more sponsors and make the event unforgettable. With your creativity and my connections, we'd be unstoppable."

"I'm not going to let you glom onto my hard work just to further your own agenda," I shoot back, my defenses still high. "If I'm going to do this, it's going to be on my terms."

His expression softens, and for the first time, I see a glimmer of vulnerability beneath the bravado. "What if I promise not to overshadow you? I just want to help make a difference. And maybe I need this as much as you do."

The honesty in his admission pulls at something deep inside me. I've spent so much time focusing on the past, on the scars left behind by my breakup, that I haven't given myself the chance to consider new alliances. "Fine," I say finally, and the word feels heavy on my tongue, like a reluctant pact. "But you need to understand: if this is going to work, I'll be in charge. My vision."

"Your vision, my connections," he replies, a playful glint in his eye. "Sounds like a solid plan."

A strange camaraderie begins to form in the space between us, the tension shifting from competition to collaboration. "Let's see if you can keep up, Blackwood. My ideas come fast and furious."

"Bring it on," he says, leaning forward, a challenge hanging in the air.

As we begin to brainstorm ideas, a strange energy crackles between us, electric and unanticipated. I pull up the proposal I've been drafting on my laptop, the vibrant colors and elaborate designs reflecting my vision. "This is where I want to start," I say, clicking through images of past events, floral arrangements bursting with color and themes that pull at the heartstrings. "I want elegance but with a touch of whimsy. Something that sparks joy."

"Joy, huh?" Nathan leans in closer, and I can't help but notice the faint scent of cedar and spice that clings to him, heady and intoxicating. "What if we added a surprise element? Something unexpected, like a flash mob or an interactive art installation?"

I can't suppress a laugh. "A flash mob? Are we in a rom-com now?"

"Why not? It'll get people talking, and when people talk, they donate," he counters, his tone earnest yet laced with mischief. "And you, of all people, should know that a little chaos never hurt anyone. Plus, it could make for some fantastic photos."

The idea dangles in my mind, tantalizing and outrageous. "You might be onto something," I admit, biting my lip as I ponder the possibilities. "But only if we can control the chaos."

"I've always fancied myself a chaos manager," he says, a smirk spreading across his face. "How else would I stay ahead in this cutthroat business?"

As we dive deeper into our planning, the atmosphere shifts. The rivalry that once felt so palpable begins to dissolve into an unexpected camaraderie, fueled by laughter and shared visions. I find myself challenged, not just by his presence but by his ideas. Nathan has a knack for thinking outside the box, a quality I can't help but admire despite my better judgment.

Just as we finish brainstorming a potential guest list, my phone buzzes, breaking the moment. It's a message from my best friend, Lily, filled with a stream of heart emojis and a simple, urgent question: Are you still alive?

I chuckle and look up at Nathan, who raises an eyebrow. "Friend in need?"

"Just my personal cheerleader," I reply, a hint of warmth creeping into my voice. "She's worried I might be holed up in here forever. Or worse, that I'm actually considering teaming up with you."

"Ah, the infamous 'team-up' concern," he quips. "You know, it's not that bad once you get used to the idea. Besides, you'll have me to blame if anything goes awry."

"Great, just what I need—someone else to shoulder the blame when I inevitably get overwhelmed." I roll my eyes, but I can't help the smile that escapes. "I'll add that to my list of reasons to hate you."

"And I'll add it to my list of reasons to charm you." He leans back, crossing his arms with an air of mock superiority.

Before I can respond, the door swings open again, this time revealing Sarah, my assistant, looking flustered. "Chloe, we have a situation," she blurts out, eyes wide.

"What now?" I ask, glancing between Nathan and Sarah, my heart racing as I brace for whatever chaos has just erupted.

"The venue just called," she continues, her voice tinged with urgency. "They're double-booked, and unless we can find a new place by the end of the day, the gala is at risk."

Nathan's eyes flash with determination. "Let's go. We can tackle this together. I know a few places that might fit our needs perfectly."

As I meet his gaze, I feel the spark of unexpected partnership ignite anew. The road ahead is fraught with uncertainty, but with Nathan by my side, perhaps it won't be so daunting after all. The pulse of adrenaline surges through me, and with a deep breath, I find myself ready to face whatever comes next.

With a shared sense of urgency, Nathan and I move through the bustling streets of Manhattan, the afternoon sun glinting off the glass facades of towering skyscrapers. The air buzzes with activity, and I feel the familiar cocktail of adrenaline and anxiety thrumming in my veins. "So, where do we start?" I ask, glancing at him as we weave through the throng of tourists and hurried locals.

Nathan grins, his confidence unshakeable as he adjusts the collar of his crisp white shirt. "I know a couple of places that aren't just venues—they have character. They'll fit the gala's vibe perfectly." His eyes sparkle with that spark of mischief, reminding me why I can't quite shake him off, despite my best intentions.

"Character, huh?" I raise an eyebrow. "You mean like the one you have? Because I'm not sure how well that translates to a venue."

He laughs, the sound rich and warm, like a summer evening. "Touché. But seriously, these places are perfect for creating a memorable atmosphere. Let's just hope they're available."

We hop into a cab, and as we drive through the heart of the city, I find myself stealing glances at Nathan. The way he seems to thrive in the chaos around us is oddly reassuring, even if I refuse to admit it. "You seem to know this city pretty well," I comment, trying to keep the conversation light. "Do you spend every waking hour charming your way into places?"

"Only the ones worth being in," he replies, a playful glint in his eyes. "But don't get used to it; my calendar is packed. Philanthropy is just one of my many hats."

"You wear quite a few hats for someone so young," I say, genuinely curious. "What's your secret? Is it just charm and good looks?"

He feigns deep thought. "A winning smile, a touch of bravado, and the occasional well-timed flattery can go a long way. But really, it's about passion, Chloe. When you love what you do, the hours are just a backdrop."

I nod, recognizing that flicker of sincerity in his voice. I've been so wrapped up in my own struggles that I've overlooked the drive that fuels others. Before I can dive deeper into that thought, we pull up outside a chic, converted loft space nestled among the art galleries of Chelsea. The facade is unassuming, yet the vibrant murals and string lights spilling out onto the sidewalk breathe life into the drab gray of the city.

"This is it," Nathan announces, stepping out of the cab with an air of confidence that makes me roll my eyes but also admire him a little.

We enter, and the atmosphere shifts instantly. The interior is vast, with exposed brick walls and beams that lend a rustic charm. Sunlight pours through large windows, illuminating a spacious area that feels both warm and alive. "Can't you just picture it?" he says, his voice rich with excitement. "A lavish banquet over there, a dance floor in the corner, and maybe an art installation on the wall. This place practically screams elegance."

"It does have potential," I admit, my mind already spinning with ideas. "But let's see if it's available first."

As we speak to the venue manager, I can't help but notice the playful banter flowing easily between Nathan and me, a stark contrast to the tension that filled my office just hours before. We make a good team. He plays the charming host, while I ask the pointed questions about availability and pricing. Just as I start to relax, the manager's expression shifts, her brow furrowing slightly.

"I'm afraid there's a bit of an issue," she says, glancing between us. "We have a tentative hold on this date, but it's not confirmed. A very high-profile client expressed interest this morning."

I feel the ground shift beneath my feet. "High-profile client? Who?" I ask, my heart sinking. I already know that in this industry, high-profile means deep pockets and relentless ambition.

The manager hesitates, glancing at her notes. "I'm not at liberty to say, but I can assure you they're a significant player in the charity scene. If they decide to proceed, we might have to look at alternate dates."

"Not an option," Nathan interjects, his tone sharp and decisive. "This date is non-negotiable. We need this venue."

The manager raises her hands in surrender. "I understand, but—"

"Who is it?" I press, my mind racing. The stakes are high, and the thought of losing this opportunity feels like a punch to the gut.

Before she can answer, Nathan steps forward, a look of realization dawning on him. "Wait. Is it Grant Miller?"

The manager nods slowly, a flicker of concern crossing her face. "Yes, his foundation is keen on hosting a gala for their latest initiative, and they're looking at this space."

A cold wave of disbelief washes over me. Grant Miller, the billionaire philanthropist known for his lavish parties and headlines, is the last person I want to compete against. "Well, isn't that just wonderful?" I mutter, my voice dripping with sarcasm. "Nothing like a little friendly competition."

"Not so friendly," Nathan replies, his gaze steely as he processes the news. "He'll sweep in and take this place like it's a game."

Suddenly, the stakes have changed dramatically. The comfort of our playful collaboration evaporates, replaced by the biting reality of our situation. "We need to act fast," I say, my mind whirling with plans and contingency strategies. "If we're going to get this venue, we have to outmaneuver him. We can't let this slip through our fingers."

"Agreed," Nathan responds, his expression shifting to one of fierce determination. "Let's strategize. We need to come up with a compelling proposal that shows them we can bring just as much—or more—to the table."

"Do you know how to get in touch with him?" I ask, my mind racing. "If we can appeal to him directly, we might stand a chance."

"I might know someone who does," he replies, the corner of his mouth lifting in a knowing smile. "But it's going to take some convincing—and possibly a little charm."

"Of course it will," I reply, rolling my eyes but unable to suppress a grin. "Your charm seems to be your go-to tactic. I'm starting to think you might be full of surprises."

With a newfound sense of urgency, we step back into the lively streets, our heads buzzing with ideas. As we brainstorm potential angles and strategies, I can't shake the thrill of adrenaline coursing through me. This is what I live for: the challenge, the intensity, the chance to rise to the occasion.

Yet, just as we plot our next move, my phone buzzes again, a notification lighting up the screen. I glance down, my breath hitching in my throat as the message unfolds: Chloe, you need to see this. It's about Nathan.

The world around me blurs, the vibrant streets of Manhattan fading into the background as the implications of the text sink in. My heart races, uncertainty and anxiety mixing in a potent cocktail of dread. "What is it?" Nathan asks, noticing my expression.

"I—" I start, but the words catch in my throat, the enormity of what I've just read overwhelming me. The game has changed again, and now, everything feels like it's hanging by a thread. The stakes have never been higher, and just when I thought I had a grasp on my path, the ground beneath me starts to crumble.

Chapter 2: Beneath the Surface

The city sprawled beneath me, a tapestry of flickering lights and whispered secrets, as I stood at the window, the cool glass pressing against my forehead. The hum of the metropolis drifted up like a lullaby—a mix of honking taxis, distant sirens, and the murmur of late-night conversations echoing through the streets. I should have felt comforted by the familiar sights, but tonight was different. My mind was a whirlwind, tangled in thoughts of the man I had just encountered.

He had walked into the conference room like a force of nature, commanding the attention of every person present with a mere glance. His tailored suit, dark and crisp, accentuated his lean frame, while his dark hair was expertly tousled, as if styled by the wind itself. I hated him for the effortless way he drew focus, like a moth to a flame. He exuded confidence—a quality that both repelled and intrigued me. As he leaned back in his chair, a sly smile playing on his lips, I felt a surge of annoyance. Did he think he could simply waltz in and take charge?

The project we were discussing, a collaboration that had brought us together, felt monumental, and yet, it was the uninvited spark that ignited during our exchange that lingered in my mind. Our arguments, heated and punctuated with sharp retorts, were more like a dance than a dispute. Each word felt charged, like electric currents zipping between us, and I couldn't help but wonder if he felt it too. I had entered the meeting determined to assert my authority, but there was something disarming about his smirk that rattled my resolve.

"Perhaps if you focused more on the facts rather than your ego, we might make some progress," I had shot back, my voice steady despite the tremor of uncertainty beneath it. His response was a low chuckle that reverberated through the room, making my cheeks flush with anger. "And perhaps if you learned to let go of your preconceived notions, you'd see the bigger picture."

The tension had hung thick in the air, and for a brief moment, I lost track of our disagreement, captivated by the intensity of his gaze. Those deep-set eyes seemed to hold a universe of contradictions—challenging yet inviting, infuriating yet strangely magnetic.

Now, hours later, as the city's glow filled my apartment, I couldn't shake the feeling that something significant had shifted within me. The adrenaline from our encounter coursed through my veins, leaving me restless and aching for clarity. I turned away from the window, pacing the length of my modest living room, the heels of my shoes clicking against the hardwood floor like a metronome, echoing my racing thoughts.

What was it about him that unsettled me so? I had spent years building my career, cultivating an image of competence and poise. Yet here I was, preoccupied with a man who seemed to thrive on chaos, teasing me with every taunt and counterargument. I needed to regain control, to carve out a space where I wasn't constantly battling this magnetic pull.

Suddenly, a loud bang interrupted my musings. I jumped, heart racing, as my neighbor's door slammed shut, and laughter spilled into the corridor. I shook my head, trying to dispel the remnants of the meeting from my mind, but the memory clung to me like a stubborn shadow. It wasn't just his infuriating charm; it was the way he had challenged my intellect, ignited my passion for the project, and somehow turned our rivalry into something exhilarating.

As if summoned by my thoughts, my phone buzzed on the coffee table, the screen lighting up with a message. I grabbed it eagerly, my heart sinking as I saw the name flashing before me—Claire, my best friend. "How did the meeting go?" she had typed, followed by a string of curious emojis that suggested she expected drama.

I typed back, fingers hesitating over the keys. Should I tell her about the unexpected thrill of our banter? About how, amidst the tension, I felt a flicker of something entirely different? I shook my head, deciding against it. I wasn't ready to dissect the chaos swirling in my head, nor to expose the vulnerability that clung to the edges of my thoughts. Instead, I settled for a simple, "It was... intense. Let's grab coffee tomorrow."

As I tossed the phone onto the couch, the nagging sense of confusion returned. I poured myself a glass of wine, hoping the rich crimson liquid would provide some semblance of comfort. The warmth of the alcohol spread through me, and I sank onto the plush sofa, allowing the soft cushions to cradle my tension-filled body. I stared at the flickering candle on the coffee table, the flame dancing wildly as if mirroring my own internal struggle.

Just then, my phone buzzed again. I glanced down, half-expecting Claire's relentless inquiries, but instead, I was met with a notification from a work email. I grimaced, torn between the desire to ignore it and the nagging need to stay on top of my responsibilities. With a sigh, I swiped open the message, instantly regretting it as I read the words that made my heart sink—another update about the project and the growing pressure to deliver results.

Beneath the surface of my professional life, a tempest brewed, and it wasn't just the project itself. It was the realization that this rivalry, tinged with attraction, had the potential to spiral into something far more complicated. As I set my glass down, I knew that my encounter with him was far from over. The spark that flickered between us had ignited a fire, one that would demand to be explored, even if it threatened to consume me whole.

Morning light spilled into my apartment, a soft golden hue that barely managed to penetrate the fog of restless sleep. I blinked against the brightness, still wrapped in the remnants of dreams filled with sharp suits and quips that had lingered from the previous evening's meeting. Pushing myself upright, I raked my fingers through my hair, the strands a wild mess that echoed my thoughts. I had never been one to lose focus, yet here I was, tangled in a web spun from a single interaction.

The coffee maker gurgled to life in the corner of my tiny kitchen, its familiar sound a comforting backdrop to the chaos of my mind. I padded across the cool tile floor, the chill a jolt that reminded me of the world outside my thoughts. As the rich aroma of brewing coffee enveloped me, I grabbed my phone, glancing at the screen to see a slew of notifications—mostly work-related, interspersed with Claire's endless barrage of texts.

"Did you dream about him? 😉" she'd messaged, followed by a string of laughing emojis. I rolled my eyes but couldn't suppress a smile. Claire had a knack for cutting through the fog, her humor a constant reminder of the world I inhabited outside of conference rooms and deadlines. I replied with a quick "You wish," then tossed my phone onto the counter, determined to focus on the day ahead.

After a quick shower, I dressed with care, choosing a vibrant red blouse that complemented my auburn hair, the color a defiant statement against the grayness of the world outside. I finished off the look with a pair of tailored trousers that had become my armor for professional encounters. As I examined myself in the mirror, I steeled my resolve, reminding myself that I was not merely a participant in this project—I was its leader.

The city bustled with energy as I stepped outside, a familiar rhythm of people rushing by, coffee cups in hand, and the distant sound of construction merging with snippets of conversation. Each day felt like an unfolding story, but today the plot was tangled in a new subplot involving him. My mind flickered to the sharp-witted responses we'd exchanged, a verbal dance that was both frustrating and exhilarating.

I navigated through the throngs of commuters, my heels tapping a staccato rhythm against the pavement, a beat that seemed to mirror my pulse. As I reached the office building, the imposing glass structure reflected the clear blue sky, and I inhaled deeply, attempting to ground myself. Inside, the cool air was a balm against the lingering tension of the past few days.

My team was gathered around the conference table, their voices a low hum of anticipation. The moment I entered, however, a hush fell over the group. I sensed their curiosity, their eyes darting to me, each one silently weighing my state of mind after the chaotic meeting with him.

"Good morning!" I declared, projecting an enthusiasm I didn't entirely feel. "Let's dive into our agenda."

As I shuffled through my notes, I caught sight of him entering the room, a ripple of energy following in his wake. The tailored suit hugged him perfectly, and the confidence radiating from him felt almost palpable. I braced myself, unwilling to let the magnetic pull distract me from my mission.

"Ready to get crushed in this meeting?" he quipped, a smirk plastered across his face, drawing the attention of our colleagues like a moth to a flame.

"Only if you're ready to finally concede that my approach is far superior," I shot back, the playful banter igniting the air around us. My heart raced as I realized we were slipping back into our rhythm, the tension crackling with a familiar energy that was both unnerving and exhilarating.

"Your approach?" he replied, feigning innocence. "You mean the one that's almost as outdated as your hairstyle?"

Laughter erupted around the table, and I felt my cheeks flush. "Oh, please! At least I don't look like I just walked off a movie set. I prefer to save the theatrics for the stage, thank you very much."

His eyes sparkled with amusement, and despite myself, I couldn't help but enjoy the banter. The room buzzed with an atmosphere of competition, but there was something more—an undercurrent of tension that had shifted from animosity to a strange camaraderie.

As we dove deeper into the project, the conversation morphed from light jabs to more serious discourse. We tossed ideas back and forth, each one building upon the last, and I began to realize how much his insights complemented my own. This unexpected collaboration felt like a dance—two rivals navigating a crowded floor, where every turn revealed a new depth to our understanding.

After the meeting, I remained at the table, thumbing through the notes, my mind racing with possibilities. Just as I was about to pack up, he sauntered over, leaning casually against the edge of the table. "I have to admit, you surprised me today. I didn't expect you to hold your ground so well."

I looked up, arching an eyebrow. "Surprised? You thought I was going to fold like a cheap suit?"

He chuckled, the sound rich and warm, laced with genuine admiration. "I didn't say that. But I'll admit, I expected a little more... flustered energy."

"Flustered?" I scoffed, crossing my arms defensively. "I'm not some damsel waiting to be rescued, thank you very much."

He leaned in slightly, a teasing glint in his eyes. "Damsel? Please. More like a knight in shining armor, ready to duel."

I rolled my eyes, but the warmth in my chest told a different story. There was something magnetic about our exchanges, an undeniable chemistry that simmered beneath the surface.

The moment hung between us, and as our colleagues filtered out of the room, leaving us alone, I felt the weight of unspoken words. "So, what now?" he asked, his voice softer, the playful banter replaced by something more sincere.

"Now?" I hesitated, glancing down at my notes. "Now we get to work. There's a lot at stake, and I refuse to let you distract me."

"Distract you?" He stepped a fraction closer, his tone teasing but with a hint of something deeper. "I'm just getting started."

A shiver ran down my spine, and I forced myself to focus on the task at hand. Whatever spark flickered between us was dangerous, and I had no intention of getting burned. Yet as I turned away, the air felt charged, and the realization that our rivalry had evolved into something far more intricate lingered, a puzzle I was both eager and reluctant to solve.

The days slid by in a blur of meetings and deadlines, each one laced with an undercurrent of tension that was both thrilling and exhausting. Each time we gathered in the conference room, it was a delicate dance, a mixture of sharp dialogue and playful barbs that only deepened the unexpected connection between us. He had a way of challenging me that ignited a fire within, pushing me to think faster, speak louder, and assert my ideas more confidently. Yet, beneath the playful facade, I could feel something else simmering, a thread that connected us in a way I had never anticipated.

It was a Thursday when it finally happened—the moment that would tip the balance from rivalry to something entirely different. We were working late, the office quiet except for the distant hum of the city outside and the occasional shuffle of papers. The atmosphere crackled as we sat across from each other, our laptops open, lost in a heated discussion over the project.

"Your plan has merit, but it's far too conservative," he declared, his gaze piercing as he leaned over the table, his intensity radiating like heat. "You need to take a risk if you want this to stand out."

"And what do you suggest, Mr. Risk-Taker?" I shot back, unable to mask my irritation. "A flash mob? Maybe a neon sign? Because those aren't really viable options."

He smirked, leaning back in his chair, his eyes dancing with amusement. "Why not? You're so focused on playing it safe that you're losing sight of what makes this project exciting. It's like trying to bake a cake without sugar. Sure, it'll look good, but no one will want a bite."

The corner of my mouth twitched upward against my will. "I didn't realize we were baking cakes now. If we were, I'd make sure to include a healthy dose of reality."

"Oh, reality. The ever-looming shadow over all our dreams," he mused, the mock seriousness in his tone making me laugh despite myself. "You know, for someone so obsessed with staying grounded, you really do have a flair for the dramatic."

"Is that your way of saying I should embrace the chaos?" I challenged, though a part of me was genuinely intrigued by the thought. What if I did push boundaries just a little?

"Chaos can lead to innovation," he replied, his voice softening slightly. "Sometimes, you need to throw caution to the wind and see what flies."

We fell into a comfortable silence, the air thick with unsaid words and the lingering spark that had become all too familiar. The moment was electric, the distance between us charged with possibility. I could feel the warmth radiating from him, a beacon drawing me closer.

"Okay, what if we compromise?" I suggested, breaking the tension with a smile. "Let's integrate some of your... chaos into my 'realistic' approach. We can find a middle ground."

His expression shifted, surprise flickering across his face before he broke into a grin. "A true diplomatic move. I'm impressed. Who knew you had it in you?"

"Don't get used to it," I replied, rolling my eyes playfully. "Let's save the celebrations for when we actually win this pitch."

We spent the next hour brainstorming, bouncing ideas off each other with newfound energy. The office was dim, shadows creeping into corners, and the city lights outside glowed like a million tiny stars. I was lost in the creative flow, my mind racing as we crafted an outline that melded our styles into something unique and exhilarating.

Then, just as the synergy reached its peak, the overhead lights flickered, plunging us into darkness. The sudden silence was disorienting, the hum of the city muffled by the unexpected blackness. "Great," I muttered, fumbling for my phone to illuminate the room.

"Perfect timing," he said dryly, his voice closer than I expected, a shadow in the dark. "Do you think this is a sign that we should wrap it up for the night?"

"Are you kidding? We're on a roll! I refuse to let a little blackout stop us," I declared, finding a spark of determination. I flicked on the flashlight, casting a beam of light across the table, illuminating the scattered papers and our expressions.

In the glow, I caught sight of him—his face softened, a hint of surprise in his eyes as they met mine. The air around us shifted, thick with something unnameable. "You really are relentless," he said, a hint of admiration creeping into his tone. "I respect that."

"Don't," I warned, but the seriousness of my tone was undercut by the playful glint in my eyes. "It'll only encourage me."

"Encouragement is key to success," he replied, his voice low. "Especially in this business."

Just then, the power surged back to life, the lights flickering on, illuminating the office in a warm glow. But as the brightness returned, I couldn't shake the feeling that something had shifted. The connection we'd forged felt palpable, and for the first time, I found myself wondering what it would be like to explore it beyond the walls of the office.

"Let's take this outside," I suggested suddenly, surprising myself with the boldness of my words. "There's a café nearby that stays open late. We could brainstorm there."

His eyebrows shot up, surprise evident on his face. "Are you inviting me to get coffee? At this hour? Is this some sort of tactic to throw me off my game?"

"Consider it an extension of our collaborative spirit," I replied, matching his playful tone. "Or maybe I just need a break from the office. Your choice."

"Ah, but I see through your clever ruse. You're trying to distract me from my master plan."

"Master plan? Is that what we're calling it now?" I laughed, shaking my head. "Fine. I'll bring the chaos; you bring the sugar. Deal?"

He hesitated for a moment, and I could see the gears turning in his mind. Then, with a grin that felt like a victory, he nodded. "Deal."

As we stepped out into the cool night air, a sense of excitement thrummed beneath my skin. The city pulsed with life, the sounds of laughter and music filling the streets as we walked side by side, the air heavy with possibilities.

But just as I was beginning to feel comfortable, my phone buzzed in my pocket, breaking the spell. I fished it out, my heart sinking as I read the message. It was from Claire, her tone unusually urgent: "We need to talk. It's important."

I glanced at him, the light in his eyes flickering with curiosity. "Everything okay?"

"Yeah, just... a friend needs me," I said, attempting to brush it off. "Let's head to the café; I'll catch up with her later."

But as we continued walking, the feeling of anticipation began to dissolve into a knot of anxiety. Claire's urgency weighed heavily on my mind, a stark reminder that beneath the surface of our newfound connection lay complications I wasn't ready to face.

"Are you sure?" he asked, sensing my distraction.

"Absolutely," I replied, forcing a smile. "Just a little late-night drama."

But as I turned to him, I caught sight of something—an expression that was both knowing and concerned. It sent a shiver down my spine. And in that fleeting moment, I realized that as we stepped deeper into the night, the fabric of my carefully controlled life was beginning to unravel, threatening to expose secrets I had long buried beneath the surface.

A sudden noise erupted from the alley beside us, a sharp crash that echoed against the walls, jolting both of us to a halt. I felt my heart race, instinctively stepping closer to him. "What was that?" I whispered, the night air suddenly feeling too close, too charged with unspoken possibilities.

His eyes narrowed as he scanned the alley, tension palpable between us. "I don't know, but maybe we should—"

Before he could finish, a figure stumbled into view, and the world shifted in an instant. The air thickened with uncertainty, and as the figure emerged from the shadows, my heart raced with dread, a realization dawning that this night was about to take an unexpected turn, one that would plunge us both into chaos.

Chapter 3: Unraveling Threads

The hum of chatter buzzed in the air, an intoxicating mix of voices layered with the sharp clink of glasses and the subtle rustle of expensive fabric. As I stepped into the grand hall, my pulse quickened, a dizzying cocktail of nerves and anticipation swirling within me. The high ceilings loomed above, draped with elegant chandeliers that cast a warm, golden glow over the polished marble floors. Each step felt like a declaration of intent; I was here to reclaim my space.

I adjusted the delicate straps of my midnight blue dress, a garment that whispered sophistication while clinging to my curves in just the right way. My reflection in the glass-paneled walls offered a flicker of reassurance. Confidence, I reminded myself, is the best accessory, even when every fiber of my being wanted to retreat. Nathan was already inside, mingling effortlessly, his presence magnetic, drawing people like moths to a flame.

I spotted him across the room, laughing at something someone had said, his head thrown back in that way that made the world seem a little brighter. His dark hair caught the light just so, and I remembered the playful banter we'd exchanged during our brief interactions, those moments where the corporate façade faded, leaving only two people behind. But the way he commanded the room tonight, it was almost as if he were the sun and everyone else were planets in orbit.

With a deep breath, I navigated through the crowd, weaving between laughter and clinking glasses, my resolve solidifying with every step. I was no longer just the diligent worker bee buried under spreadsheets and presentations. I was a woman with something to say, and more importantly, someone who wanted to hear what Nathan had to offer beyond the boardroom.

"Is it me, or do you look more radiant every time we meet?" His voice, smooth as silk, broke through the ambient noise, a subtle thrill racing down my spine.

"Nathan," I replied, a playful smile dancing on my lips, "you say that to all the women."

"Only the ones who matter," he countered, his eyes glinting with mischief. I felt the warmth of a blush creep up my cheeks, but I pushed it aside. Tonight was not about falling for flattery; it was about connection.

"Are you still working on that project in marketing?" he asked, genuinely interested, which surprised me. Most people would have feigned interest before steering the conversation back to safe topics, like the latest tech gadgets or the best golf courses.

"Yes, it's been a whirlwind," I confessed, gesturing toward a small buffet table. "I almost had to hire a personal assistant to keep my schedule from exploding."

"Ah, but wouldn't that take away the fun? I hear the chaos is where the magic happens," he remarked, leaning closer as if sharing a delightful secret.

I laughed, a sound that felt refreshing against the backdrop of tension. "True, but a little order never hurt anyone. I could use a break from the whirlwind."

His gaze lingered, and I could see the wall he typically wore beginning to slip, revealing glimpses of the man behind the corporate veneer. "You know," he said, his tone shifting to something more contemplative, "I've always found that balance is key. My childhood was a bit chaotic, so I tend to gravitate toward structure now."

This admission surprised me. Nathan was always so composed, a quintessential professional, radiating confidence and competence. "What do you mean by chaotic?"

He chuckled softly, as if wading through memories. "Let's just say there were times when I'd come home to a mess of my parents' arguments instead of a home-cooked meal. It taught me early on to keep my life organized."

A knot formed in my throat, a pang of empathy swelling within me. "I'm sorry to hear that. It sounds like you had to grow up fast."

"Not as fast as some," he replied, a hint of vulnerability cracking through his polished exterior. "But I learned to fend for myself, you know? Got pretty good at making instant ramen before I could tie my shoelaces."

I couldn't help but smile at the image. "Nothing quite like a gourmet meal made in the microwave."

"Exactly! It's an art form, really." His laughter danced in the air, infectious and warm.

But before I could respond, the atmosphere shifted, like the moment before a storm. A figure stepped into the room, casting a shadow that seemed to darken the air around us. It was Viktor, a familiar presence in our corporate landscape, his reputation preceding him like a thunderous drumroll. Known for his ruthless tactics and calculated maneuvers, he thrived on creating discord. The moment he approached, the laughter dimmed, and the vibrant chatter stilled, the lightness of our exchange dissipating like smoke.

"Nathan," Viktor's voice cut through the tension, smooth but with an undercurrent of menace. "I see you've found a new friend."

I felt my heartbeat quicken, the exhilaration of our earlier conversation replaced by a wave of unease. Nathan straightened, an almost imperceptible shift in his demeanor as he faced Viktor.

"Just catching up, Viktor. You know how networking events can be." Nathan's voice was steady, but the undertones hinted at a deeper friction between them.

"Oh, I do indeed. The real question is whether this delightful evening is worth your time, or if you'd rather focus on the bigger picture?" Viktor's eyes flicked to me, and I suddenly felt like a pawn on a chessboard, my presence both noticed and dismissed in the same breath.

"Every connection matters," Nathan replied, his jaw tightening slightly. "Even the unexpected ones."

There was an electric tension in the air, a palpable shift that seemed to invite the crowd to watch, as if we were all mere spectators in a high-stakes game. I could feel the weight of Viktor's gaze, the scrutiny that seemed to peel back layers of who I was and what I represented. The warmth of the evening faded, replaced by a chill that whispered of danger lurking just beneath the surface.

As I stood there, caught in the crossfire of their silent battle, I realized that this networking event was no longer just about ambition; it had morphed into something far more complex—an arena of alliances, unspoken histories, and the potential for unforeseen consequences.

The tension thickened, a palpable force that held the air hostage. Viktor's presence was a cold splash of reality, and I could feel the hairs on the back of my neck rise as he continued to assess us, his smirk widening. "I wouldn't want you to lose sight of what really matters in this industry, Nathan," he said, each word wrapped in a velvet-lined threat. "We both know there's no time for frivolities."

I caught Nathan's glance, a fleeting flicker of uncertainty that deepened my concern. "Right," he replied, his voice steady, though I could sense the undercurrent of irritation bubbling beneath the surface. "I believe in nurturing every connection. It's what makes us more than just a name on a business card."

"Cute," Viktor retorted, leaning closer as if to shield his words from the eavesdropping crowd. "But remember, it's the connections that count—those that can actually advance your career." He gestured dismissively at me, and a hot wave of indignation surged through me.

"Funny you should say that, Viktor," I interjected, my voice slicing through the tension. "Sometimes, the unexpected connections can lead to the best opportunities. Don't you think?"

His expression soured, but I pressed on, unwilling to let my moment of confidence slip away. "Besides, if you only focus on what's 'useful,' you might miss out on a brilliant idea or a unique perspective. After all, isn't that why we're here?"

The room fell silent, all eyes glued to our little standoff. Nathan raised an eyebrow, a hint of amusement breaking through his earlier tension. Viktor opened his mouth to retort but instead settled for a tight-lipped smile, clearly annoyed that I had derailed his game.

"Well, it seems our newcomer has a voice," he said, forcing a laugh that did nothing to mask his irritation. "Just don't confuse enthusiasm with practicality, darling."

The way he addressed me as "darling" felt like a calculated jab. I wanted to hurl back a witty comeback, but instead, I steeled myself, the adrenaline coursing through me transforming indignation into resolve.

Nathan stepped in, his tone turning sharp. "Viktor, we both know the value of fresh ideas. And I'd rather not stifle someone's potential for the sake of your antiquated views." The tension crackled, and I could see the battle lines drawn as the stakes escalated.

Viktor straightened, the bravado slipping slightly. "You should know better than to pick a fight you can't win, Nathan. I've seen careers crushed by misplaced loyalties."

"I'd take my chances, thanks," Nathan shot back, his gaze unwavering.

And just like that, the conversation turned from idle banter to an arena of unspoken histories and veiled threats. I felt like an unwitting spectator in their duel, caught in the crossfire of their unyielding rivalry. Suddenly, I wished I could disappear, to retreat into the shadows of the room where I could observe without being the focus of their scrutiny.

But before I could retreat, Viktor waved his hand dismissively, redirecting his attention toward the more socially advantageous crowd forming behind us. "Good luck, Nathan," he said, his tone dripping with sarcasm. "I'm sure this charming conversation will yield dividends." With that, he sauntered off, his presence still lingering like a bad smell, leaving a cold silence in his wake.

I turned to Nathan, my heart racing. "Did I just make things worse?"

He chuckled, shaking his head as if to dispel the tension. "Not at all. You held your ground, and I appreciate that." There was a warmth in his voice, a gratitude that made me feel momentarily buoyant. "Besides, if anyone can handle Viktor's barbs, it's you."

"Great, so I'm the brave knight against the dragon of corporate despair?" I quipped, trying to lighten the mood, though my pulse still raced from the encounter.

Nathan laughed again, and the sound was like a balm for my frayed nerves. "More like a clever strategist, outmaneuvering an old foe."

For a moment, we simply stood there, the tension between us easing into something more comfortable. "I must admit," he began, "I wasn't expecting you to engage with him like that. Most people just let Viktor have his say and scuttle off."

"I've always had a flair for the dramatic," I replied, smirking. "Not all of us can blend into the wallpaper."

Nathan looked at me, his expression shifting into something more serious. "I admire that. It's easy to lose ourselves in the corporate grind, to become someone else. But staying true to who you are—that's the real challenge."

His words hung in the air, and I found myself searching his eyes for more of the vulnerability he had briefly shown earlier. "It can be exhausting, though. I often feel like I'm playing a part instead of living my life."

His brow furrowed, and for a moment, it felt like we were the only two people in the bustling room, the world around us fading into a blur of noise and activity. "You're not alone in feeling that way," he said softly. "But it's those moments, those real conversations, that remind us of what matters."

Just then, a loud burst of laughter from a nearby table shattered the bubble we had created. I glanced over to see a group of colleagues from my department, a few of whom were already in various states of inebriation. They waved enthusiastically, beckoning me over.

"Looks like my backup has arrived," I said, forcing a smile. "I should probably go rescue them from drowning in champagne."

"Don't let them drag you into the fray too quickly," Nathan warned, an endearing seriousness in his tone. "You're more than just their designated driver."

"Thanks for the reminder, knight of the corporate roundtable," I teased, stepping back to give him space. "But I think I can manage a little fun while still being myself."

His expression softened, and a glimmer of admiration danced in his eyes. "I'll hold you to that."

As I turned to join my colleagues, I couldn't shake the feeling that our exchange had shifted something profound between us. The earlier tension felt like a distant memory, replaced by an exhilarating promise. Yet, I couldn't ignore the nagging doubt that lingered in the back of my mind.

Navigating this corporate labyrinth was no small feat, and as I blended back into the crowd, I realized that alliances were as delicate as the finest porcelain. I'd thrown my hat in the ring, but the game was far from over. Every interaction would count, every decision, every twist of fate. And as the night wore on, I couldn't help but wonder just how deep the currents ran beneath the surface of our corporate lives.

The chatter surged and receded like ocean waves, a symphony of laughter and clinking glasses filling the air. I managed to steer my group of colleagues toward the bar, where a cheerful bartender was crafting cocktails with an enthusiasm that seemed to cut through the corporate haze. My friends clapped each other on the back, and the tension that had held me captive a moment ago began to dissolve in a swirl of camaraderie and good-natured teasing.

"Did you see the way you challenged Viktor?" Ava, one of my closest friends from work, grinned at me, her eyes sparkling with mischief. "I thought you were going to set off fireworks with the way you two were going at it!"

"More like a slow-burning fuse that might explode at any second," I quipped back, stirring my drink with a cocktail straw. "I just didn't want to let him walk all over me. Someone has to remind him he's not the only player in this game."

"Love it! You've got to teach me your ways," she laughed, giving me an affectionate nudge. "Honestly, I'm surprised you didn't throw a drink in his face."

"Well, we all know how much Viktor loves a good scene," I replied, suppressing a grin as I remembered his hawk-like gaze and clipped remarks. The tension of that earlier encounter lingered in the back of my mind, but the levity of the moment swept me into its embrace.

Just as I began to relax, however, a familiar figure loomed at the edge of the bar, his dark silhouette sharp against the flickering lights. Nathan had woven back into my periphery, the easy smile returning to his face as he approached, effortlessly drawing attention. I noticed the way the crowd parted for him, as if he carried an invisible banner that declared his significance.

"Hey there," he said, a hint of warmth threading through his voice as he leaned casually against the bar. "Looks like you've found your entourage."

"Just doing my best to keep the peace," I replied, raising my glass in a mock toast. "And trying not to get sucked into the whirlwind of Viktor's next power play."

Nathan chuckled, the sound rolling out like a comforting balm. "A noble pursuit. Though it seems you handled yourself quite well. I didn't know you had it in you."

"Oh, I'm full of surprises," I said, matching his playful banter. "I also bake an exceptional chocolate cake, should you ever need a sweet treat to celebrate your corporate victories."

"Chocolate cake and corporate strategy? Quite the combination," he teased. "Maybe I should take you up on that offer."

As we exchanged playful barbs, I felt the earlier tension melt away, replaced by a connection that sparked like electricity between us. Yet, beneath the surface of our banter, I sensed a deeper current at play, something that made my heart race faster than the friendly conversation warranted.

Then, a voice rang out across the room, slicing through the warmth like a knife. "Nathan, there you are! I've been looking for you."

It was a woman with sharp features and an aura that seemed to command attention even in the midst of a crowded bar. She wore a sleek black dress that draped elegantly over her figure, and her hair was styled into a polished chignon that seemed to radiate authority. She approached with purpose, her gaze fixed firmly on Nathan, completely bypassing the rest of us as if we were mere wallpaper.

"Ah, Claudia," Nathan said, his expression shifting subtly. I caught a flicker of something in his eyes—a tension, perhaps. "What can I do for you?"

"We need to discuss the Montgomery project. I have some new data that requires your immediate attention."

"Right now?" He glanced at me, an unspoken apology lingering in the air.

Claudia's voice was smooth, but there was an edge to it, a determination that left little room for negotiation. "Yes, Nathan. Now."

I felt a sinking sensation in my stomach, the buoyancy of the evening's camaraderie deflating like a balloon losing air. Here was another layer of corporate complexity I hadn't anticipated. This was no ordinary business matter; there was an urgency in Claudia's tone that spoke volumes.

"Of course," he said, his tone shifting back into that professional register I had first encountered. "I'll be right there."

He turned back to me, a shadow of frustration flitting across his features. "I'm sorry. Duty calls, I guess."

I nodded, forcing a smile that felt more like a mask. "Go. I wouldn't want to hold you back. Business first, right?"

"Right." He hesitated for a moment, his gaze lingering on me, the warmth of our earlier conversation still crackling in the air. "We'll pick this up later?"

"Absolutely," I replied, though a tiny voice in my head whispered doubts that I couldn't shake. As he walked away with Claudia, a hollow feeling settled in my chest, one that seemed disproportionate to the fleeting moment we'd shared.

Ava nudged me gently, her expression a mixture of concern and amusement. "You okay? You looked like you were about to throw your drink at her."

"Just peachy," I replied, though my mind raced with questions. What was their relationship? What project could be so urgent that it interrupted a networking event? I could feel the fabric of the evening unraveling, the threads of what I thought I understood beginning to tangle.

As I turned back to my colleagues, the lively atmosphere faded into background noise, and I couldn't help but glance over at Nathan and Claudia. They stood together, heads close, discussing something that appeared far too serious for the setting. I felt a sharp twist in my gut, the unwelcome sting of jealousy sparking to life.

But then a sudden shout cut through my thoughts, drawing attention back to the main floor. "Look out!"

Everyone turned in unison, just in time to see a waiter stumbling, a tray of drinks tumbling through the air. The glasses spun in a dramatic arc before crashing down to the ground, a chaotic symphony of shattering glass and spilled liquid. Gasps erupted from the crowd as people recoiled, instinctively stepping back to avoid the incoming wave of calamity.

I glanced back at Nathan, who had instinctively moved to help, a look of determination etched across his face. In that moment, as he rushed to assist the waiter, I could see the very essence of who he was—a man who didn't shy away from chaos, who dove into the fray even when the stakes were high.

But before I could process the scene fully, the lights flickered ominously overhead, casting shadows that danced like specters across the walls. A hush fell over the crowd, and I felt a chill creep up my spine, the air thickening with a tension that had nothing to do with spilled drinks.

Then, the unmistakable sound of shattering glass echoed once more, but this time it was different, sharper, like the crack of thunder. I turned to see Claudia's face pale, her eyes wide as she stumbled back, clutching her arm, a flicker of red staining her pristine dress.

"Claudia!" Nathan's voice pierced the air, filled with an urgency that sent a shockwave through the crowd.

And just like that, everything shifted once again. The night had unraveled in a way I never saw coming, and as I stood there, caught between the remnants of our earlier laughter and the ominous turn of events, I couldn't shake the feeling that this was just the beginning.

Chapter 4: Shadows from the Past

The night was heavy with the scent of rain-soaked earth, the lingering aroma of petrichor mingling with the sweetness of blooming jasmine from the garden outside. I stood at the window of my small apartment, the glass cool against my fingertips, gazing out into the blurred lights of the city. It was one of those evenings when the streets shimmered with a slick glaze, and the promise of adventure danced just beyond the glow of the lampposts. Yet, all I could think about was Nathan and the unsettling presence of the man who had appeared in our lives like a shadow creeping from a past better left undisturbed.

Nathan had always been an enigma, a complex puzzle wrapped in charisma and brooding intensity. The way he leaned against the doorframe when he arrived, drenched from the downpour yet looking somehow like he had just stepped out of a magazine, sent a flutter through my stomach. I loved that he could carry an air of mystery, but that very mystery was beginning to feel like a riddle I could no longer decipher. Tonight, something in his eyes—a flash of recognition or perhaps regret—made my heart quicken. It was as if he were standing on the precipice of revealing something monumental, yet he hesitated, as if afraid of the weight of the truth.

"Who is he, Nathan?" I asked, my voice barely above a whisper, the gravity of my question hanging heavily between us. I had caught a glimpse of the man earlier, a fleeting moment as he passed by the café where Nathan and I often met for our late-night discussions. Dark hair slicked back, his presence radiating a certain dangerous charm that made the hairs on the back of my neck stand on end. He had laughed too easily, a sound that grated against my instincts, and as he'd approached Nathan, I felt an almost palpable shift in the atmosphere. The warm, inviting space had turned cool, as if a winter breeze had swept through, ushering in unease.

Nathan's expression hardened, his jaw tightening as if I'd slapped him. "You don't need to worry about him," he replied, his tone clipped, dismissive. The way he turned away from me felt like a wall rising between us, one built from unspoken words and buried secrets. I fought the urge to reach out and pull him back, to bridge the distance growing like a chasm in the silence that followed. Instead, I crossed my arms, a defensive posture that mirrored my swirling emotions—frustration, concern, and something else I couldn't quite place.

"What do you mean, I don't need to worry? Nathan, he clearly knows you, and not in a casual acquaintance sort of way." I could feel the heat rising in my cheeks, the indignation flaring at his nonchalance. "This isn't just a random encounter. You're acting like you're not even affected by it." The tension was a taut string pulled to its limit, and I was terrified it might snap at any moment.

Nathan sighed, running a hand through his hair, a gesture I had come to recognize as a signal of his growing agitation. "It's complicated, and I—" he began, but I cut him off, the urgency in my voice overriding my concern for tact.

"Complicated? Complicated is what my laundry looks like after a week of procrastination! This is more than that. You can't just brush it off." I stepped closer, my heart racing as I searched his eyes for the truth. "You need to tell me, Nathan. I deserve that much."

The flicker of vulnerability that crossed his face was quickly smothered by a veil of determination. "Trust me. I'm trying to protect you." His voice softened, the tension between us crackling with unspoken feelings. I could see the conflict raging within him, and it mirrored the turmoil in my own heart. How could he protect me by keeping me in the dark? My instincts were screaming that the man from his past was a danger lurking just outside our door, waiting for the right moment to strike.

"Protect me? Or protect yourself?" The words slipped out before I could stop them, the accusation hanging in the air like an unwelcome guest. Nathan's eyes darkened, a flash of anger cutting through the haze of concern.

"You don't understand," he shot back, his voice rising slightly. "This isn't just some old grudge. It's bigger than you think. I can't involve you in this."

"And yet, here I am, standing right in the middle of it!" I stepped back, my heart pounding not just from anger but from the cold realization that the man I cared for might be involved in something dangerous. "You've pulled me into this mess without my consent, and I have a right to know what's happening."

The silence that followed felt like an eternity, the air thick with tension and unacknowledged emotions. Nathan's gaze dropped to the floor, and I could see the battle raging within him. "This man... he's not just anyone. He was involved in things I had to walk away from—things I thought I had left behind." The words were barely a whisper, but the weight of them pressed heavily against my chest.

"Then let me help you," I urged, feeling the stirrings of determination rise within me. "Whatever it is, we can face it together. You don't have to shoulder this alone."

He looked up, surprise flickering in his eyes, and for a moment, I thought I saw a glimmer of hope there. But then it was gone, replaced by that familiar guardedness. "You don't know what you're asking for. This isn't a fairy tale, and I can't risk your safety."

"Maybe I'm willing to take that risk," I countered, my heart racing. "Maybe I'm more than just the girl you think you can protect. You've got to trust me, Nathan, just as I'm trying to trust you." The words tumbled out, each one an arrow aimed straight for his heart, and I hoped he could feel the sincerity woven into them.

His expression softened momentarily, the walls around him crumbling just enough for me to glimpse the real Nathan beneath the layers of mystery. "I wish it were that simple," he murmured, stepping closer, the warmth radiating from him grounding me in the storm of emotions swirling around us.

"Sometimes, the hardest paths are the ones that lead to the most beautiful destinations," I said softly, a smile teasing the corners of my lips despite the gravity of our conversation. The flicker of amusement in his eyes suggested he appreciated my attempt to lighten the mood, even if just for a moment.

But the moment was fleeting, and reality intruded once more as the shadows of Nathan's past loomed over us, reminding me that the fight was only beginning.

The soft patter of rain against the window was a comforting reminder of the world outside, a world where chaos was softened by nature's gentle touch. I could hear the distant hum of traffic and the occasional laughter from the café across the street, but within these four walls, it felt like a different realm—one tangled in secrets and shadows. Nathan leaned against the kitchen counter, arms crossed, the sharp lines of his silhouette cutting through the dim light like a dagger. I could sense the unresolved tension vibrating in the air, thick enough to slice with a knife.

"Why won't you tell me?" I pressed again, my voice steadier than I felt. The truth hung between us, a palpable weight that threatened to pull us both under. "If he's such a threat, don't you think I deserve to know what I'm getting into?"

His brow furrowed, eyes darkening like storm clouds gathering on the horizon. "It's not just about you. It's about everything that came before." The corners of his mouth twitched as if he were struggling to keep a secret that was more than just the situation at hand; it was his past, wrapped in layers of regret and unresolved conflict.

"Everything that came before?" I echoed, pushing myself to remain calm despite the rapid-fire beat of my heart. "You mean like shady deals and dangerous people? Because, Nathan, I think I deserve more than that vague explanation."

He sighed, running a hand through his damp hair, which was still a little wild from the rain. "You don't understand how deep this goes." His voice softened, a hint of vulnerability peeking through his guarded facade. "This isn't a storybook where we get to choose the characters. I've made choices that put me in this position."

"Choices, sure. But what about me?" I shot back, the frustration bubbling up again. "I'm not asking for a fairy tale. I'm asking for honesty. If you care about me, then why would you keep me in the dark?"

He stared at me for a long moment, a battle waging in his eyes between a desire to protect and an urge to share. Finally, he spoke, his voice low, almost reverent. "Because if I let you in, I might have to admit that I'm scared. Scared of what this could mean for us."

"Scared of what? Of me getting hurt? Nathan, I've faced worse things in life than some ghost from your past," I replied, surprising myself with the ferocity in my tone. "You've seen me tackle my own monsters. Don't underestimate my ability to handle whatever this is."

A flicker of something crossed his face—admiration, perhaps? Or was it simply recognition of my stubbornness? "This man..." he began hesitantly, "his name is Jaxon. We used to work together, but things... they went south. Fast. He's not someone you want to get tangled up with. He's involved in some dangerous dealings, and he doesn't play nice."

"Like I said, welcome to my life," I quipped, trying to inject humor into the heavy air. "So, what, we just throw caution to the wind and pretend he doesn't exist?"

Nathan's expression hardened again, but his eyes flickered with something softer. "No, we confront it. Together, if you're really up for it."

"Of course I am," I declared, a rush of adrenaline coursing through me. "But we need a plan. We can't just wait for him to show up again. We should gather information, find out what he wants."

A slow smile broke across Nathan's face, though it didn't reach his eyes. "Now that's the spirit. I knew I liked you for a reason."

"Oh, really? You mean I'm not just a pretty face?" I shot back, crossing my arms with a playful huff. "I'll have to remember that when I'm brewing your morning coffee."

"Trust me, it takes more than a pretty face to keep up with the likes of you." His eyes sparkled, the momentary lightness brushing aside the shadows that clung to him. It was refreshing, a brief reminder of why I had fallen for him in the first place.

But as quickly as the moment of levity had appeared, it was gone, replaced by the weight of our situation. "What does he want, Nathan? Do you know?"

Nathan shook his head, frustration etched in his features. "I don't know. He's always been ambitious, but I never thought he would sink this low. If he's involved in something shady, it could be dangerous for everyone—especially those close to me."

"Close to you," I echoed, my heart sinking as I considered the implications. "You mean like me?"

He nodded, the gravity of his acknowledgment pulling us both back into the seriousness of our circumstances. "I can't bear the thought of anything happening to you because of me. I won't let that happen."

"Then we need to be proactive. This isn't just about staying in the dark and hoping he'll go away." I took a deep breath, drawing on the resolve that had always been a part of me. "Let's dig deeper. Maybe I can help."

"You really want to be involved in this?" Nathan asked, skepticism lacing his tone.

"Not just involved; I want to be by your side. I won't let you face this alone."

He studied me, the tension in his shoulders easing slightly. "Alright, but we need to be careful. I can't afford to put you in any more danger than you might already be."

"Danger is my middle name," I quipped, attempting to lighten the mood. "At least, it should be, considering the last few months. But let's be real; I've got my fair share of experience in navigating tough situations."

A slow grin spread across his face. "Okay, then. Let's figure this out together. But I want you to promise me something."

"Depends on what it is," I replied, raising an eyebrow.

"Promise me that you'll listen. If things get too dangerous, I need you to walk away. No arguments. Just trust me to keep you safe."

"Fine, I promise," I said, though I felt the familiar stir of rebellion at the thought of being told what to do. "But I have to warn you, Nathan, my idea of safety might differ from yours. I'm not one to sit idly by."

His eyes softened, and for a brief moment, I could see the glimmer of admiration mixed with affection. "That's what makes you so infuriatingly compelling."

Before I could respond, a sharp knock on the door echoed through the apartment, jolting us both from our momentary truce. My stomach dropped as a familiar tension gripped me, tightening like a noose around my chest. Nathan's eyes narrowed, and I could sense the tension crackling anew, a warning that something significant was about to unfold.

"Stay here," he said, moving toward the door with a determination that made my pulse quicken.

"Wait! Who is it?" I called out, a sense of foreboding creeping in as I stood frozen in place.

"Don't move," he replied, his voice low, almost protective.

But the insistent knock came again, louder this time, demanding an answer. I felt the air thicken with the weight of uncertainty, and as Nathan paused before opening the door, I knew that whatever awaited us on the other side would change everything.

The moment Nathan turned the knob, the door creaked open, revealing a figure silhouetted against the hall light. I held my breath, bracing for a confrontation, or perhaps some shattering revelation that would unravel everything I thought I knew about him. The man standing in the doorway, however, was not Jaxon. Instead, he was someone I recognized but hadn't seen in years—a familiar face that ignited both memories and dread.

"Marcus," I breathed, disbelief tumbling from my lips as the name slipped into the charged air. He had been a staple of our social circle back in college, charismatic and effortlessly charming, the kind of guy who could talk his way into—or out of—just about anything. But there was a reason I hadn't thought about him in years; he had slipped into the background of my life after a few too many reckless nights and questionable decisions. Now, he stood before us, his grin wide and easy, but his eyes held a glimmer that made me uneasy.

"What brings you back to this side of town?" I asked, my voice sharper than I intended, but I couldn't shake the sense of something amiss. I could feel Nathan tense beside me, a subtle shift that signaled his own discomfort.

"Nice to see you too, Mia," Marcus replied, his tone smooth as honey, completely unbothered by the chill that hung in the air. "I was just in the neighborhood and thought I'd drop by. Heard you were back in town, Nathan." His gaze shifted to Nathan, and the warmth in his expression evaporated, replaced by something darker and more calculating.

"Not a great time, Marcus," Nathan said, his voice low, his protective instinct kicking in. I could almost hear the unspoken warning: Don't let him in.

Marcus stepped forward, brushing past Nathan as if he were an inconvenient shadow. "Oh, come on! Don't be like that. I'm just here to catch up, see how life has been treating you." His smile faltered as his eyes darted toward me, curiosity mixed with something more dangerous lurking beneath the surface.

"I'm fine, thanks," I said, standing a little taller, feeling the urge to shield Nathan from whatever this was. "What exactly do you want?"

"Straight to the point, I like that," Marcus replied, raising an eyebrow in amusement. "Just a friendly visit, I promise. I hear you've been busy making waves in your little corner of the world. Thought you might appreciate a bit of company."

"Waves? More like ripples," I replied, trying to sound unfazed, though my heart raced with the unsteady rhythm of apprehension. "If you're looking for something, you should know Nathan and I are in the middle of—"

"—something important," Nathan interjected, cutting me off with a glare that communicated both urgency and irritation. "We don't have time for social calls, Marcus."

Marcus shrugged, unperturbed. "Fair enough. But you know how the world works, don't you? Information is currency, and I happen to know a thing or two about the shadows lurking around here." He leaned in, eyes sparkling with mischief. "Especially regarding a certain someone who's been making headlines lately."

I glanced at Nathan, whose expression had darkened further, jaw clenched tight. "What do you know?" he asked, a low growl that sent shivers down my spine.

"Oh, just enough to know that old friends can sometimes become old foes," Marcus replied casually, the tension crackling in the air. "And that certain associates have a way of resurfacing when you least expect it. Like ghosts from the past, if you will."

The way he spoke sent a jolt of alarm through me. I couldn't shake the feeling that he was playing a dangerous game, weaving words with precision, aiming to draw us into a trap. "You're not being very specific," I said, trying to keep my voice steady. "What exactly are you implying?"

"Just a warning," he said, raising his hands in mock surrender. "If you're going to play in the big leagues, you'd better know what's at stake. Jaxon is not just a name from Nathan's past; he's a tempest. And he's coming for what he wants."

Nathan took a step closer, his intensity growing. "And what is it he wants?"

Marcus's smile widened, revealing too much confidence. "You know what they say—money makes the world go round, and power can be a beautiful thing." He leaned against the wall, casual and deceptively nonchalant. "If you're not careful, you might find yourselves caught in the crossfire."

The implications hung heavy in the air, each word wrapping around me like a vine, suffocating and tight. "What do you stand to gain from this?" I asked, unwilling to let him steer the conversation any further without a purpose. "You don't care about us."

"Ah, but that's where you're mistaken," he replied, his tone light but his eyes calculating. "I care deeply about what happens to my friends. Especially when they find themselves entangled in someone else's chaos." He shifted, his demeanor shifting from casual to predatory. "And trust me, Nathan, chaos is what you'll find if you continue to ignore the signs."

"Enough," Nathan snapped, and I could feel the electricity crackle in his voice, a warning that resonated deep within me. "We don't need your cryptic warnings. If you have something to say, say it clearly."

"Alright, then," Marcus replied, tilting his head slightly as if savoring the moment. "Let's just say that Jaxon is not done with you yet. He has plans, and those plans might involve people who care about you." He turned to me, his gaze piercing. "You might want to keep your distance. It's a dangerous game you're playing, and the stakes are higher than you realize."

My heart thudded in my chest, his words heavy with foreboding. "And you think just dropping by with this information is helping?" I shot back, anger rising. "This isn't a game for us. This is my life."

"Oh, darling, life is always a game," Marcus said with an exaggerated flourish. "It's just a matter of who's holding the cards."

With a flick of his wrist, he pulled out a sleek, black business card, placing it on the counter with a flourish. "If you ever change your mind, you know where to find me."

Before I could respond, he turned on his heel and walked out, leaving behind an unsettling silence that reverberated through the room. I felt the air shift, the gravity of his visit settling like a lead weight in my stomach.

"Do you think he knows something?" I asked, the question heavy with implication.

Nathan ran a hand through his hair, frustration radiating from him. "He always knows something," he replied tersely. "But the question is, how much of it is true?"

I took a deep breath, my mind racing. "This isn't just going to blow over, is it? Jaxon is going to come after you, after us."

Nathan turned to face me, determination flashing in his eyes. "We're not going to let that happen. We need to take control of this."

"But how? We don't even know what we're dealing with," I said, anxiety gnawing at the edges of my resolve.

Nathan stepped closer, his intensity grounding me. "We start by digging deeper, finding out who's really behind Jaxon's return. There's always a thread to pull, and we'll unravel this together."

As the words hung between us, I felt a surge of both fear and exhilaration. We were standing on the brink of something monumental, the weight of the unknown stretching before us like a vast ocean.

Just then, a soft ping from my phone drew my attention. I glanced down at the screen, my stomach sinking as a message from an unknown number flashed before my eyes:

"I know where you are. I know what you're doing. You're playing a dangerous game, and I'm watching."

I looked up, my heart racing. Nathan caught the look on my face, a dawning realization washing over him. "What is it?" he asked, his voice suddenly taut with concern.

I swallowed hard, the air thick with anticipation. "It's from someone who knows. They're watching us, Nathan."

A tense silence settled over us, and in that moment, I realized that we had stepped into the shadows, deeper than I ever anticipated. The stakes were rising, and the danger was no longer just a whisper—it was breathing down our necks.

Chapter 5: The Dance of Deception

The grand ballroom of the Crescent Moon Hotel shimmered under a cascade of twinkling chandeliers, each crystal facet catching the light like tiny stars held captive. A low hum of conversation floated through the air, punctuated by the soft clink of glasses and the rustle of silk dresses. It was a night dedicated to charity, but it had become a battleground—a splendidly extravagant arena for a rivalry that felt both exhilarating and exhausting.

As I surveyed the scene, I caught a glimpse of him across the room. Lucas Thorne, clad in a tailored navy suit that fit him as if it had been stitched by the hands of a master craftsman. His dark hair was artfully tousled, and that infuriatingly charming smile was flashed at a small group of admirers gathered around him like moths drawn to a flame. He was the very embodiment of effortless confidence, while I, on the other hand, was practically vibrating with the thrill of competition.

"You look like you're about to burst into flames," my friend Jess teased, nudging me with her elbow. She was dressed in a flowing emerald gown that contrasted sharply with my bold crimson ensemble. "You know this is supposed to be for charity, right?"

"Oh, it is," I replied, trying to suppress the smile tugging at the corners of my mouth. "But it's also an opportunity to show Lucas that I'm not just the second-best event planner in the room."

"Are we still doing this?" Jess rolled her eyes, a playful grin spreading across her face. "I thought we had moved past this whole 'one-upmanship' thing."

"Sure, we have," I said, unable to contain the mischievous glint in my eyes. "But you must admit, watching him squirm a little is worth the price of admission."

With an exaggerated sigh, Jess surrendered. "Fine. But try not to set the place on fire—figuratively, of course."

As the night unfolded, the air thickened with the scent of expensive perfumes and the rich aroma of gourmet hors d'oeuvres, mingling to create an intoxicating atmosphere that almost masked the competitive tension swirling around us. I busied myself with my designated tasks—adjusting table settings, checking on the auction items, and ensuring the champagne flowed freely. Each time I crossed paths with Lucas, our exchanges danced between playful barbs and pointed insults, a tightrope walk that left the air crackling with energy.

"Ah, Emily," he drawled, leaning against a table draped in satin. "I see you've chosen to wear the color of victory tonight. How predictable."

"And I see you've opted for 'dashing rogue' instead of 'successful businessman,'" I shot back, unable to hide the smirk that crept onto my face. "I suppose it's good for your brand."

"Always thinking ahead, aren't you?" His eyes sparkled with mischief. "But you do know this is a charity auction, right? Might want to focus on the cause instead of your overblown ego."

"Easy for you to say, considering you practically live for the spotlight." I turned away, but not before catching the flicker of something more in his expression—an intensity that sent a shiver of doubt through me.

As the night progressed, the moment came when we were both called to the stage to introduce the live auction items. The microphone felt heavy in my hand as I stepped up beside him, the crowd's anticipation palpable. Lucas leaned in, his voice low and teasing. "Let's give them a show, shall we?"

I suppressed a laugh, my heart racing. "Only if you don't trip over your own charm."

The bidding began, and the atmosphere shifted from playful banter to a more serious tone as we highlighted the causes behind each item. Lucas's enthusiasm was infectious, his passion for philanthropy shining through. I caught glimpses of the man beneath the bravado—a man who cared deeply about making a difference, even while cloaked in a facade of competition. It was a side of him that I hadn't fully appreciated, and I found myself drawn in.

"Last item up for bid," I announced, excitement bubbling in my chest as I revealed a stunning piece of art, its colors swirling like a tempest. "Proceeds from this painting will go towards funding local youth programs. We're hoping to inspire the next generation."

Lucas stepped closer, his tone turning earnest. "Art has a way of sparking imagination and igniting dreams. This piece could do just that." His gaze locked onto mine, and for a heartbeat, the rivalry dimmed. There was something electric in the air, a vulnerability that lingered just beyond our witty repartee.

Then, without warning, he took a step back, the walls around him snapping back into place. "Let's see how much these people are willing to pay for their conscience," he quipped, masking the moment with a grin that didn't quite reach his eyes.

I swallowed, the weight of his guardedness settling over me like a shroud. What lay beneath the surface of this man who seemed so confident? The question lingered, and I could almost feel the cracks forming in my own carefully constructed barriers.

As the auction reached its crescendo, we found ourselves standing together, the energy of the room swirling around us. "You're good at this," I said, my tone softer now. "You know how to connect with people."

He hesitated, a shadow passing over his face. "It's all just a game, Emily. You learn to play your part."

"What if you don't want to play anymore?" The question slipped out before I could stop it, a whisper of sincerity in the midst of our games.

For a moment, the air felt thick with unspoken words. His gaze flickered to the ground, then back to me, and I saw a glimpse of the man battling with his past—a man haunted by the darkness that lurked just outside our glamorous lives.

"Sometimes you don't have a choice," he replied, his voice low, laden with a weight I could barely comprehend.

I felt a pang in my chest, a sharp ache of empathy that broke through the competitive facade. "You're not alone in this, Lucas."

But before I could delve deeper, the applause of the audience erupted, jolting us back to the present. The rivalry roared back to life, and the moment of connection slipped away like smoke in the wind. As we resumed our banter, I couldn't shake the feeling that beneath the playful exchanges lay a labyrinth of fears and vulnerabilities, threads waiting to unravel. The dance of deception continued, and I wondered just how deep the layers ran.

The night unfolded like a perfectly choreographed dance, each moment punctuated by laughter and applause, yet tinged with an undercurrent of tension. As the final auction item was sold, I felt the adrenaline still thrumming in my veins, an electric reminder of the vibrant exchange between Lucas and me. Despite our relentless competition, the evening had taken on a life of its own, twisting and turning in ways I hadn't anticipated.

I slipped away from the crowd, needing a moment to breathe. The balcony offered a stunning view of the city skyline, twinkling like a sea of diamonds against the velvet sky. I leaned against the wrought-iron railing, letting the cool breeze tousle my hair and settle the frayed edges of my nerves. It was a surreal escape, one that allowed me to reflect on the man I had been sparring with all night. Just as I started to gather my thoughts, the soft crunch of footsteps interrupted my reverie.

"Out here sulking, are we?" Lucas's voice carried a hint of teasing, but his eyes, illuminated by the soft glow of the moonlight, betrayed a deeper curiosity. He stepped closer, the scent of his cologne mingling with the cool night air, filling the space between us with an intoxicating mix of warmth and challenge.

"Not sulking, just... enjoying the view," I replied, trying to maintain my bravado. "This city looks much better from a distance, don't you think?"

"Everything looks better from a distance," he said, leaning on the railing beside me. "Including us." The way he said it sent a ripple of surprise through me. He had a knack for stripping away the layers, revealing the vulnerable truth hidden beneath the surface.

I turned to face him fully, intrigued by the shift in our dynamic. "What do you mean by that?"

He chuckled softly, the sound rich and warm, creating a momentary cocoon between us. "Just that when you're caught up in the chaos of it all, sometimes it's hard to see clearly. It's easy to get lost in the competition, the glitz, and forget what really matters."

"Is that what you do? Get lost in the competition?" I challenged, arching an eyebrow. "I assumed you thrived on it."

His gaze turned serious, an intensity in his eyes that made my heart race. "Maybe I do, but it's exhausting. Sometimes, I wonder if I've built this persona to hide from the things that scare me."

"Scared? Of what? Losing?" My words were laced with playful skepticism, yet I felt a sincerity brewing beneath the surface.

"Of becoming irrelevant. Of being just another face in the crowd." He turned to look at the skyline, as if searching for answers among the stars. "You wouldn't understand."

"Try me," I urged, my voice softer, coaxing him to share more. "You might be surprised."

He sighed, a sound heavy with unspoken fears. "There's a darkness in my past, Emily. It's not something I wear on my sleeve, but it lurks just beneath the surface." He paused, glancing back at me, and I could see the turmoil etched into his features. "It's like the shadows of this city. Beautiful from a distance but hiding secrets that can swallow you whole."

For a moment, the rivalry melted away, leaving just two people standing on a balcony, vulnerable under the vastness of the night sky. I felt a swell of compassion for him, the sharp edges of our playful competition blurring into something more meaningful. "You know, we all have shadows. We all have things that scare us," I said gently. "It's part of being human."

His lips twisted into a half-smile, gratitude flashing in his eyes. "You make it sound so simple."

"It can be," I insisted, my heart racing as I stepped a bit closer. "The trick is to let others see those shadows instead of hiding behind them."

Lucas looked thoughtful, the gears in his mind visibly turning. "Maybe that's why I'm drawn to you," he mused, the spark of connection igniting something unexpected between us. "You're not afraid to be unapologetically yourself."

"Flawed and all?" I teased lightly, desperate to keep the mood from tipping into seriousness. "You should really be more selective about your admirations."

"Who says I'm not?" He met my gaze, his eyes glinting with playful defiance. "After all, it takes one to know one, right?"

A soft laugh escaped my lips, and the moment hung between us, delicate yet charged with a sense of understanding that felt unfamiliar yet welcome. But just as I thought we were reaching a pivotal moment, the abrupt clang of the hotel's grand doors shattered the intimacy. A swarm of our colleagues poured onto the balcony, drinks in hand and laughter echoing into the night.

"Lucas! Emily! Come on, we're about to start the after-party!" one of them shouted, drawing us back into the thrumming heart of the event.

With a reluctant glance, Lucas straightened up, a familiar mask slipping back into place. "Duty calls," he said, his voice laced with a hint of disappointment that mirrored my own.

"Looks like we're back to being rivals," I quipped, trying to rein in the strange connection we had just forged. "Don't think I'll go easy on you just because we shared a moment."

"Wouldn't dream of it," he replied, that trademark smirk returning, his playful bravado at the ready once again.

As we stepped back inside, I felt the weight of unspoken words hanging in the air between us, like an unfinished conversation waiting to be revisited. The ballroom buzzed with laughter and music, the energy electric, but something had shifted in me. No longer just competitors, we were two souls drawn together by our complexities, our vulnerabilities intertwined beneath the sparkling veneer of the evening.

Throughout the night, as we navigated the crowded floor filled with laughter and clinking glasses, every glance, every quip took on a new layer of significance. I was acutely aware of the way he moved through the crowd, a magnetic force, and I couldn't shake the feeling that there was more to uncover beneath our playful banter.

"Do you think anyone noticed?" I asked him later, after one particularly competitive exchange had left us both breathless, the energy in the room shifting as colleagues began to murmur and laugh.

"Not yet, but they will," he replied, the mischief dancing in his eyes. "It's only a matter of time before they realize we're not just sparring partners anymore."

"Maybe it's time to change the game," I suggested, an idea forming in my mind. "What if we team up instead? Show them that rivals can be more than just competition."

His brows shot up, clearly intrigued. "You really think we can pull that off?"

I smiled, a conspiratorial glint lighting up my eyes. "Why not? We can outshine everyone, together."

He chuckled, the warmth of his laughter washing over me like a balm. "Now that sounds like a challenge worth taking. Just know, I won't hold back."

"Neither will I," I shot back, excitement bubbling within me. The night felt like it was spinning toward something new and uncharted, a thrilling promise of what might lie ahead.

In that moment, surrounded by the flickering lights and the vibrant pulse of the evening, I knew that the dance of deception we had been performing together had transformed into a far more intricate and exhilarating choreography. And as we moved forward, I couldn't help but wonder what layers we would uncover next, beneath the surface of our rivalry, and how the shadows of our pasts would entwine with the light of our future.

The energy of the after-party buzzed like a live wire, weaving its way through the room and electrifying the air. As Lucas and I moved seamlessly through the throng, our banter danced on the edge of flirtation and competition. I could feel the eyes of our colleagues watching, a mix of amusement and curiosity swirling in their gazes as they tried to decipher the evolving dynamic between us.

"Alright, partner," I said, raising my glass in a mock toast, "let's show them how a true team operates."

"Team?" Lucas echoed, an eyebrow arched. "Isn't that a bit too... cooperative for you? I thought you thrived on chaos."

"Chaos can be fun, but teamwork can be even more thrilling," I shot back, my heart racing at the possibility of shifting our rivalry into something more collaborative. "Besides, I want to outshine everyone, not just you. I have standards to maintain."

"Standard? Please, you're already on another level," he said, smirking as he took a sip from his glass. "But fine, let's see if we can set a new record for dazzling our colleagues. I'm in."

As we brainstormed ideas, the atmosphere around us shifted, the air thickening with an energy that felt charged. Lucas's presence was magnetic, drawing me closer and igniting a fire within me that I had barely acknowledged before. His laughter was infectious, and with each shared glance, I sensed the rivalry morphing into something altogether different—a thrilling partnership that bore the promise of deeper connections.

"Let's kick things off with the centerpiece," I proposed, motioning to the extravagant floral display at the center of the room. "We can do something outrageous."

"What do you have in mind?" he asked, eyes glinting with mischief.

"Let's turn the flowers into a scavenger hunt. Guests can bid on bouquets, and the ones who find the rare blooms hidden among them get a chance to win a mystery prize," I suggested, feeling a surge of excitement at the idea.

He grinned, his features lighting up. "That's brilliant! But we need something else to really get them hooked."

As we plotted our next moves, the rhythm of the night began to shift once again. Laughter floated in and out like the gentle lapping of waves, and the music pulsed through the crowd, creating an atmosphere thick with anticipation. But just as our plans took shape, a sudden commotion erupted at the entrance, slicing through the revelry.

A woman with striking auburn hair and an air of authority swept into the room, her heels clicking sharply against the polished floor. The chatter stilled, eyes darting toward her as if she were a lighthouse cutting through fog. My pulse quickened as I recognized her—the formidable Veronica Hastings, the chairwoman of the charity we were working for.

"Where's Emily?" she demanded, her voice commanding the room's attention. The silence that followed felt oppressive, a heavy curtain drawn across the festivities.

"I'm here!" I called out, stepping forward, the confidence I'd built up in my partnership with Lucas suddenly feeling fragile.

"Good," she replied, striding towards me, her heels echoing ominously. "We need to talk about the donations. I'm concerned about the final figures."

I forced a smile, trying to maintain my composure. "Of course, everything is on track. We've raised more than last year—"

"That's not enough," she interrupted, her sharp gaze piercing through my bravado. "We need a strong finish. I want this event to make headlines."

I nodded, feeling the pressure rise. "We'll deliver, I promise. Lucas and I have some exciting ideas to keep the momentum going."

Her gaze flicked to Lucas, sizing him up, and I sensed the tension coiling between us. "I hope so. This charity needs more than just a flash; it needs results. If I don't see a significant increase in donations, heads will roll."

As she turned on her heel and strode away, a wave of apprehension washed over me. I had been swept up in the thrill of our partnership with Lucas, and now the stakes felt painfully high. The pressure to not only perform but to impress Veronica was like a vise around my chest, squeezing tighter with each passing second.

"Wow, she really knows how to deflate a mood, huh?" Lucas commented dryly, trying to inject some levity into the moment.

"Tell me about it," I said, my voice tight. "I need to come up with something spectacular. We can't let her down."

"Or let this opportunity slip through our fingers," he added, his tone shifting from playful to serious. "What if we staged a dramatic reveal? Something that highlights not just the donations but the cause itself?"

"A reveal?" I echoed, my mind racing. "You mean like an unveiling?"

"Exactly! We could present a symbolic item representing what we're raising funds for. Something grand, something that captures the heart of the cause," he explained, excitement igniting in his voice.

I nodded, feeling a spark of inspiration. "How about a live art installation? We could have an artist create something on-site, showcasing the power of community and creativity."

Lucas's eyes lit up. "That's brilliant! And we can encourage guests to participate, creating a collaborative piece that reflects the spirit of the night."

"Exactly! It'll draw people in and show them what their contributions mean," I said, enthusiasm bubbling to the surface. "Let's make it a moment they won't forget."

As we discussed the details, our connection deepened, the tension from earlier dissipating into a shared excitement. However, in the back of my mind lingered the shadow of Veronica's expectations, gnawing at my confidence.

The rest of the night flowed seamlessly, filled with laughter and creativity as we worked together to bring our vision to life. We buzzed around the venue, arranging the space, gathering materials, and rallying the guests with our newfound sense of teamwork.

As we approached the final stretch, I caught a glimpse of Lucas watching me with a mix of admiration and something deeper, something that sent butterflies fluttering wildly in my stomach.

"You know," he said, stepping close, "I never expected this night to turn out like it did. Working together like this... it feels good."

"It really does," I replied, my heart racing as our eyes met. "I think we make a pretty good team."

The moment lingered, filled with unspoken possibilities, until the lights dimmed slightly, signaling the start of our big reveal. I glanced at Lucas, a rush of adrenaline coursing through me.

"Ready?" I asked, my voice barely above a whisper.

"Ready," he replied, a confident smile breaking across his face.

We moved to the front, and I took a deep breath, ready to captivate our audience with the culmination of our hard work. But just as I opened my mouth to speak, the doors burst open again, this time with more urgency.

A man in a crisp suit rushed in, eyes wide with panic. "Veronica! We have a problem!"

My stomach dropped, the festive energy plunging into a void of uncertainty. As whispers surged through the crowd, I exchanged a glance with Lucas, the thrill of victory suddenly slipping from our grasp.

"What now?" I muttered, a feeling of dread curling in my gut.

"We need to find out," he said, determination flashing in his eyes.

The man continued speaking urgently to Veronica, and as I stepped closer, trying to catch snippets of their conversation, the world around us faded. My mind raced with questions. What could possibly be wrong? The night had been going so well.

But the way Veronica's face paled and the rising tension in the room told me we were on the brink of something unforeseen, a storm brewing just beyond the horizon. And as the atmosphere thickened with uncertainty, I realized our night of celebration had morphed into a night of revelation, one that could change everything we thought we knew.

Chapter 6: The Tipping Point

The fluorescent lights hummed overhead, casting a sterile glow over the cluttered office, but all I could feel was the thrum of impending chaos in my chest. The deadline for our project loomed like a storm cloud, threatening to break at any moment. My fingers danced nervously over the keyboard, the clatter of keys a frenetic symphony underscoring my anxiety. I had always thrived under pressure, but today felt different. Today, as I poured over the last-minute revisions, the air was thick with the weight of secrets.

Nathan was sprawled across the desk opposite mine, his usual smirk replaced by an intensity that made my heart skip a beat. He was the kind of man who could command a room with just a glance, his dark hair tousled, eyes glinting with mischief. But today, there was an edge to him, something lurking beneath the surface that I couldn't quite place. "You look like you've seen a ghost," he quipped, breaking the tension. "Or maybe just a particularly bad spreadsheet."

"Very funny," I shot back, trying to inject some levity into the situation. Yet, I could sense he was just as unnerved as I was. The project had become a whirlwind, a blend of long nights and caffeine-fueled brainstorming sessions, and it was taking a toll on both of us. "We've got more pressing matters than your attempts at stand-up comedy, Nathan."

He leaned forward, elbows resting on the desk, and narrowed his eyes, his gaze sharp as a knife. "Maybe I'm just trying to lighten the mood. You've been so serious lately, and it's killing the creativity." There was a teasing lilt in his voice, but the tension lingered, a taut string ready to snap.

"Creativity?" I laughed, but it came out as a half-hearted attempt to dismiss the rising unease. "I'd say we're teetering on the brink of a disaster, not a breakthrough. If we don't get this proposal together by end of the day—"

"Then we'll figure it out," he interrupted, his tone abruptly serious. "It's what we do, right? We're good at turning chaos into something beautiful." He leaned back, a glimmer of confidence flashing across his face, but beneath that bravado, I caught a flicker of vulnerability. For a moment, I wanted to believe him, to bask in the idea that everything would turn out fine. But the truth was, I couldn't shake the feeling that something was about to change, and not just for our project.

As I turned back to my screen, a ping echoed in the air. My email had dinged, and I glanced down, curiosity piqued. It was from an unknown sender. With a mixture of apprehension and intrigue, I opened the message, the words swimming before my eyes like an ominous warning: You need to know the truth about Nathan.

My heart raced, adrenaline coursing through my veins. Who was this person? What truth could possibly be lurking in Nathan's past? Just when I thought the day couldn't get any more chaotic, a whole new layer of uncertainty descended. I shot a quick glance at Nathan, who was obliviously scrolling through his phone, his brows furrowed in concentration. The easy banter that had just flowed between us felt like a distant memory, replaced by a heavy, suffocating silence.

I took a deep breath, trying to steady my nerves. The email could be a prank, a cruel joke by someone who thrived on stirring trouble, but the pit in my stomach told me otherwise. I had to know more. "Nathan," I began, my voice unsteady. "We need to talk."

"About what?" He looked up, brow raised, the hint of a challenge in his tone.

I hesitated, torn between my growing feelings and the need to protect myself. "About... us." I didn't know how to phrase the whirlwind of thoughts swirling in my mind, the emotions battling for dominance.

His expression shifted, a mix of surprise and curiosity, and he set his phone down, leaning forward as if he sensed the weight of my words. "Us? What do you mean?"

"Your past. I received an email... someone seems to think I should know more about it."

Nathan's expression hardened, his playfulness evaporating like mist in the morning sun. "What did it say?"

I hesitated again, not wanting to lay out the jagged pieces of a puzzle that I hadn't yet fully deciphered. "Just that there are things you haven't shared with me."

A flicker of anger flashed across his features, but just as quickly, it was replaced by something softer, more vulnerable. "Look, I—"

Before he could finish, the office door swung open with a bang, and our manager entered, a storm of frantic energy. "Guys, we have a problem!"

The interruption shattered the moment, but the unresolved tension hung between us like a fragile thread. I exchanged a glance with Nathan, and in that instant, I knew we were caught in a web far more complicated than a mere project deadline. The stakes were rising, and we were both part of a dangerous game neither of us had anticipated.

"Let's handle this, and then we can talk," Nathan said, his voice steady despite the chaos encircling us. I nodded, even as the lingering question of his past nagged at me, pulling me deeper into the vortex of uncertainty.

As we jumped into action, the earlier lightness faded into the background, replaced by the heavy anticipation of what lay ahead. The office transformed into a battleground, filled with papers flying and frantic discussions, but beneath it all, I felt the undeniable pull towards Nathan. In the heart of the turmoil, amid deadlines and unspoken truths, I was falling for him—an undeniable connection that was as thrilling as it was terrifying.

The chaos swirled around me like autumn leaves caught in a whirlwind, each gust threatening to sweep me off my feet. I navigated the cluttered office, adrenaline sharpening my senses. Papers flitted through the air like startled birds, and voices rose above the low thrum of fluorescent lights buzzing overhead. Nathan, ever the master of distraction, was engaged in a heated discussion with our manager, his hand gesturing animatedly as he fought to calm the storm of panic that had erupted.

"Just breathe, folks! We've been in worse situations," Nathan urged, his voice a steady anchor amid the tumult. But I could see the tension etched in the corners of his mouth, the way his jaw tightened as he spoke. I wanted to reach out, to ground him just as he was trying to ground everyone else, but the nagging email in my inbox pulled at my thoughts like a relentless tide.

"Look, we can fix this," Nathan continued, his tone softening as he directed his attention toward the team. "If we all pitch in and focus, we'll make this deadline." His confidence radiated, and for a fleeting moment, I felt that sense of camaraderie that often emerged during crises. But as I joined the fray, trying to sift through the panic to find solutions, my mind flickered back to that ominous message. It was like a puzzle with missing pieces, and the more I thought about it, the more I felt the ground shift beneath my feet.

As we split off into smaller groups to tackle the various issues, I found myself working closely with Clara, our graphics guru. Her vibrant hair was tied into a messy bun, paint-stained fingers flying over her tablet as she whipped up visuals to accompany our pitch. "What's eating you?" she asked, glancing up from her work, perceptive as ever. "You look like you just saw a ghost—or worse, your ex."

"Nothing like that," I replied, forcing a smile. "Just... office drama. Nathan's got this air of mystery about him today."

Clara raised an eyebrow, her expression shifting from curiosity to mischief. "Oh, Nathan? He's like an enigma wrapped in a designer suit. What did you uncover?"

I hesitated, weighing my words. The truth about Nathan was like a ticking clock, its echoing chimes reminding me that time was running out. "I got an email that suggested there's more to his past. It's probably nothing, just someone trying to stir the pot."

"Or it's everything," she shot back, grinning. "That's the best part about office romances—there's always a secret lurking beneath the surface. You're just one 'who is he really?' away from a total soap opera."

"Great, just what I need—a romantic subplot with all the drama," I scoffed, but a flicker of excitement danced within me. Clara was right; the more I thought about it, the more I was drawn to the complexity of Nathan. There was a thrilling tension between us, ignited not just by the project but by the undercurrent of mystery. I was beginning to wonder if uncovering the truth would bring us closer or tear us apart.

As the hours ticked by, our team worked feverishly, the atmosphere charged with energy and purpose. Even in the midst of chaos, I caught Nathan's eye, and he offered a slight nod, a silent acknowledgment of our shared struggle. My heart quickened, a betraying flutter of warmth spreading through me. Was I really falling for him, or was it merely the thrill of our precarious situation?

Just when I thought I had compartmentalized my swirling emotions, the email pinged in my inbox again, this time more insistent. I couldn't ignore it. "Clara, can you hold down the fort for a second? I need to check something."

She waved me off, her focus back on her screen. "Go, sleuth! Get that gossip!"

I stepped away from the frenetic energy of our workspace and into the quieter corridor, the sound of muted conversations fading behind me. I opened the email, heart racing as I read the cryptic message again: You need to know the truth about Nathan. This could change everything. My fingers trembled slightly over the keys, and I felt the weight of those words pressing down on me.

Before I could second-guess myself, I hit reply, a sense of urgency pushing me forward. "Who are you? What do you know about him?"

Just as I clicked send, a shadow fell over me. I turned, startled to find Nathan standing there, his expression a blend of concern and curiosity. "What's going on? You disappeared," he said, his voice low, a softness that disarmed me.

"I just—needed a moment," I stammered, the email I'd just sent hovering in the back of my mind like an unwanted specter. "You know how it is. The deadline stress and all."

He studied me, his brow furrowing. "You don't seem like you're handling it well. Is it really just about the project?"

The question hit harder than I expected, forcing me to confront the whirlwind of emotions swirling within me. "There's a lot at stake here, Nathan. I've put my heart into this project, and the thought of failing... it's terrifying."

"And if I told you that I understand that fear?" He stepped closer, the intensity of his gaze making it difficult to breathe. "I've got my own demons to battle. You know that, right?"

"Do I?" The challenge was unwittingly sharp in my voice, and I regretted it the moment I saw the flicker of pain cross his features. "You're the one who's kept your past under wraps. If we're going to get through this, I need you to be honest with me."

His expression shifted, revealing the weight of something unspoken. "I'm not hiding from you; I just... it's complicated. There are things you wouldn't understand."

The tension in the air thickened, charged with unresolved feelings and hidden truths. My mind raced with possibilities. What if the email was true? What if there was something about Nathan that I didn't know—something that could change everything between us?

Before I could voice my concerns, his phone buzzed, cutting through the moment. He pulled it out, glancing at the screen. His face paled, a quick flash of anxiety crossing his features. "I need to take this," he muttered, stepping back, the connection between us fraying like an old rope.

"Sure," I replied, my heart sinking. As he walked away, I felt the weight of uncertainty settle over me like a cloak. The world had shifted again, and I was left grappling with questions I didn't have answers for.

The rest of the day unfolded in a blur of activity, but my thoughts remained tangled around Nathan and the impending revelation about his past. As the clock ticked down to our deadline, I felt the tension thickening, each second drumming a relentless beat in my chest. The deeper I delved into my feelings for him, the more afraid I became of what lay beneath the surface. The game was shifting, the stakes climbing higher, and as the pieces of our lives intertwined, I couldn't help but wonder if we would emerge victorious or if we were destined to be caught in the crossfire of secrets and betrayal.

The air in the office had thickened with tension, the deadline looming like a thunderhead ready to burst. I sat at my desk, glancing at the clock as if willing the hands to move faster. Each tick echoed in my ears, reminding me of how precariously close we were to disaster. Yet, even amid the frantic energy of my colleagues, my thoughts were tangled around Nathan, his mysterious past, and the cryptic email that had unsettled me to my core.

I glanced up, catching Nathan's eye across the room. He was deep in conversation, his brows knitted as he strategized with Clara about the visuals she was crafting. Despite the surrounding chaos, he exuded an undeniable charm, but there was a shadow behind his smile that gnawed at me. I wanted to trust him, to believe in the connection we shared, but every moment of doubt felt like a chasm opening between us, threatening to swallow me whole.

"Hey, earth to my favorite workaholic!" Clara's voice jolted me back to reality. "You've been staring at Nathan like he's the last slice of pizza at a party. Care to share?"

"Maybe I was just pondering life's mysteries," I replied, attempting a nonchalant smile, but the corners of my mouth betrayed me, twitching upward. "Or, you know, the imminent collapse of our project."

"Life's mysteries, huh?" She raised an eyebrow, smirking. "I can think of one mystery you might want to solve before our project gets dragged down with it."

"Clara!" I exclaimed, feigning outrage. "We're supposed to be focusing on work, not my budding romantic interests."

"Budding?" she snorted, her laughter ringing like a bell. "That sounds like a delicate flower. More like a full-blown greenhouse with all the drama attached."

As I rolled my eyes, a familiar, fiery sensation ignited in my chest, one that had grown too familiar when it came to Nathan. I stole another glance his way, watching him lean in closer to Clara, their laughter ringing in the air. It struck me then that while I was caught up in my worries, they were actively collaborating, making the best of our dwindling time. But the moment felt almost tainted, and I couldn't shake the feeling that there was more to Nathan's charm than met the eye.

"Do you think Nathan's ever going to let anyone in?" I blurted, the words escaping before I could rein them back in. "I mean, does he have a past we should know about?"

Clara's expression shifted to one of consideration. "With guys like Nathan, it's usually a rollercoaster. But the ride can be worth it, right? You should just ask him."

Before I could respond, Nathan approached, his gaze lingering on me with an intensity that made my heart race. "Can we talk?" he asked, his voice low, a hint of urgency threading through the words.

"Uh, sure," I managed, my pulse quickening as I followed him to a quieter corner of the office, the world around us fading into a blur. "What's up?"

He leaned against the wall, his body language shifting from confident to vulnerable in the span of a heartbeat. "I received a text earlier, and I need to tell you something before this gets out of hand."

My stomach twisted into knots, dread pooling at the pit of my belly. "What kind of text?"

"It's about the email you got," he said, his tone grave. "I didn't want to involve you in my mess, but it looks like I don't have a choice anymore."

The world spun, the air thickening with unspoken truths. "You mean it's connected to you?"

He nodded, the weight of his admission hanging heavily between us. "Someone from my past has resurfaced, and they know things—things I thought were buried for good."

A myriad of emotions flooded through me—anger, fear, and something that resembled concern. "Why didn't you tell me before? Why keep me in the dark?"

"I was trying to protect you," he replied, his voice strained. "I didn't want to drag you into this. It's not just my past; it's dangerous."

"Dangerous?" I echoed, my heart racing. "How dangerous?"

His gaze hardened, the lightness that usually danced in his eyes extinguished. "You have no idea what I'm dealing with. This person—let's just say they have a knack for causing chaos."

Just then, the office phone rang, shattering the moment. Nathan stepped back, frustration flickering across his features. "I have to take this," he said tersely, his tone leaving no room for argument. "Just... stay safe, alright?"

He turned and strode away, the tension between us unresolved, a heavy door left ajar with shadows lurking behind it. I stood there, my heart pounding in my chest, caught between the need to confront him and the urgency of our deadline.

When I returned to my desk, Clara was waiting, her eyes alight with curiosity. "What was that about? You two looked like you were about to star in your own drama."

"Just a little... crisis management," I replied, my voice barely above a whisper. "Nathan's got some baggage he didn't mention."

Her expression shifted, sympathy etched across her face. "You're worried about him. But you also need to protect yourself, you know?"

"I know," I said, the weight of her words settling over me. "But it's complicated. He's not just a co-worker anymore. There's something about him, something that pulls me in."

"Just don't lose yourself in it. Stay grounded," she advised, her voice laced with concern. "You can't forget that this is a workplace, and feelings can complicate everything."

I nodded, but deep down, I felt the gravity of our connection—a thrilling, dangerous pull that ignited something within me. Just then, another email pinged in my inbox, slicing through the tension like a knife. I hesitated before opening it, the familiar sense of dread creeping back. The message was from the same anonymous sender, and as I read the words, my breath caught in my throat.

I hope you're ready for the truth. Nathan's past is closer than you think. Trust me, it's about to get real. Meet me at the old diner on Main Street. You have until midnight to make a choice.

My heart raced, a chilling wave of apprehension coursing through me. This wasn't just about our project anymore; this was a countdown, a threat dangling precariously over everything I held dear. I glanced at the clock—less than two hours remained. My mind swirled with possibilities, fear intermingling with a strange exhilaration.

I needed to confront Nathan, to uncover the truth behind his guarded facade, but the clock was ticking. With every second that passed, the shadows lengthened, and I could feel the ground shifting beneath me. This wasn't just a game anymore; it was a high-stakes gamble, and the stakes were rising. Would I unravel the truth, or would I find myself trapped in a web of secrets far darker than I ever anticipated?

As I pondered my next move, a familiar voice called out behind me, and I turned, my heart racing at the sight of Nathan standing at my side. The resolve in his eyes was unmistakable, but so was the uncertainty, and in that moment, I knew we were on the cusp of something monumental—something that could change everything. Just then, the lights flickered ominously, casting a shadow over us both, and I couldn't shake the feeling that we were not alone in this office. Something was lurking just beyond the edge of our understanding, waiting for the perfect moment to strike.

Chapter 7: Torn Apart

The air was thick with tension, a suffocating mixture of unspoken words and half-formed accusations, as I faced Nathan in the dim light of my living room. Shadows danced across the walls, flickering like the doubts swirling in my mind. I could feel the heat of my anger coursing through me, a raw energy that begged to be unleashed. "You can't just brush this off like it's nothing!" I said, my voice rising in volume and intensity. It was a reflex, a desperate attempt to claw back some semblance of control.

Nathan leaned against the doorway, arms crossed, his brow furrowed in that way that always made me feel like he was peeling away my layers, exposing my vulnerabilities for everyone to see. "I'm not brushing anything off, Maya. You're overreacting."

"Overreacting? Really?" I laughed, a sharp sound that surprised even me. "Is that your go-to response? Because let me tell you, it's not working." Each word felt like a pebble hurled at a glass window, threatening to shatter the fragile peace we'd constructed around us.

He pushed away from the door, taking a step closer, the air between us crackling with an energy that was both intoxicating and infuriating. "You don't understand what I'm dealing with. You have no idea what's really going on."

"No idea?" My voice dripped with sarcasm, and I took a step forward, closing the gap. "You've been hiding everything from me, Nathan. If I'm supposed to be your partner, then I deserve the truth." The way his expression shifted—a mixture of frustration and something softer, almost pained—only ignited my resolve further.

"You think it's easy for me to talk about my past?" His eyes flickered with something raw, something buried deep that I had only glimpsed before. "You think I enjoy keeping secrets?"

"Secrets?" I scoffed, waving a hand dismissively. "This isn't just about secrets anymore. It's about trust. Do you even realize how much I've shared with you? And yet you stand there, guarding your heart like it's some ancient treasure."

"Maybe it is," he shot back, his voice low, but the intensity was palpable. "Maybe I don't want to hand over the keys to a kingdom that might crumble at any moment."

His words were like a dagger, slicing through the air, leaving behind a gaping wound. I could feel my heart pounding in my chest, the weight of his fear pressing down on me. "You think I'm going to run away just because things get tough? I thought we were in this together!"

"Together? What does that even mean if you can't accept my past?" The sharpness of his words was matched only by the vulnerability in his gaze, and for a fleeting moment, I felt a pang of empathy for the walls he'd built around himself.

But anger was a potent drug, and I was high on it, addicted to the rush of standing my ground. "You know what? Maybe I should just take your advice and stop trying to pry open those gates," I spat, my voice trembling with the force of my emotions. "Maybe I should just walk away and let you keep your precious secrets."

And just like that, the words were out, stark and unyielding. I turned on my heel, each step echoing in the charged silence that followed. The door creaked as I flung it open, the cool night air washing over me like a refreshing wave. The world outside was dark, the streetlamps casting a yellow glow that felt both inviting and ominous.

As I stepped into the night, the reality of my actions crashed over me like a cold wave. My heart raced—not just from the argument, but from the unsettling awareness that I was on the brink of something I couldn't fully understand. I was angry, yes, but beneath that anger was a layer of confusion and hurt that gnawed at my insides.

I needed comfort, a familiar embrace that could help me piece together the shards of my shattered emotions. My friends had been there for me before, their laughter and easy banter a balm for my wounds. I pulled out my phone, my fingers trembling as I typed a quick message to Lily, asking her to meet me at our usual spot, the cozy café down the block.

The street felt eerily quiet as I walked, the echoes of our argument trailing behind me like shadows. Each step felt heavy with doubt, the weight of Nathan's words lingering in my mind. Did he really believe that sharing his past would somehow make me walk away? I was strong enough to face the truth, wasn't I? But the deeper question loomed, one I couldn't shake: how could I stand by a man whose life felt like it was spiraling out of control?

The café's warm glow beckoned as I approached, the comforting aroma of coffee enveloping me like a soft blanket. Inside, the chatter of patrons blended with the clinking of cups, a symphony of everyday life that felt achingly normal. I spotted Lily in our usual corner, her bright smile cutting through my turmoil like a beacon.

"Maya!" she exclaimed, waving me over with an enthusiasm that nearly knocked the wind out of me. "You look like you've been through a tornado."

"More like a hurricane," I muttered, sliding into the seat opposite her. "It was bad, Lils. Really bad."

She leaned in, her brow furrowing with concern. "What happened? Did you guys have another one of those talks?"

I sighed, rubbing my temples as I recounted the heated exchange, my emotions spilling out in a chaotic jumble. "He just won't open up, and it's driving me crazy. I feel like I'm on the outside looking in, and I don't know if I can keep doing this."

"Maybe he's scared," Lily offered gently, her gaze steady. "Sometimes people think that keeping their past hidden will protect the ones they love."

"Protect them from what?" I asked, the frustration bubbling to the surface again. "The truth? We're supposed to be a team, not a collection of secrets."

"That's fair," she conceded, "but you know, sometimes people need a little push to let those walls down. It's not always easy to show vulnerability, especially when it feels like it could destroy everything."

Her words hung in the air, heavy and laden with truth. The ache in my chest shifted, morphing into a tumult of uncertainty and longing. I could feel the edges of my resolve beginning to fray as I pondered what it really meant to trust someone with your heart, to share the weight of your past with another soul.

As I sat across from Lily, the warmth of friendship offered a momentary reprieve from the storm swirling inside me. But even as she spoke, I felt that familiar pang of doubt creeping back in, gnawing at my thoughts like a hungry beast. What if Nathan's past was too much to bear? What if my desire to uncover the truth led us both to a cliff from which we might not return?

The café bustled around me, a soothing hum that contrasted sharply with the chaos whirling in my mind. I took a deep breath, inhaling the rich aroma of freshly brewed coffee mingling with the sweetness of pastries. Lily's animated chatter filled the space between us, but my thoughts were elsewhere, spiraling through the remnants of my argument with Nathan. Every sip of my caramel macchiato felt like a distraction, a way to quiet the noise in my head, but I knew it wouldn't last.

Lily leaned in closer, her eyes sparkling with the kind of concern that only true friends can muster. "So, what's next? Are you going to talk to him again?" She nibbled on a croissant, crumbs dotting her lips, but her expression was serious.

I shrugged, trying to play it cool. "I don't know. It's exhausting, Lils. I want to help him, but he makes it so damn hard." My frustration spilled over, and I could feel the familiar heat rising in my cheeks. "Why can't he see that I'm not going anywhere? Why can't he just trust me?"

"Maybe it's not about you," she offered gently, pausing to wipe her hands on a napkin. "Some people have a hard time letting others in, especially if they've been hurt before. It's like trying to break through a brick wall with a feather."

"Great," I replied dryly, "so I need a sledgehammer? Should I just march over and knock down the walls?"

Lily laughed, a bright sound that sliced through my mood like a knife through butter. "Only if you're prepared for the debris. Relationships can be messy, you know? Not everyone comes with a manual."

"I feel like I need one," I admitted, taking another sip of my drink, savoring the way the warmth spread through me. "How do I even know if I can trust him? What if his secrets are too big to handle?"

"Sometimes, trust is a leap of faith. You have to believe that the person you're with will catch you, even if they're struggling to hold on to themselves." Her words hung in the air, weighty and profound, and I found myself contemplating their truth.

The conversation swirled around us, voices rising and falling like the tide, but I felt tethered to my own thoughts. Nathan's past loomed over me like a thundercloud, threatening to burst at any moment. Just as I was beginning to wrap my mind around it, my phone buzzed, startling me out of my reverie.

I glanced down, my heart skipping a beat as I saw Nathan's name flashing on the screen. My stomach twisted as I contemplated answering. What could he possibly want? Hadn't we just torn each other apart?

"Are you going to get that?" Lily asked, arching an eyebrow.

I hesitated, the phone vibrating ominously in my hand. "What if it's just him wanting to argue again?"

"Or maybe it's him finally ready to talk," she replied, her tone encouraging. "You'll never know unless you pick it up."

With a deep breath, I swiped to answer, my pulse quickening. "Hello?"

"Maya," Nathan's voice came through, low and tentative, wrapping around me like a favorite sweater. "Can we talk?"

I bit my lip, torn between the desire to hear him out and the instinct to protect my heart from more hurt. "Now? I'm kind of busy."

"Please," he pleaded, and something in his tone made me pause. "I just... I need to explain."

The sincerity in his voice was a beacon, pulling me in. "Okay," I found myself saying, before I could second-guess myself. "Where?"

"Can you meet me at the park? The one by the river?"

I agreed, and after hanging up, I felt a mix of dread and anticipation bubbling within me. "He wants to talk," I told Lily, watching her expression morph from curiosity to concern.

"Be careful," she warned, her eyes narrowing slightly. "You know how volatile things are right now. Just... keep your guard up, okay?"

"Yeah," I replied, but deep down, I felt the weight of uncertainty pressing on my chest.

The walk to the park was almost surreal, the world outside bustling with life while I felt suspended in my own emotional quagmire. The leaves rustled softly in the cool autumn breeze, painting the ground in hues of orange and gold, but I barely noticed the beauty around me. All I could think about was what Nathan might say, and whether the truths he revealed would help or hurt me more.

When I arrived at the park, Nathan was already there, standing by the edge of the river. His back was to me, broad shoulders tense, hands shoved deep into his pockets. I hesitated for a moment, taking in the way he looked so lost in thought, as if he were battling demons only he could see.

"Maya," he said without turning around, his voice barely above a whisper. "Thank you for coming."

I approached cautiously, the ground crunching beneath my feet as I stepped into the space beside him. "What's going on?" I asked, trying to keep my voice steady, despite the uncertainty churning in my gut.

He finally turned to face me, his expression a mixture of vulnerability and resolve. "I've been an idiot, trying to keep you at arm's length when all I really want is for you to be here with me. I need to be honest about my past. I should have done this a long time ago."

"Okay," I said slowly, unsure of how to respond. "What do you need to tell me?"

His gaze faltered, then drifted back to the river, the sunlight glinting off the water like scattered diamonds. "It's about my family. About what happened before I moved here."

The words hung in the air, heavy with unspoken pain. I could feel my heart race as he took a deep breath, gathering the fragments of his story. "I was involved in some... not-so-great things. My family had some issues that went deeper than I ever let on."

"Like what?" I prompted gently, sensing the struggle within him.

"Criminal stuff, mostly," he admitted, his voice cracking slightly. "I got wrapped up in it, and when things went south, I decided I needed a clean break. So I left everything behind. My family, my past. It was my only option."

The confession hit me like a slap. I stared at him, trying to process what he was saying. "You mean you were in trouble?"

"Not just trouble," he said, shaking his head, frustration flaring in his eyes. "I was involved with people who did things I'm not proud of. I didn't want that life anymore, but it's like shadows from my past keep creeping back in."

"Why didn't you tell me?" I asked, my voice barely above a whisper. The revelation spun in my mind, weaving together my feelings of betrayal and understanding.

"I didn't want you to see me that way," he said, anguish coloring his words. "I wanted you to see the man I'm trying to be, not the boy who ran away from his family and his mistakes. I thought if I kept it hidden, I could protect you."

"Protect me?" I echoed, incredulous. "By lying to me?"

Nathan closed his eyes, running a hand through his hair in frustration. "I see how that sounds, but I thought it was for the best. I thought I could handle it myself."

A wave of anger surged within me, hot and suffocating. "Handle what? The fact that you've been living with these ghosts? You're not alone in this, Nathan! I want to help you, but I can't if you keep shutting me out."

He looked at me, a flicker of something in his eyes—regret, perhaps? "I know. I see that now. But I've been scared, Maya. Scared that if I let you in, I'll drag you down with me."

"Do you honestly think I'd walk away just because things get complicated?" I shot back, my voice steadier now. "I'm here, aren't I? But I can't do this alone. You have to let me in."

His gaze held mine, the tension between us electric, crackling with the weight of unspoken emotions. The world around us faded, and in that moment, I realized that our connection ran deeper than the surface chaos. There was love there, threaded with pain and uncertainty, and it was stronger than the shadows threatening to engulf us.

"Then help me," he said finally, his voice low and sincere. "Help me find a way out of this mess. I don't want to lose you."

And just like that, the conversation shifted. The air around us seemed to brighten, filled with the possibility of something more, something that transcended our fears. I could feel the walls I had built around my heart begin to crack, and beneath them lay a willingness to embrace the unknown. Together, we could navigate the storms ahead, our paths entwined like the branches of the trees lining the riverbank.

The river flowed lazily beside us, the water glinting in the afternoon sun like shards of glass, reflecting the tumult of emotions swirling in my heart. Nathan's gaze was steady, but I could see the storm brewing beneath the surface. The weight of his confession hung between us, dense and heavy, as if we stood at the edge of a precipice, teetering on the brink of something monumental.

"I never wanted to drag you into this mess," he said, his voice barely above a whisper. "I thought I could leave it behind, but it seems the past doesn't forget so easily."

"Neither do I," I replied, my own voice firmer than I felt. "But you're not alone in this, Nathan. We can face it together. But you have to let me in."

He nodded slowly, the corners of his mouth twitching into a fragile smile that didn't quite reach his eyes. "I want that. I really do."

But as he spoke, a sudden chill swept through the air, stealing the warmth from our shared moment. I instinctively pulled my cardigan tighter around me, feeling an unease creep in, a sense of foreboding that something was still amiss.

"Are you sure there's nothing else you're keeping from me?" I pressed, searching his eyes for the truth. "Because if there is, you need to tell me now."

The flicker of uncertainty that crossed his face was enough to send my heart racing. "Maya, I swear I'm not trying to hide anything from you."

"Then why do I feel like there's a storm cloud looming just out of sight?" I challenged, the frustration bubbling back to the surface.

Before he could respond, a sudden shout echoed across the park, breaking through the tension that wrapped around us. "Nathan!" A voice boomed, sharp and commanding, cutting through the calm like a knife.

We both turned to see a tall figure striding towards us, his demeanor radiating authority. I recognized him instantly—Detective Harris, the officer who had been a constant presence in Nathan's life, a shadow looming over everything he tried to rebuild.

"Detective," Nathan said, his posture stiffening as he faced the man. "What are you doing here?"

"Just came to have a word with you," Harris replied, his tone all business, his gaze shifting to me with a flicker of curiosity. "And it seems you have company."

"I'm fine, Detective," Nathan shot back, his irritation palpable. "We were just talking."

"Yeah, I can see that," the detective replied, unimpressed. "But I need to speak with you about the investigation. It's time we had a serious discussion."

My stomach twisted at the word "investigation." The implication hung heavily in the air, and I could feel a knot forming in my throat. "What investigation?" I asked, my voice tinged with unease.

Harris glanced at me before turning back to Nathan. "You know exactly what I'm referring to. Your past is catching up with you faster than you think."

The weight of his words pressed down on me, suffocating and chilling. "Nathan, what is he talking about?" I demanded, my heart racing as I searched his face for answers.

"It's nothing," Nathan insisted, but his voice lacked conviction. The way his eyes darted between Harris and me told a different story, one filled with secrets and unspoken truths that felt like a dam about to burst.

"Nothing?" I echoed, incredulous. "You call this nothing?"

"Listen, Maya," Nathan said, taking a step closer to me, his expression desperate. "You don't need to worry about this. It's just some old business that has nothing to do with you."

"Old business?" I repeated, a bitter laugh escaping my lips. "Nathan, this is a police detective. How can you possibly think I'm not going to worry?"

Harris interjected, his patience clearly thinning. "This is serious, Nathan. We've received new information regarding your case. It's time to come clean."

A muscle in Nathan's jaw tightened as he looked back at the detective, and I could see the conflict raging within him. "What information?" he asked, his voice suddenly low, cautious.

"Enough to warrant a further investigation," Harris replied, his tone matter-of-fact. "And if you're not careful, this could escalate quickly. You need to be ready for what's coming."

The words hung in the air like a guillotine waiting to drop, and my heart sank further into despair. I looked at Nathan, and for the first time, I saw the fear etched across his features, a stark contrast to the bravado he often wore like armor. "What does that mean for us?" I whispered, barely able to voice the question as my mind raced with possibilities.

Nathan opened his mouth to respond, but before he could say anything, his phone buzzed in his pocket, cutting through the tension like an unexpected clap of thunder. He pulled it out, his eyes scanning the screen before they widened in shock.

"What is it?" I asked, my heart pounding as I reached out to him. "Is it about the investigation?"

He didn't answer, his face going pale as he continued reading whatever message had just come through. My stomach twisted tighter, a sense of dread washing over me. "Nathan, please talk to me."

"I... I need to go," he finally said, his voice shaky. "Something's happened."

"Go?" I echoed, disbelief flooding my system. "You can't just leave! Not now, not when—"

"Trust me," he interrupted, the urgency in his tone cutting through my protests. "I'll explain everything, but I need to deal with this first."

Before I could respond, he turned and began walking away, each step feeling like a betrayal. "Nathan, wait!" I called after him, panic rising in my chest. But he didn't look back, disappearing down the path, leaving me standing there with the detective, my heart in my throat.

"Why does it feel like I'm losing him?" I muttered, a surge of frustration boiling within me.

Harris regarded me for a moment, his expression softening slightly. "He's in a tough spot. The past has a way of resurfacing when you least expect it. Just keep your head down, and don't get involved in whatever is about to unfold."

"Get involved?" I scoffed, frustration boiling over. "I'm already involved! I care about him!"

"That's exactly why you need to be careful," he replied, his tone suddenly stern. "Sometimes, the people we love can lead us into darkness we never anticipated. Just remember that."

I stared at him, my emotions in turmoil, caught between anger and fear. "You think I can just walk away?"

"No," he said, his eyes narrowing slightly. "But you should be prepared for what might come next."

Just then, Nathan's phone buzzed again, and this time, it rang loudly in the silence. I instinctively reached for it, my heart racing. "What if it's him? What if he needs me?"

Harris shook his head, stepping closer to me. "You shouldn't."

Ignoring him, I swiped to answer, my voice trembling. "Nathan?"

Silence greeted me, and I felt a chill creep down my spine. "Hello?" I repeated, but just as I was about to hang up, a voice crackled through the line, cold and foreboding.

"Maya? You need to listen carefully. Nathan's in trouble, and time is running out."

The world around me blurred, my heart racing as the implications of those words crashed over me. "What do you mean?" I managed to stammer, panic surging through me.

"Just stay away from him. Trust me, you don't want to get involved in this."

And then, the line went dead. I stared at the phone, my heart pounding in my ears, the air around me growing thick with tension. I felt the ground shift beneath my feet, the fear of the unknown wrapping around me like a vise, squeezing tighter with each breath.

"Who was that?" Harris demanded, his eyes narrowing as he took a step closer, sensing the shift in the atmosphere.

"I don't know!" I cried, my voice rising in desperation. "But they said Nathan is in trouble!"

Before I could process the weight of those words, my phone buzzed again, this time with a message from Nathan. I opened it, my heart pounding as I read the words that appeared on the screen, chilling me to the bone.

"I'm sorry, Maya. I have to protect you, even if it means leaving you behind."

And just like that, my world unraveled as a deep, gnawing fear took hold, a feeling that I was about to be dragged into a storm I wasn't prepared to face.

Chapter 8: In the Eye of the Storm

I could feel the weight of the moment pressing down on me, each breath heavy with the unspoken words that danced just beyond the reach of my lips. Nathan stood before me, his dark eyes swirling with a tempest of emotions that mirrored the storm brewing outside. Rain lashed against the windows, each drop a reminder of the chaos encroaching on our fragile world. It was as if the universe had conspired to match our internal turmoil with the ferocity of the elements.

"Do you even realize what's at stake here?" I challenged, my voice sharper than I intended. I watched as he ran a hand through his tousled hair, the movement both frustrated and exasperated. I wanted to reach out, to reassure him that I was on his side, yet the fear of what lay ahead held me firmly in place.

"I'm trying to protect you," he said, the weight of his words resonating like thunder in the distance. There was a sincerity in his tone that made my heart stutter, a reminder that beneath the bravado, Nathan was just a man trying to navigate a labyrinth of shadows.

"Protect me? Or keep me in the dark?" I stepped closer, feeling the heat radiating from his body, the proximity amplifying the tension. "What happened with your past? Why can't you just tell me?"

His jaw tightened, and I saw the flicker of something—guilt, perhaps? "Because it's not just my past anymore. It's ours, whether you want it to be or not."

That struck a chord. The very idea that our fates were intertwined was both exhilarating and terrifying. I wanted to reach out and touch him, to bridge the gap between us and erase the uncertainties looming overhead. But the question lingered like a cloud, dark and heavy: could I truly trust him?

The thunder outside roared in response, punctuating my thoughts. Just then, a flash of lightning illuminated Nathan's face, revealing a vulnerability that made my heart ache. He was not just the confident, infuriating man who had captivated me with his charm and wit; he was also a man grappling with demons I could barely comprehend.

"You need to understand," he continued, his voice low and urgent. "There are people out there who want to hurt us. This isn't just about you and me anymore; it's bigger than that."

"Then let me in," I urged, the desperation creeping into my voice. "You can't keep me at arm's length and expect me to be okay with it. I care about you, Nathan. I'm falling for you."

The silence that followed felt like a held breath, suspended in time. His expression shifted, and for a fleeting moment, I thought I saw something akin to hope flicker across his features. But then, just as quickly, it was gone, replaced by the familiar mask of guardedness.

"Caring about me is a dangerous proposition," he said, stepping back, the distance between us stretching like an insurmountable chasm. "You have no idea what I'm capable of, what I've done."

"And you have no idea what I'm capable of either," I shot back, surprised by the fierceness of my own resolve. "I'm not some delicate flower waiting to be saved, Nathan. I can handle myself. But I can't do it alone."

He looked at me then, really looked, and for a moment, the chaos outside faded away, leaving just the two of us. I felt the storm of his emotions swirling around us, heavy and electric. It was a connection deeper than any I had ever felt, and yet the fear of what lurked beyond our door threatened to pull us apart.

Before he could respond, a sharp rap on the door shattered the tension, a sound that echoed ominously through the room. My heart raced as Nathan's expression shifted from contemplation to alarm. "Stay here," he ordered, his tone leaving no room for argument.

"Are you kidding me?" I protested, indignation flaring within me. "I'm not just going to hide while you deal with whatever is out there."

"I don't have time for this!" he snapped, though his voice softened slightly as he glanced back at me. "Please, just trust me this once."

I bit my lip, the unyielding desire to protect him clashing with my need for self-preservation. "Fine," I relented, though every instinct screamed for me to follow him, to not let him face the darkness alone.

He nodded, but his expression was grim as he moved toward the door, every muscle in his body taut with tension. I watched him, heart in my throat, wishing I could rip apart the barriers he had built around himself. Nathan was so much more than his past; he was the man who made me laugh in the darkest moments, who held me close when the world felt overwhelming. Yet here he was, ready to confront the shadows without me.

The door swung open, revealing a figure cloaked in the shadows of the hallway, silhouetted by the flickering light from the storm. My heart plummeted as recognition hit like a gut punch. The man standing there was someone I had seen only in fleeting glances and whispers—a ghost from Nathan's past, someone whose very presence could unravel everything we had started to build.

"Nathan," the figure said, a smooth, chilling voice that dripped with malice. "We need to talk."

In that instant, the world around us shifted, the air thickening with tension as reality crashed in. I felt the weight of what was about to unfold, and suddenly, every choice I had made—the love I felt, the defenses I had lowered—hung in the balance. The stakes had never been higher, and as I stood there, watching the storm rage both outside and within, I knew I was caught in the eye of it all, with nowhere to go but forward.

The figure in the doorway seemed to pulse with darkness, each moment stretching as though time itself had caught its breath. I didn't recognize him at first, the shadows cloaking his features like a cloak of malevolence. Nathan's entire demeanor shifted, muscles tensing as he instinctively positioned himself between me and the intruder. The storm outside raged louder, as if nature itself conspired to amplify the tension hanging thick in the air.

"Derek," Nathan said, his voice a low growl that held both recognition and disdain. It was clear he wanted no part of this reunion, yet here we were, trapped in a tempest that had nothing to do with the weather. I swallowed hard, uncertainty flooding my mind as I took a step back, heart hammering against my ribs.

"Long time, no see," Derek replied, his smile razor-sharp, cutting through the tension with an unsettling ease. He stepped into the room, and I caught a glimpse of something that sent a shiver down my spine—a glint of something metallic at his side, partially obscured but unmistakable.

I could feel the adrenaline surging through my veins, spurring me to take action. "What do you want?" I demanded, my voice steadier than I felt. "We don't have anything to discuss."

"Oh, but we do," he said, glancing at me with a predatory gleam in his eye. "Your little affair with Nathan complicates things. You've stirred up quite the mess, haven't you?"

The air crackled with menace, and I felt a surge of defiance rise within me. "I'm not afraid of you," I retorted, even as I felt a cold dread creeping along my spine. I glanced at Nathan, who remained rigid, his jaw set in a hard line. There was an intensity in his gaze that told me he was calculating his next move, and it left me breathless.

"Ah, but fear is a delightful companion in times like these," Derek drawled, his voice dripping with mockery. "You see, Nathan and I go way back. He's got secrets, and secrets tend to have a way of unraveling, especially when they're tied to a pretty little thing like you."

The implications of his words hung between us like a blade poised to drop. I wanted to shout that he didn't know me, that he had no power here, but the truth was, I felt like a pawn caught in a game I didn't understand.

Nathan stepped forward, placing himself protectively in front of me. "You're not welcome here, Derek. I suggest you leave before this gets ugly."

"Uglier than the storm? I doubt that," Derek chuckled, taking a leisurely step closer. "But you know me, Nathan. I thrive on chaos. Besides, I have no intention of leaving without what I came for."

"What you came for?" I echoed, confusion twisting in my gut. I glanced at Nathan, who looked as though he were battling a storm of his own.

Derek's gaze turned icy, focusing solely on Nathan. "You know exactly what I mean. The package. The information. You owe me, and I'm here to collect."

With each word Derek uttered, the weight of the situation pressed down harder, and I felt a spark of fear mix with anger. "You're not getting anything from him," I interjected, a fierce resolve swelling within me. "Whatever it is, you can take your threats and leave."

Derek laughed, a low, mirthless sound that echoed off the walls. "Oh, sweetheart, it's adorable that you think you can protect him. But this isn't just about you two playing house. It's bigger than both of you, and I've got plans that will unfold whether you like it or not."

A heavy silence fell over the room, broken only by the relentless patter of rain against the window. I could feel Nathan's tension radiating off him, and it struck me then that we were both in over our heads. I had thought our rivalry had transformed into something deeper, but now it seemed like the storm was just beginning.

"Derek, you need to leave. Now," Nathan said, his voice low but firm, each word laced with a threat I didn't fully grasp. "You don't want to make this worse than it already is."

"Worse?" Derek scoffed, shaking his head as if Nathan's words amused him. "You misunderstand. This is just the beginning. I've got a score to settle, and you're in the way."

"Settle your score somewhere else," Nathan snapped, fists clenching at his sides. "I won't let you hurt her."

Hurt me? The implication sent a chill coursing through my veins. I turned to Nathan, searching his eyes for reassurance, but all I found was a darkness that matched the storm raging outside. Just then, a flash of lightning illuminated the room, casting an eerie glow on Derek's face.

"See? He's already worried about you," Derek said, leaning back slightly, satisfaction gleaming in his eyes. "You should consider how much danger you're really in. But don't worry, I'll take good care of you if things go south."

"Enough!" Nathan's voice boomed, startling me. I could feel the intensity of his resolve, a desperate need to shield me from the encroaching threat. "If you want something, you'll have to go through me first."

"Oh, I intend to," Derek replied, his tone suddenly serious. He straightened, eyes narrowing as he surveyed Nathan with a calculated gaze. "But I'm not the only player in this game, Nathan. There are others who will come for what you owe. You can't run forever."

The words hung in the air, heavy with a promise of impending chaos. I could see Nathan's expression flicker, a brief crack in his armor revealing the turmoil beneath. "You're bluffing," he shot back, but I could hear the uncertainty lacing his voice.

"Am I?" Derek said, stepping closer, the smirk fading. "Just remember, Nathan, you can't protect her from the past forever. It'll catch up to you, and when it does, you'll wish you had made different choices."

With that, he turned on his heel, retreating back into the shadows from which he had emerged. The door creaked shut behind him, and I felt the rush of breath leave my lungs, as if the very act of his departure had pulled a weight from my chest.

But the reprieve was short-lived. Nathan stood there, his shoulders tense, eyes dark with an emotion I couldn't quite decipher. "Are you okay?" he asked, though it felt like a formality. The question hung in the air, echoing with unspoken fears.

"I don't know," I admitted, struggling to piece together my thoughts. "What just happened? What does he mean by 'the past'?"

Nathan's silence stretched, heavy with secrets, and I felt the walls closing in once more. "There's so much I haven't told you," he murmured, stepping closer, vulnerability seeping into his voice. "But I promise, I'll explain everything. Just give me time."

Time. The word felt heavy, a promise weighted down by uncertainty. I searched his face, desperate for reassurance, but all I found was a man caught in a web of his own making, the shadows still looming ominously behind him. As the storm continued to rage outside, I knew this was only the beginning of a battle neither of us was truly prepared for.

Nathan's eyes held a tempest of emotions, a mixture of fear and determination that mirrored the storm raging outside. The remnants of Derek's threat lingered like a bad aftertaste, and I could see that he was grappling with the weight of whatever burden he had been carrying alone. "You need to understand," he began, his voice a whisper that somehow cut through the stillness left in Derek's wake. "Derek isn't just some ghost from my past. He's... complicated. And now he's involved you."

The sincerity in his gaze sent a jolt through me, igniting the protective instinct I'd been trying to stifle. "Then let me help you," I urged, the urgency in my tone wrapping around us like a taut string. "Whatever this is, we can face it together."

He opened his mouth to respond, but his expression faltered. For a heartbeat, I could see the desire to let me in, to share the secrets that had twisted like vines around his heart. "I wish it were that simple," he said, the words a mix of frustration and longing. "But it's not just about me. It's about everyone I've ever cared about."

"Then maybe you should stop pretending you're a lone wolf, Nathan. People need to hear the truth." The words spilled out of me, raw and honest, fueled by a mixture of fear and defiance. "I'm not going anywhere, and if Derek thinks he can intimidate me, he has another thing coming."

His lips twitched upward in a fleeting smile, but it quickly faded, overshadowed by the gravity of the moment. "You don't know what he's capable of," he warned, his voice low, nearly trembling with urgency. "He plays games, and lives are at stake. Yours, mine... everyone's. I can't let you get hurt because of my choices."

"Then let me make my own choice." The words felt like an incantation, a promise I had to make for both of us. "I want to stand by you, Nathan. But I can't do that if you keep pushing me away."

The silence between us crackled with unspoken thoughts, the air thick with tension that made it hard to breathe. Just then, the lights flickered ominously, and I felt a sudden chill sweep through the room as the storm outside seemed to respond to our emotional tempest. The howling wind pressed against the windows like a thousand whispered secrets, and I had the eerie sensation that we were teetering on the edge of something monumental.

Then, as if the universe had decided to intervene, Nathan's phone buzzed violently on the counter. He glanced at the screen, tension radiating off him like heat from a fire, and I felt a surge of apprehension. "It's my contact," he muttered, his brow furrowing as he tapped the screen to answer.

I held my breath, feeling the weight of the moment push down on my chest. "Nathan?" a voice crackled through the receiver, sharp and urgent. "We need to talk. It's about Derek."

"Talk?" Nathan replied, his voice suddenly icy. "You think talking is going to make this better?"

"It's about more than just you two," the voice insisted. "You need to listen. Derek's made his move, and it's not just a warning. He's serious this time. You have to get out now."

The gravity of the situation sank in, the air thickening with an electric charge. I could see the realization dawn on Nathan's face, his earlier bravado fading like smoke in the wind. "What are you talking about? What does he want?"

"It's a setup. He's leveraging your past to draw you out, and he won't stop until he gets what he wants," the voice continued, urgency escalating. "If you care about her—"

Nathan cut off the call, his expression darkening as he turned to face me. "We need to leave. Now."

"Leave? Where?" I demanded, feeling the ground shift beneath me. "What's happening, Nathan?"

"There's a safe house—someone I trust. We can figure this out there."

"Safe house?" The word sent a jolt of unease through me. "What do you mean? Why are we in danger?"

His eyes darted around the room as if the shadows themselves were creeping closer. "Because Derek's not just a threat to me; he's a threat to everyone who gets too close. If he thinks you're a weakness, he'll use you to get to me."

The implication hung between us, a shroud of darkness that threatened to swallow everything whole. "So what are we supposed to do? Run away?" I shot back, defiance rising in my chest. "I won't hide. Not again."

"It's not hiding; it's survival," he said, his voice taut with tension. "And right now, I need you to trust me. Please."

"Trust you?" I echoed, feeling a tempest of emotions swirl inside me. "You're the one who keeps secrets! How can I trust you if you won't share anything?"

"Because I care about you!" His voice broke, a raw edge seeping through his calm facade. "I've already lost too much, and I won't lose you too."

The desperation in his eyes made my heart ache. But before I could respond, the sound of a heavy thud echoed from the hallway, slicing through the thick tension in the room like a knife. I jumped, instinctively moving closer to Nathan, who was already positioning himself protectively in front of me.

"We need to go. Now," he urged, his voice low and commanding. I nodded, adrenaline flooding my system, but just as I turned to reach for my bag, the door burst open, and there stood Derek again, flanked by two imposing figures cloaked in darkness.

"Going somewhere?" he taunted, a wicked smile playing on his lips. The air thickened with dread, and the oppressive weight of danger settled around us like a thick fog. "I wouldn't be in such a hurry if I were you."

My heart raced as I glanced at Nathan, whose face was set in a grim expression of determination. But the dread pooling in my stomach threatened to drown out the resolve. This was it—the line had been drawn, and there was no retreating from the storm now. I held my breath, the tension snapping like a taut wire, as Derek stepped inside, the shadows behind him shifting like predators poised to strike.

"Let's see how much you really care about each other when the stakes are this high," he said, his voice dripping with malice as the door swung shut behind him, sealing our fate in an unyielding grip.

Chapter 9: Beneath the Surface

The soft hum of the fluorescent lights filled the office, their glow casting long shadows that danced across the walls, mingling with the fading light of the late evening. I sat hunched over my desk, surrounded by mountains of paperwork that seemed to multiply like rabbits in the quiet. The clack of my keyboard punctuated the silence, each keystroke a desperate attempt to distract myself from the swirling thoughts about Nathan. The man was an enigma, a puzzle with pieces that stubbornly refused to fit together. My heart, once a steady companion, now raced in a chaotic rhythm, torn between longing and trepidation.

As I rifled through a stack of client files, an envelope slipped out, landing with a soft thud on the polished surface of my desk. Its edges were frayed, yellowed with age, and the ink was smudged, barely legible. My heart stuttered; this was not a document I recognized. With cautious curiosity, I picked it up, feeling the weight of secrets hidden within. Unsealing the envelope, I carefully extracted a series of documents, their crispness contrasting sharply with the worn exterior of the envelope.

The first page was a memorandum from a law firm, referencing an investigation into Nathan's former associates. My breath caught in my throat as I skimmed through names that echoed with whispers of betrayal and criminal undertones. Each subsequent page unveiled a darker tapestry: financial discrepancies, mysterious disappearances, and a web of connections that twisted like a serpent, tightening around the very core of Nathan's life before I had entered the picture. I felt as if I had stumbled upon the remnants of a shattered mirror, each shard reflecting a piece of a world I had never known.

With each paragraph, my stomach knotted tighter. The implications were staggering, but the one that lingered like a ghost at the back of my mind was the thought that Nathan had been enmeshed in something sinister, something that could seep into our lives if I wasn't careful. My instincts buzzed like a swarm of angry bees, warning me that the danger wasn't merely confined to his past. I set the pages aside, my pulse thrumming against my skin, and buried my face in my hands, fighting the whirlwind of emotions that threatened to drown me.

It was late, the office silent except for the occasional rustle of papers and the distant hum of traffic outside. I could no longer deny that I had to confront Nathan. Clarity eluded me, slipping through my fingers like grains of sand, and the only way to grasp it was to face him, to pull back the layers of mystery that surrounded him. But would he be honest? Would he share the truth behind the shadows that loomed over us, or would he weave another tale, crafted to protect me from a past that might still be breathing down our necks?

The idea of confronting him filled me with dread and anticipation. What if the answers were worse than I feared? I shook my head, trying to clear the fog that clouded my thoughts. He was here in the city, living among us, but what part of him still belonged to that dark world? The question hung heavy in the air as I gathered the documents, tucking them into my bag, the weight of my decision pressing down on my shoulders like an unwelcome cloak.

I glanced at the clock on the wall; it was nearly midnight. The office was deserted, the hum of the fluorescent lights becoming a monotonous lullaby, urging me to leave, to retreat into the safety of my home. But my feet felt like lead, rooted to the floor as my mind raced with possibilities. As I walked towards the exit, I imagined Nathan's face when I confronted him, the spark in his eyes that had once ignited something within me now a source of uncertainty. Would he see my love or my fear?

The streets were empty as I made my way to his apartment, the cool night air biting at my skin, each breath a reminder of the tumult within. As I approached the building, the familiar scent of the city wrapped around me—a blend of asphalt, the distant sea, and the ever-present hint of coffee. I paused, my heart pounding in my chest, uncertainty battling with determination. I knocked, the sound echoing in the stillness, and waited, my palms clammy against the cool metal of the door handle.

When Nathan finally opened the door, I was struck by the contrast between his casual demeanor and the storm swirling inside me. He wore an old T-shirt, the fabric soft and faded, and his hair was tousled, as though he had just rolled out of bed. "Hey, I didn't expect to see you this late," he said, his voice a low, inviting rumble that sent a shiver down my spine.

"I found something at the office," I managed, my voice barely above a whisper as the tension hung between us, thick as fog. The invitation to step inside hung in the air, and for a moment, I hesitated, the comfort of the familiar clashing with the urgency of my newfound knowledge.

"Come in," he urged, stepping aside. "You look like you've seen a ghost."

As I entered, the warmth of his space enveloped me, but the flickering shadows seemed to dance in mockery of the turmoil in my heart. I glanced around, taking in the scattered remnants of his life—books piled high on the coffee table, the remnants of dinner in the sink, and a guitar leaning against the wall, waiting for fingers to strum its strings. But beneath the surface of that coziness lurked the undercurrents of the secrets I had unearthed.

I took a deep breath, my heart racing as I faced him. "We need to talk."

The weight of my words hung in the air, palpable and heavy, as I faced Nathan. He leaned against the doorframe, the warm light from the living room spilling around him, softening the angles of his face but doing nothing to ease the tension pooling in my stomach. "Talk?" he echoed, raising an eyebrow with that familiar smirk that often melted my resolve, but this time, it felt more like a challenge than an invitation.

I crossed my arms, half a step closer to the doorway and half a step back, caught in a limbo of uncertainty. "Yes, Nathan, we need to talk about what I found." The words tumbled out, sharp and accusing, before I could second-guess myself.

"Alright," he said, pushing himself away from the door and gesturing toward the couch. "Let's sit." He led the way, his relaxed posture betraying none of the storm brewing behind his deep brown eyes. I couldn't help but notice how comfortable he looked, his feet bare against the wooden floor, jeans slung low on his hips, radiating an effortless charm that had once drawn me in like a moth to a flame.

Settling into the couch, I felt like I was balancing on the edge of a precipice, every fiber of my being thrumming with the urgency of what I needed to say. "I found documents at work," I began, hesitating as I watched the flicker of confusion dart across his face. "They mentioned people you used to work with—associates involved in some... questionable activities."

Nathan's expression hardened, the warmth in his eyes replaced by a guarded flicker. "Questionable activities?" he repeated, his tone now laced with caution. "What exactly did they say?"

I leaned forward, feeling the urge to reach out and touch his hand, to bridge the chasm that had suddenly opened between us. But I refrained, knowing I had to stay focused. "There were names, connections to financial fraud and other... darker dealings. It feels like there's a part of your life that you haven't shared with me. A part that might still be coming back to haunt you—or us."

Silence enveloped the room, thick enough to cut with a knife. Nathan's gaze dropped to the floor, and for a moment, I feared I had shattered something fragile between us. "I didn't want to bring that into our lives," he finally murmured, his voice barely above a whisper. "It's in the past for a reason."

"Is it really in the past?" I pressed, a mix of frustration and fear propelling my words. "I can't just ignore the fact that there might be people still looking for you, or even looking for answers. What if this comes crashing down on us?"

"Don't you think I know that?" His voice raised slightly, tinged with a mix of hurt and defiance. "I've spent years trying to escape that world. I thought I had left it behind." He ran a hand through his hair, a gesture of exasperation that tugged at my heartstrings. "But clearly, I was wrong."

The shift in his demeanor was unsettling. It was as if I had pulled a thread, unraveling a tightly woven fabric that had once seemed so secure. I could sense the emotions churning within him, the frustration of a man who had fought hard to bury his past, and the regret of a relationship now shadowed by the specter of secrets. "Nathan," I began, wanting to bridge the gap, wanting him to know I was on his side, but he cut me off.

"Please, just let me explain." He took a deep breath, his eyes locking onto mine with a fierceness that sent a shiver down my spine. "A few years ago, I was involved with a group that operated in a gray area. We thought we were untouchable, but you can't play in the shadows without getting burned. When things started to go south, I walked away. I thought I was free."

I opened my mouth, searching for the right words to soothe the sharp edge of his confession, but the air felt too thick, too charged. "Did you ever think you'd have to face it again?" I asked, my voice trembling with the weight of what I was about to say. "Or that it might come back to put us both at risk?"

Nathan shifted in his seat, his jaw clenched as he considered my words. "I hoped I wouldn't have to. But I didn't expect you to dig up that part of my life. You have to understand, I never wanted you to know."

"And now I do," I replied, my heart hammering in my chest. "I'm not going to pretend this doesn't exist. We can't build something real on secrets."

His expression softened, the sharp lines of his face becoming more vulnerable. "I want to protect you," he said quietly, the sincerity in his voice tugging at the edges of my resolve. "That's why I kept it from you."

"By keeping me in the dark?" I shot back, the frustration bubbling over. "That's not protection, Nathan. That's manipulation."

He leaned forward, his intensity palpable. "And what would you have done if I told you? Would you have walked away? Would you have wanted nothing to do with me?"

The question hung between us like a pendulum, swinging with the weight of the truth I hadn't wanted to confront. I felt cornered, the walls of my own emotions closing in. "I don't know," I admitted, feeling raw and exposed. "But I do know that we can't move forward without honesty."

"Then let's move forward," he said, his voice a low growl, determination replacing the previous tension. "I'm willing to face whatever comes our way, as long as you're by my side."

His words echoed in my mind, a mix of warmth and trepidation. There was something undeniably fierce about his willingness to confront the darkness that loomed over us. But the lurking shadows still whispered doubts, each one more insistent than the last.

"Okay," I said slowly, a sense of resolve creeping into my voice. "But if we're going to do this, we need a plan. I refuse to let your past dictate our future."

The fire in Nathan's eyes reignited, a spark of hope mingling with the lingering uncertainty. "You're right. We can't let it control us. But I need you to trust me. Whatever happens, I'll protect you."

"Just promise me you won't shut me out," I replied, my heart aching with the weight of the words.

He reached out, capturing my hand in his, grounding me in that moment. "I promise," he said, the warmth of his grip wrapping around my resolve like a shield. In that moment, beneath the glow of the soft lighting, I felt a flicker of hope amidst the chaos, a possibility that perhaps together we could navigate the tangled web of his past and emerge stronger on the other side. But deep down, an unsettling feeling lingered—what if the shadows had already begun to reach for us, threatening to engulf the fragile light we had kindled?

The air in Nathan's apartment buzzed with a tension that felt almost electric, each heartbeat echoing the uncertainty that had settled between us. I could still feel the warmth of his hand around mine, grounding me in this moment as if to remind me of the fragile connection we were forging amidst the chaos. Yet, every time I glanced at the documents nestled in my bag, the chill of dread crept back in, a haunting reminder that we were standing on the edge of a precipice.

"Okay, so what's the plan?" I finally asked, pulling away slightly to search his eyes for assurance. "You said you'd face it, but what does that actually mean?" My voice came out sharper than I intended, but the question hung in the air, demanding an answer.

Nathan leaned back, a flicker of hesitation crossing his features. "First, we need to understand what we're dealing with. If these people are indeed connected to my past, we have to be smart about it. I need to reach out to someone who can help."

"Who?" I asked, curiosity piqued, although the idea of him contacting someone from that world made my skin crawl. "Do you have a contact you trust? Someone who won't just throw you to the wolves?"

His gaze drifted for a moment, and I could almost see the gears turning in his mind. "There's a woman I used to work with, Eliza. She was always the brains behind the operations—sharp, resourceful, and not easily intimidated. If anyone can provide insight, it's her."

"Does she know about your past?" I probed, trying to gauge how deep the roots of his former life stretched.

"She knows enough," he replied, his voice low. "But it's been a while since we last spoke. I'm not sure how she'll react to my reaching out now. It's risky."

"Risky seems to be the theme of the evening," I muttered, the reality settling in like an unwelcome weight. "How do you plan on contacting her?"

"I'll send a message through a secure channel," he said, his tone firm. "She's meticulous about her privacy, and I'll need to tread carefully. I don't want to draw attention to myself—especially not from the wrong people."

A knot of unease twisted in my stomach at the thought of him stepping back into that world, even just to make a phone call. "And what if someone's watching? What if they find out you're trying to reach her?"

"Then we'll have to be smarter than them." His voice had taken on a fierce edge, a spark igniting in his eyes that I couldn't help but admire. "We'll create a distraction. Something to draw attention away while I make contact."

"Like what? A street performance? A flash mob?" I couldn't keep the sarcasm from dripping into my words, a poor attempt to mask my anxiety.

"Something more subtle," he replied, a small smile playing on his lips, the first sign of levity in an otherwise tense conversation. "How about we throw a party? Invite a few friends, create a buzz. While everyone is focused on the festivities, I can slip away to make the call."

"A party?" I blinked, the absurdity of the idea cutting through my worries. "You think our best move is to throw a shindig? What are we, amateur spies?"

"Amateur spies with flair," he quipped, the tension easing just a fraction. "It'll give us the chance to gather information without drawing attention. Plus, it'll be fun."

"Fun," I echoed, skepticism lacing my tone. "Right. Because a bunch of strangers celebrating is exactly what I need right now." Still, I felt a reluctant grin tugging at my lips. "Are we supposed to put on party hats and blow noisemakers while you're off uncovering your past?"

"Why not?" He leaned closer, his eyes glinting mischievously. "It's not like we can just sit here and wait for something to happen. We need to take control. Besides, what's life without a little chaos?"

His enthusiasm was infectious, and despite my better judgment, I felt a spark of excitement stirring within me. "Alright, let's do it," I said, the words escaping before I could stop myself. "But if things go south, you're the one explaining to our guests why the cops are showing up."

Nathan chuckled, and for a moment, the weight of the world seemed to lift, replaced by the warmth of camaraderie and shared purpose. "Deal. We'll get everything ready for Saturday. I'll reach out to Eliza in the meantime, and we'll see what happens."

As we began mapping out plans for the gathering, the initial thrill of action morphed into a cloud of uncertainty looming just beyond the horizon. But amid the lighthearted banter and the gentle teasing, a deeper concern gnawed at my thoughts. I couldn't shake the feeling that whatever we were igniting was more than just a party. It felt like a match struck against the tinder of a world we were both desperate to escape.

By the time we had settled on a loose outline for the evening, I felt a sense of camaraderie swelling between us, one that drowned out my earlier doubts. "We'll need snacks," I declared. "And good music. And maybe a secret escape route if all hell breaks loose."

Nathan raised an eyebrow, amusement dancing in his gaze. "Already planning the getaway, are we? You know me too well."

"Or maybe I just don't trust the people you used to associate with," I shot back, my tone light but my heart heavy with the truth that underlined it.

As the conversation continued, weaving through logistics and potential guests, the laughter and connection soothed the edges of my anxiety. However, when Nathan stepped into the kitchen to grab us both a drink, my gaze flicked back to the stack of documents still hidden in my bag. The reminders of the world we were attempting to confront loomed over us, but the normalcy of our planning felt like a temporary balm for my worry.

Just as Nathan returned, a sound outside caught my attention—a soft thud, followed by the crunch of gravel. I frowned, instinctively leaning closer to the window to peer out, but the street was dark, shadows dancing in the glow of the streetlight. Nothing seemed out of place, yet the unease that had settled in my gut returned with renewed vigor.

"What's wrong?" Nathan asked, concern etched across his features.

"I thought I heard something," I replied, still scanning the street. "Maybe it's just a cat or something. But I don't like it."

Nathan stepped beside me, looking out into the night as well. "Probably nothing. But we should stay vigilant. If there's anything I've learned, it's that danger can come from unexpected places."

And just as those words slipped into the air, my phone buzzed on the table. I glanced at it, my heart leaping into my throat as I saw an unknown number flashing across the screen. My instincts screamed at me, a voice in the back of my mind insisting this was no ordinary call.

"Who is it?" Nathan asked, his curiosity piqued, but I remained frozen, unable to move.

The phone buzzed again, more insistent this time, and I finally reached for it, my hand trembling as I accepted the call.

"Hello?" I answered cautiously, my heart hammering in my chest.

A low, gravelly voice responded, sending chills racing down my spine. "We need to talk about Nathan. He's in deeper than you think."

The line crackled before going silent, leaving me standing there, frozen in shock as Nathan turned to me, confusion etched across his face. "What was that?"

"I... I don't know," I stammered, but the look in his eyes told me he was already realizing something was very, very wrong.

And just like that, the night unraveled, shadows creeping closer, threatening to engulf us both.

Chapter 10: The Unveiling

The air was thick with unspoken words, a silence heavy with the weight of Nathan's revelations. We sat in his small, dimly lit living room, the flickering candle casting playful shadows on the walls. He leaned forward, elbows resting on his knees, his hands clasped as if trying to hold onto the very essence of his past. The scent of burnt cinnamon lingered, remnants of the candle's earlier promise of warmth, now a mere whisper against the chill that crept in from the cracked window.

"Things weren't always like this for me," Nathan said, his voice low, barely above a murmur. I could see the way his jaw tightened, the flicker of a memory playing behind his dark eyes. It was a look I recognized—a vulnerability masked by bravado, a dance between the shadows of regret and the flickering hope for redemption. "I got caught up with people who...well, they didn't care about the consequences."

I shifted in my seat, suddenly aware of how the room seemed to constrict around us, wrapping us in a cocoon of shared secrets. "What do you mean? What kind of people?" The question slipped out before I could stop it, curiosity laced with the thrill of danger.

He hesitated, a shadow crossing his face, as if grappling with demons that were too numerous to name. "You know the stories you hear in whispers? The kind of stories that make you shiver at night? I lived those. I was involved with a crew that didn't take kindly to outsiders, and I learned quickly that loyalty came at a steep price."

His confession hung in the air, a tangible entity that pressed against my chest. I could almost feel the weight of his past bearing down on him, the burdens of guilt and fear etched into the lines of his face. The rivalry we had once shared seemed trivial now, a game of chess in a world that had turned to a brutal survival of the fittest. The corners of my mind began to race—was this the Nathan I had known, or was there an entirely different man hiding beneath layers of bravado?

"I had to make choices, choices that haunted me," he continued, his eyes locking onto mine with an intensity that both captivated and unsettled me. "I turned my back on them, but they don't easily let go. They have a way of reaching out from the darkness when you least expect it."

A chill swept through me, my heart quickening. "Is that why you've been so secretive?" I asked, my voice barely above a whisper. "Why you keep pushing me away?"

He rubbed the back of his neck, the tension in his shoulders rising like a storm. "I didn't want to drag you into my mess. You deserve better than that."

My instincts flared at the implication. "Better? Or is it that you're afraid I might actually care?" The words were sharp, a playful jab wrapped in underlying truth. I leaned closer, feeling a sudden surge of courage. "You're not the only one with shadows, Nathan. We all have our ghosts."

For a heartbeat, we lingered in that space, where the air was charged with unsaid confessions and the unsteady rhythm of our breathing filled the silence. I could see the conflict in his eyes, the flicker of something deeper, something that threatened to unravel the walls he had carefully constructed around himself.

But just as he opened his mouth to speak, my phone buzzed against the table, shattering the moment like glass. I reached for it, my heart sinking as I glanced at the screen. The message was terse, chilling in its simplicity: "I know about Nathan. You should watch your back."

The world shifted, colors dulling as the weight of the message settled in. "Who is it?" Nathan asked, his voice suddenly sharp, pulling me from the fog of shock.

"I don't know," I stammered, my fingers trembling as I stared at the screen. "Just a number I don't recognize. But...what if they're serious?"

His expression darkened, eyes narrowing as he processed the implications. "They shouldn't be able to find you," he said, an edge of frustration creeping into his tone. "I thought I had covered my tracks."

"Clearly, someone knows more than we thought." My voice came out steadier than I felt, though the tremor in my gut threatened to unravel me. The vibrant tapestry of our conversation had frayed, leaving only the stark, harsh reality of danger and deception in its wake.

"I'll handle it," Nathan asserted, his tone resolute as he stood, the shadows of his past seemingly melding with the present. "I can't let them get to you."

"And what about you?" I shot back, rising to match his intensity. "You think I'll just stand by while you fight your battles? This is bigger than you or me now."

We faced each other, the room pulsating with unspoken tension, the flickering candlelight now casting elongated shadows that danced menacingly on the walls. The bond we had formed began to shimmer with a fragile resilience, yet the undercurrent of fear threatened to fracture it.

"We need to figure this out together," I insisted, my heart pounding in my chest as I stepped closer. "Whatever is coming, we'll face it head-on. I'm not leaving you to fend for yourself."

He paused, studying me with a mix of surprise and admiration, as if the resolve I displayed had cut through the gloom surrounding him. "You're not like anyone I've ever met," he admitted, his voice softer now, an unexpected warmth threading through the edges of our precarious situation.

"Don't let it go to your head," I quipped, a grin breaking through the tension, even as my heart raced. But the uncertainty lingered, a specter hovering over us, reminding us that this fragile alliance was built on the shifting sands of trust and betrayal.

The candle flickered again, and for a moment, the light danced in the darkness, illuminating the potential that lay before us—both in the dangers we faced and the unexpected bond that had begun to blossom amid the chaos.

The air crackled with an energy that was almost electric, and as Nathan stared at the message on my phone, I felt an urgency rise between us. This wasn't merely a story of danger anymore; it was our story now. I could see the gears in his mind turning, calculating risks like a chess master assessing the board. "We need to find out who sent this," he said, the steel in his voice offering a strange comfort amidst the chaos.

I nodded, my pulse quickening with both fear and excitement. "Right. But how do we do that? I don't even know where to start." I glanced back at the screen, the numbers blurred in my peripheral vision, as if they were taunting me with their anonymity.

"Let me take a look at it," he said, extending a hand. His fingers brushed against mine, and for a fleeting moment, I felt the warmth radiate from him, igniting a strange mixture of adrenaline and something softer beneath the surface. I relinquished my phone, and he studied the message, his brow furrowing in concentration.

"First things first, we can't panic," he said, his voice steady, a tone that suggested he had navigated darker waters than this. "I need to see if I can trace the number. There are ways."

"Like hacking into the phone company?" I teased, trying to lighten the mood, but his serious expression didn't waver. "Or maybe just a friendly chat with your old criminal friends?"

A flicker of a smile broke through his intensity, but it vanished as quickly as it appeared. "I'd rather not. I've burned those bridges for a reason." He ran a hand through his hair, tousling it into a mess that somehow made him look more approachable. "Let's just say they don't take too kindly to their former associates."

"Can't blame them for that," I quipped, crossing my arms. "But if you're going to be all mysterious, how do I know you're not still involved in some underground society?"

"Wouldn't you like to know?" he shot back, his smirk playful, but the intensity in his eyes warned me that this was no game.

As he began to type furiously on my phone, I took a step back, glancing around the dimly lit room. The flickering candlelight danced, casting shadows that felt like secrets whispering against the walls. Outside, the wind howled like a restless spirit, rattling the window panes and causing the hairs on my arms to stand on end. This was not just about Nathan anymore; it was about me too, whether I wanted to acknowledge it or not.

"Okay, here's a thought," I said, interrupting the silence. "What if we go to the police?" The suggestion felt like a loaded gun, the kind of idea that could backfire spectacularly.

Nathan stopped, his fingers hovering above the screen. "And tell them what? That you got a mysterious message about me? That I used to run with the wrong crowd? No, thank you."

His response left a bitter taste in my mouth. "But what if it's serious? What if they're coming after you—and by extension, me?" I pressed, my voice rising. "I refuse to be your collateral damage. I may not have a past like yours, but I'm not without my share of battles either."

His expression softened, the lines of tension around his mouth easing slightly. "I know that. You're not just some damsel in distress, and I wouldn't treat you like one." He paused, looking deep into my eyes, as if searching for something. "But you have to understand, I'm not just protecting myself. I'm protecting you."

A warmth spread through my chest at his concern, but I shook my head. "Protecting me from what? The truth?" I stepped closer, a fierce determination brewing inside me. "You can't keep running from your past forever, Nathan. If you don't face it now, it'll only catch up to you."

He sighed, the weight of my words hanging in the air like a thick fog. "And what if it does? What if it's worse than I can imagine?" His voice was raw, and I could see the battle lines drawn across his features, the uncertainty weighing heavily on him.

"Then we face it together," I replied, my heart pounding with conviction. "I'm not going to sit back and let you shoulder this alone. You've let me in, whether you meant to or not. So let's figure this out, Nathan."

Just then, a loud knock echoed through the room, startling us both. The sound reverberated against the walls, breaking the fragile bubble we had created. My heart raced as I exchanged a quick glance with Nathan. "Do you think it's them?" I whispered, anxiety curling around my stomach.

"Only one way to find out," he replied, his voice low and cautious.

"Right. Because the best way to handle a threat is to answer the door," I muttered, rolling my eyes even as dread coiled tighter within me.

"Just stay behind me," he ordered, a protective glint in his eye. He moved toward the door, his presence commanding and watchful, as if he were preparing to confront a wild animal rather than a mere visitor.

As he reached for the doorknob, I took a deep breath, my senses heightened, acutely aware of every sound—the rustle of the wind, the creak of the floorboards beneath us, and the thundering beat of my heart. I wished I could project a sense of calm, but with each passing second, the tension spiraled.

With a decisive motion, Nathan opened the door, and the harsh light from the hallway poured into the room like an intruder. My breath caught in my throat as a figure stepped into the threshold, silhouetted against the bright backdrop.

It was a woman, her long dark hair cascading like a waterfall over her shoulders, her presence both commanding and unsettling. "Nathan," she said, her voice a melodic yet ominous whisper that sent chills racing down my spine. "We need to talk."

"Lila," he replied, the surprise in his voice unmistakable.

The atmosphere shifted instantly, the air thickening as the room grew charged with unspoken histories and unresolved tensions. I could feel my heart thudding in my chest, a wild animal trying to escape as Nathan's expression turned from surprise to something darker, more guarded.

The woman stepped further inside, eyes darting between us, a predator assessing her territory. "I didn't think you'd still be in town," she said, her gaze locking onto mine, a subtle challenge flickering in the depths of her dark eyes. "And I certainly didn't expect you to be here."

"I don't think this is a good time," Nathan said firmly, but the steel in his voice faltered slightly, revealing a crack that suggested his past was indeed closing in on him.

"Time's not the issue," she replied, a hint of a smirk playing on her lips. "It's the truth you're avoiding."

My mind raced with questions, a storm of confusion swirling within me. Who was she? What did she know? And more importantly, what did she want with Nathan? The fragile alliance we had built in those fleeting moments seemed to unravel before my eyes, replaced by a new layer of tension that promised to expose even more secrets lurking in the shadows.

The air grew thick with tension as the woman stepped over the threshold, her presence as commanding as a thunderstorm on the horizon. Nathan's body stiffened, and I could see the subtle shift in his demeanor as he faced Lila. Her gaze swept across the room before settling on me, a calculating glint in her dark eyes that made my skin crawl.

"Who's this?" she asked, her tone deceptively casual, like she was inquiring about the weather rather than the sudden presence of a stranger in a charged situation.

"Nobody you need to worry about," Nathan replied, his voice low but firm. There was an edge to it that felt like a protective barrier, yet it cracked ever so slightly under the weight of unspoken history.

"Right," she countered, an eyebrow arched. "Because it's never a good sign when your old life comes knocking." She glanced at me again, her lips curving into a smile that didn't reach her eyes. "You really should know what you're getting into, sweetie."

I felt a surge of indignation. "Excuse me? Sweetie? This isn't some petty rivalry we're caught up in; this is real, and I have every right to be here," I shot back, feeling the fire within me flare. If Nathan was going to protect me, I needed to prove I could stand my ground too.

Lila laughed softly, a sound as smooth and cold as polished marble. "Feisty. I like that." She turned back to Nathan, her expression shifting from playful to serious. "But you're playing with fire, Nathan. And sooner or later, you're going to get burned."

"Enough with the cryptic warnings, Lila," he replied, a tension threading through his voice that suggested a history filled with more than just friendly banter. "What do you want?"

"Simple," she said, stepping deeper into the room, her heels clicking against the wooden floor. "I want you to know that your past isn't done with you. It's just waiting for the right moment to rear its ugly head."

The words hung between us like a dark cloud. I felt a shiver dance down my spine, the weight of her declaration settling in. "What do you mean? What's going to happen?" I demanded, my voice trembling with a mix of fear and curiosity.

Lila's smile widened, her gaze shifting back to me. "You really want to know? It's all very exciting, really. You have no idea how thrilling it is to watch the inevitable unfold."

"Enough games," Nathan growled, stepping protectively in front of me. "If you have something to say, just say it."

Lila tilted her head, assessing him as if he were a puzzle she couldn't quite solve. "You're still trying to play the hero, huh? It's charming, in a way. But you should know—your heroics can't save you from the choices you've made. Your little friend here is caught in the crossfire whether you like it or not."

"Stop calling me a friend," I retorted, taking a step forward, emboldened by the protective stance Nathan had taken. "I'm not just some bystander in your twisted drama."

"Drama?" Lila repeated, feigning shock. "This isn't drama, darling. This is life and death. And you're dancing on the edge of a knife."

A tense silence enveloped us, the weight of her words pressing down like a physical force. Nathan glanced at me, and in that fleeting moment, I could see the conflict playing out in his mind. He was torn between protecting me and facing the ghosts of his past. I could practically feel the tempest brewing within him, an amalgamation of rage and regret.

"Why are you really here, Lila?" he asked, his voice low and threatening, a stark contrast to her casual demeanor. "What do you want from me?"

Her smile vanished, replaced by a look that seemed to pierce straight through him. "I'm here because I'm your link to the past you thought you could outrun. You know as well as I do that the people you abandoned don't take kindly to betrayal. And they're ready to collect."

"What does that mean?" I interjected, my heart racing as anxiety clawed at my insides. "What's going to happen?"

She turned her gaze back to me, amusement dancing in her eyes. "Ah, you're the curious type. That's cute." Then her expression hardened. "But let's just say you're about to find out. The shadows of his past don't just threaten him; they threaten anyone close to him."

The walls of the room seemed to close in, the reality of her words settling like a stone in my stomach. Nathan was in deep, and I had unwittingly plunged into his world of chaos. I wanted to scream at him, to demand answers, but the uncertainty of our situation paralyzed me.

"Get out," Nathan said, his voice steady yet edged with barely restrained fury. "You have no right to come here and threaten her."

Lila shrugged, feigning nonchalance, but the gleam in her eye betrayed her excitement. "You'll see me again, Nathan. Count on it." She turned to me, her smile returning but now twisted with something darker. "And you might want to brush up on your self-defense skills. You'll need them."

With that, she slipped back out the door, the shadows swallowing her whole. The moment the door clicked shut, the room erupted into silence, an echo of her words reverberating in the air. I felt the weight of dread wash over me, the reality of our situation crashing in like a tidal wave.

"What the hell was that?" I breathed, turning to face Nathan, my voice a mixture of anger and confusion. "Is this what you meant by your past catching up to you?"

He ran a hand through his hair, his expression torn between frustration and something deeper—fear. "She's right, in a way. I've made choices that have consequences, and I thought I had left it all behind."

"Clearly, you were wrong." The accusation slipped out before I could hold it back, the anger boiling to the surface. "And now I'm in the crosshairs too?"

Nathan stepped closer, his eyes searching mine, a plea wrapped in unspoken emotions. "I didn't want this for you. I thought I could protect you."

"Protect me? By hiding the truth?" I shot back, my heart racing as the reality of the situation set in. "I can't believe you thought that would work."

He opened his mouth to reply, but before he could speak, a loud thud reverberated from the door, rattling the frame. We both turned sharply, the air growing thick with tension once more. "What was that?" I whispered, my throat tightening as my pulse raced.

Nathan's expression hardened, shifting from concern to determination. "Stay behind me," he instructed, moving toward the door with a sense of purpose that sent a thrill through me, but also a wave of dread.

"Like that worked out for us the last time," I muttered, feeling the weight of uncertainty settle over us both.

He shot me a quick glance, a flicker of a grin breaking through the tension. "Touché."

Before I could respond, the door burst open, and a figure stumbled in, breathless and wide-eyed, panic etched across their face. "They're coming!" the newcomer shouted, the urgency in their voice slicing through the silence like a knife.

The world around us spun on its axis, and as my heart sank, I realized we were about to be thrust into the chaos I had been so desperate to avoid. The room filled with a palpable sense of impending danger, and the last thing I saw before the shadows engulfed us was Nathan's determined gaze, a storm brewing behind his calm facade.

In that fleeting moment, I understood—this was no longer just Nathan's battle; it was ours, and the stakes had never been higher.

Chapter 11: Into the Abyss

The air crackled with tension as Nathan slammed the cabin door behind us, the sound echoing through the quiet expanse of the Adirondacks. A part of me felt as though I had crossed an invisible threshold, stepping into a world where reality blurred and shadows breathed life into my every fear. The rustic charm of the cabin belied its unsettling history, the wooden beams standing witness to secrets kept too long, stories half-told. I could smell the faintest hint of pine and woodsmoke, but beneath that was an undercurrent of something darker, a lingering essence of heartache.

Nathan's shoulders were taut, and his jaw clenched with an intensity that was both alarming and oddly magnetic. I caught a glimpse of vulnerability in his eyes, a flicker of the man behind the shield he wore like armor. He was used to the weight of the world resting on his shoulders, yet in this moment, it was clear that he carried more than just his own burdens. "You shouldn't have to worry about anything," he said, his voice low and gravelly, as though the words were dragged from the depths of a dark well. "Just let me handle this."

I swallowed hard, the words catching in my throat. I wanted to believe him, to surrender to the safety he promised, but doubt flickered at the edges of my mind. "Handle what, exactly? The whispers in the dark? The shadows that seem to watch us?" My voice trembled slightly, a betraying echo of the fear that gripped my heart.

He stepped closer, the heat radiating from his body a stark contrast to the cool cabin air. "It's just the woods playing tricks on us. You know how they are." His attempt at reassurance felt flimsy, as if the shadows themselves mocked our fear. The very walls of the cabin, adorned with the ghosts of laughter and despair, seemed to hold their breath, as though waiting for a story to unfold.

I glanced around the room, the cozy yet cluttered space telling its own tale. Photographs lined the mantle, sepia-toned memories of Nathan as a child, his small hands cradling a fishing rod, the delight captured on his face. They were tender snapshots of innocence that contrasted sharply with the grim reality of our present. There was a rusted fishing lure, a couple of old novels with dog-eared pages, and a heavy quilt draped over the back of a worn couch, all serving as fragments of a life lived in the beauty and brutality of nature.

The sunlight filtered through the thick canopy of trees outside, casting dappled patterns on the floor, but the shadows felt longer, as if the sun was being swallowed whole. I found myself drawn to the large window that framed a breathtaking view of the surrounding wilderness, yet the serene landscape held an unsettling quality. It was beautiful, yes, but it was also a place where the earth felt alive and watchful.

"Why did you bring me here, Nathan?" I asked, my voice barely above a whisper, the weight of my question thickening the air between us. "You could have gone anywhere." The truth was, the cabin was a refuge, but it was also a reminder of all that had been lost, and I could see it etched in the lines of his face.

He hesitated, his gaze turning inward as if he were searching for the right words among the chaos in his mind. "Because it's safe here. For now," he finally said, an edge of uncertainty creeping into his tone. "I thought if we could just be away from everything for a while, maybe—"

"Maybe what?" I pressed, feeling a surge of frustration. "Maybe we can pretend everything is okay?"

He stepped back, running a hand through his tousled hair, frustration evident in his posture. "It's not about pretending! It's about surviving long enough to fight back." His eyes sparked with determination, yet beneath that was a flicker of fear that felt almost palpable. "I won't let anything happen to you. I promise."

I felt the heat of his promise enveloping me, a fierce warmth that battled the chill of the unknown looming just beyond the trees. "What if I don't want to be a pawn in someone else's game?" I shot back, emboldened by the raw energy between us.

"That's not what this is! You're not a pawn; you're..." He paused, searching my eyes for something, perhaps a sign that I understood the depth of the stakes involved. "You're more important than that. I can't lose you."

His words hung in the air, a thread woven with unspoken fears and the weight of history. As he spoke, I felt an unfamiliar flutter in my stomach, a blend of hope and trepidation. Did he really mean that? Was I truly that significant in the vast, tangled web of his life? Just as the thought settled, the wind howled outside, a mournful sound that sent a shiver racing down my spine. It felt like a warning, a reminder that even in this haven, danger lurked.

"Do you hear that?" I asked, my voice barely a whisper, as I instinctively stepped closer to him, seeking solace in his presence.

"Probably just the wind," he replied, though his eyes darkened, a shadow crossing his face. "But we should stay alert."

With that, we settled into an uneasy quiet, each of us grappling with our thoughts as the sun dipped lower in the sky, the fading light a stark reminder of the encroaching darkness. The atmosphere thickened, laden with unspoken fears, and I couldn't shake the feeling that we were caught in a web spun from our pasts, one that tightened with every passing moment.

The cabin, once a sanctuary, now felt like a cage, the walls closing in as the outside world slipped further from view. Whispers danced just beyond my reach, and I wondered if the past would finally come crashing down on us in this secluded corner of the world, or if perhaps, in this fragile cocoon, we might find a way to emerge, stronger and more resolute than ever before.

The darkness draped itself over the cabin like a heavy curtain, muffling the sounds of the outside world and amplifying the ones that lingered just beyond the walls. I was acutely aware of every creak of the floorboards beneath my feet, the soft sigh of the wind as it slipped through the cracks, and the distant call of a lone owl echoing through the night. It was as if the very house had come alive, whispering secrets in a language I couldn't quite understand. I turned my attention to Nathan, who stood by the window, the last rays of twilight casting shadows across his face.

"Do you always stand there like a brooding romantic?" I quipped, trying to infuse some levity into the heavy atmosphere. "Because if so, you might need to work on your 'mysterious stranger' routine. A little less 'brooding' and a bit more 'charming' would do you wonders."

He turned to me, the corners of his mouth lifting slightly, though his eyes retained that serious glint. "I thought you liked the brooding type."

"Only when they're not trying to hide secrets behind their carefully constructed walls," I shot back, enjoying the brief banter that punctured the tension swirling around us. "Or when they don't seem one step away from throwing themselves into the abyss. You know, details."

Nathan chuckled softly, the sound warm yet tinged with a hint of unease. "Fair point. I'm still working on that part." He stepped away from the window, the space between us narrowing as he moved closer. "But I promise you, I'm not the type to leap into the dark without a plan. I just need you to trust me."

"Trust isn't exactly a currency I have in abundance right now," I replied, my heart thudding against my ribs as I met his gaze. "Especially not with everything swirling around us."

He reached for my hand, his grip firm yet gentle, grounding me amid the tumult. The warmth of his touch sent a cascade of unexpected shivers down my spine, and I felt an involuntary flutter deep within. It was an enticing contradiction, the way danger danced around us while his presence felt like a lifeline.

"Let's get through tonight, one way or another," he said, his voice low and soothing, like a balm on an open wound. "How about we make a little noise ourselves? Drown out the whispers for a while."

"Ah, yes, the age-old tradition of distracting oneself from impending doom through...what? A rousing round of charades?" I raised an eyebrow, a smirk playing at my lips.

"I was thinking more along the lines of food," he replied, his eyes twinkling with a mix of mischief and warmth. "The kitchen is stocked, and I make a mean grilled cheese. Nothing chases away the gloom like melted cheese and crispy bread."

"Now you're speaking my language. But I'm fairly certain the darkness isn't afraid of dairy products," I teased, the levity easing the knots in my stomach. "Still, I'll take any distraction I can get."

We moved to the kitchen, a cozy nook that smelled of aged wood and old spices. As Nathan rummaged through the cabinets, I couldn't help but admire the way he moved—confident, purposeful. It was a stark contrast to the chaos that had brought us to this moment. The thought of him darting in and out of shadows, trying to keep me safe, sent a rush of warmth through me. I found myself drawn to the familiar rhythm of his actions, the comfort it provided in this strange landscape of uncertainty.

"So, what's the story behind this place?" I asked, my curiosity piqued as I leaned against the counter. "It must have some history if you're using it as a hideout."

Nathan paused, turning to me with a somber expression that belied his earlier lightheartedness. "It belonged to my grandparents. They brought the family here for summers, fishing and hiking, telling stories around the fire. But..." His voice faltered, the weight of unspoken memories thickening the air between us. "It wasn't all sunshine and laughter. This place has its ghosts."

"Ghosts? Are we talking metaphoric or literal?" I asked, unable to resist the wry smile tugging at my lips. "Because if it's the latter, I might have to rethink my cheese-filled comfort strategy."

"Literal, actually." He leaned against the counter opposite me, crossing his arms as if to shield himself from the memories. "My brother...he didn't come back one summer. Just disappeared into the woods, and we never found him."

The levity drained from the room, replaced by a heavy silence that seemed to throb with the intensity of his words. My heart ached at the vulnerability he revealed, the loss shadowing his eyes. "I'm so sorry," I whispered, the gravity of the moment wrapping around us like a shroud.

"Yeah, it's something we've lived with for a long time." He let out a shaky breath, the fragility of his expression breaking my heart. "Every creak, every gust of wind feels like a reminder. Some days are worse than others."

I nodded, the warmth of his earlier bravado replaced by a shared understanding of grief. "I can't imagine what that must be like," I said, my voice soft. "But I can promise you one thing: you're not alone in this."

He studied me, his gaze searching, and for a moment, the air around us felt electric. It was as if we were balancing on a precipice, teetering between sorrow and something more—a connection that had forged itself amid the chaos of our lives.

Just then, a sharp sound pierced the quiet, a crack like a twig snapping outside. We both froze, eyes wide, our hearts pounding in unison. I felt a chill race down my spine, the air suddenly thick with a sense of dread. Nathan's expression hardened, the lightness evaporating in an instant. "Stay here," he instructed, his tone a fierce command.

"What? No way!" I protested, adrenaline surging through me. "I'm not about to be a damsel in distress while you go off to battle...whatever that is."

"Nobody's going off to battle anything," he replied, urgency threading through his voice. "Just stay put. I'll check it out."

I opened my mouth to argue further, but a flicker of movement caught my eye just outside the window. A shadow darted past, disappearing into the underbrush, and the world outside felt suddenly sinister. "Okay," I said, my resolve wavering. "But I'm coming with you."

With a nod, Nathan moved toward the door, and I followed, our earlier banter lost in the urgency of the moment. The chill in the air wrapped around us, a stark reminder that the woods were not merely a backdrop but a character in our unfolding story—a living entity with its own secrets, one that demanded respect and, perhaps, a bit of caution. As we stepped outside, I could feel the weight of unseen eyes watching, and for the first time, I realized we were not just hiding from our pasts; we were confronting something far more present and dangerous.

The air outside the cabin felt electric, charged with an unspoken tension that set my nerves on edge. Nathan moved silently, his senses sharpened, scanning the shadows that danced along the tree line. I matched his intensity, every whisper of the wind seeming to carry a message just out of reach. My heart raced as I strained to listen, the world narrowing down to the rustle of leaves and the distant call of a night bird.

"Nathan, what if it's just an animal?" I whispered, trying to dismiss the fear that crept up my spine. "I mean, we are in the woods. There are bound to be squirrels and raccoons out here."

He shot me a sideways glance, a mix of amusement and seriousness etched on his face. "Squirrels don't typically snap twigs like that. Plus, they don't have the creepy habit of stalking people."

"Right, because that's definitely a raccoon thing." I attempted a teasing smile, but the tension in my chest only tightened. He took a cautious step toward the edge of the clearing, the cabin's soft glow dimming behind us. I took a deep breath, willing myself to stay calm. If I couldn't poke fun at the absurdity of the situation, I'd lose my mind.

"I need you to stay close," he murmured, the protective instinct in his tone making my heart flutter. "If anything happens, you run back inside."

"Me? Run? Please. I'm more of a 'stand my ground and yell obscenities' type," I quipped, though my pulse quickened as he moved farther away.

"Maybe that should change," he replied, his voice a low growl as he turned back to the dark forest. "Just... stay alert."

With every step he took, I felt the weight of uncertainty press down on me. Shadows seemed to elongate, merging into each other, blurring the line between reality and imagination. Nathan crouched down, peering into the underbrush, and I couldn't help but wonder what haunted him in these woods. The echoes of his past whispered through my mind, and I felt a sudden urge to reach out, to bridge the gap between his fears and my own.

"I know this might sound silly," I began, my voice breaking the heavy silence. "But what if we treated this like a ghost story? You know, instead of being terrified, let's get creative with it. I mean, if we're going to be stalked by something, it might as well have a backstory, right?"

Nathan straightened, a bemused expression crossing his face. "You really think a ghost will get distracted by a backstory?"

"Hey, if the ghost wants to haunt us, it might appreciate a little character development," I retorted, a spark of courage igniting within me. "Plus, I could use a good laugh right now."

"Okay, so let's say it's the ghost of my brother," Nathan said, his tone lightening ever so slightly. "He's wandering the woods looking for a lost fishing rod and a sandwich he left behind."

"Perfect! What's his name? Rod the Lost?" I shot back, grinning despite the darkness that surrounded us. The playful banter seemed to lighten the mood, if only for a moment.

Nathan chuckled, but the laugh faded quickly as another sound pierced the stillness—a rustle followed by a low growl. My heart plummeted as we froze, the humor evaporating in an instant. "That doesn't sound like a sandwich thief," I whispered, my breath hitching in my throat.

"I think it's time we get back inside," he said, his expression now one of focus, the playful veneer stripped away.

Before I could respond, a shadow lunged from the trees, a dark figure bursting into the clearing. I barely had time to process the sight before Nathan was in motion, moving to shield me. The creature—large and menacing, with piercing eyes that glimmered in the moonlight—snarled as it advanced toward us.

"Stay behind me!" Nathan commanded, his stance protective as he positioned himself between me and the advancing threat.

"What the hell is that?" I exclaimed, instinctively clutching his arm.

"I think we're about to find out," he muttered, eyes locked on the creature, muscles coiled like a spring ready to unleash.

The beast halted, sniffing the air, and for a moment, everything felt suspended in a breathless hush. I could feel Nathan's heartbeat pulsing through his arm, a steady rhythm that contrasted with the chaos around us. I swallowed hard, forcing myself to remain rooted despite the urge to flee.

"Maybe it's just a really big dog?" I suggested, my voice barely above a whisper, though I knew it was a feeble attempt at reassurance.

"I'm pretty sure that's not the kind of dog anyone wants as a pet," he replied, his gaze unwavering.

The creature took a step closer, its growl resonating in the silence, a sound that rattled the very bones of the earth beneath us. It seemed to glow in the moonlight, its fur matted and wild, eyes burning with an intelligence that sent chills racing down my spine. I couldn't tell if it was an illusion or if the woods had truly birthed something nightmarish.

"Run," Nathan said suddenly, urgency flooding his voice.

And just like that, instinct took over. I didn't hesitate; I bolted toward the cabin, my feet pounding against the ground as I raced past Nathan. I could feel the creature behind us, the heat of its breath sending a shockwave of terror through my body.

The cabin door loomed ahead, an oasis in the chaos, but as I reached for the handle, a deep, rumbling growl echoed behind us. I turned just in time to see Nathan, still locked in place, his muscles tense as he prepared to confront whatever nightmare stalked us.

"Get inside!" he yelled, his voice piercing through the darkness.

But as I pushed the door open, a deafening crack split the air, and the earth trembled beneath us. The shadows shifted, coiling around Nathan like tendrils, and I froze, a scream trapped in my throat.

The night had transformed into a battleground, with the cabin standing as our last line of defense. But before I could process the horror unfolding before me, the ground gave way, a chasm opening beneath Nathan's feet, pulling him down into the abyss.

"No!" I screamed, lunging forward as the world tilted, my heart breaking as I reached for him, desperate to bridge the chasm that had suddenly yawned between us. But as my fingers brushed his, the darkness enveloped him, and I was left alone in the storm of shadows and uncertainty, my world crashing down as I stood at the edge, terrified of what lay below.

Chapter 12: Haunted by Shadows

The night wrapped around us like a velvet cloak, heavy and thick with the scent of rain-soaked earth. I had always loved the serenity that came with these quiet hours, the world outside slumbering, each whisper of the wind a lullaby coaxing the stars to stay a little longer. But on this particular evening, tranquility had morphed into something sinister. As I stirred from a restless sleep, I found Nathan standing by the window, a silhouette against the muted glow of the streetlight. His shoulders, usually so relaxed, were drawn tight, and I could sense the turmoil radiating from him.

"Hey," I murmured, my voice still thick with sleep. "What are you doing?"

He didn't turn to look at me immediately. Instead, he stared out into the darkness, his jaw clenched, the muscles in his neck taut. I shuffled to his side, the cool wooden floor sending shivers up my spine. Outside, the rain began to fall again, each drop a tiny percussion against the window, echoing the anxiety thrumming in my chest.

"Nathan?" I tried again, a little louder this time. The concern in my tone seemed to finally pierce through whatever haze had settled over him. He turned slowly, revealing the shadows beneath his eyes, shadows that hinted at something deeper than mere sleeplessness.

"I've been getting these messages," he said, his voice barely above a whisper. "Strange texts that make no sense. They taunt me about my past... and threaten anyone close to me."

A chill skated down my spine, cold and unsettling. "What do you mean, taunting?"

He ran a hand through his hair, frustration mingling with fear in his dark gaze. "It's as if someone knows everything—every mistake, every regret. They want me to know that they're watching, waiting. It's... it's terrifying."

I took a step back, processing the weight of his words. The past was supposed to be a shadow that faded with time, not a vengeful spirit ready to drag us back into its grasp. "What kind of messages?"

"Vague threats, mostly," he replied, swallowing hard. "Just enough to unnerve me. Last night, it said, 'The past never forgets. Watch your back.'"

"Who do you think it is?" I asked, but I already feared the answer. Our sanctuary, which had felt so secure, now pulsed with an ominous energy, as if the walls themselves were listening in, sharing secrets with the creeping darkness outside.

"I don't know," he admitted, rubbing the bridge of his nose as if trying to erase the weight of dread that had settled there. "But it feels personal."

I nodded, feeling a sense of determination rising within me. "We need to investigate this together. I refuse to let some anonymous coward haunt us in our own home."

He looked at me then, the tension in his posture easing just a fraction. "You really want to get involved in this?"

"Absolutely," I said, a fire igniting in my heart. "You're not alone in this. We'll figure it out."

Nathan hesitated, his vulnerability flashing across his face like lightning. "You might regret that. I have a lot of baggage, and I don't want to drag you into it."

"Regret?" I scoffed, forcing a smile that I hoped was more convincing than it felt. "The only thing I might regret is not standing by you. Besides, I'm the queen of baggage—just ask my last three relationships."

He chuckled softly, the tension in the air easing ever so slightly. But I could still see the flicker of unease behind his eyes. "Okay, then. Let's start digging. But promise me you'll stay safe."

"Safe?" I grinned, leaning closer. "I plan to be downright reckless."

As the rain continued to tap softly against the window, we set to work. Our first step involved combing through Nathan's old emails, a digital archive of his past that had begun to unravel like a frayed thread. Sitting side by side at his laptop, the glow of the screen illuminated the lines of worry etched on his face. I fought the urge to reach out and squeeze his hand, knowing the intimacy would only deepen the shadows we were navigating.

Scrolling through, we found little of interest until a name surfaced—a name that sent a jolt through my system. "Wait. This person... I've heard of them before." I leaned closer, my heart racing. "It's that journalist who was obsessed with your case. The one who wouldn't let it go."

Nathan's expression darkened, a storm brewing behind his eyes. "Lila Carter. She wrote those articles years ago, painting me as a monster. But I thought she'd moved on. Why would she be reaching out now?"

"Maybe she hasn't moved on," I suggested, my mind racing. "If she's been following you—watching you—it could be her. But why would she threaten you?"

"I have no idea," he replied, the frustration evident in his voice. "But we need to confront this head-on. I won't let her play with my life any longer."

The determination in his voice sent a rush of adrenaline through me. We were standing on the precipice of something big, something dangerous. And yet, the thrill of the unknown intertwined with the fear was intoxicating. It was a reckoning we both needed, a confrontation with our respective pasts that loomed like a specter.

"Let's find out what she knows," I said, my voice firm and resolute. "And together, we'll face whatever comes next."

The shadows shifted around us, but I could sense a spark igniting between us, binding our fates together. Whatever haunted our pasts, we would unearth it, drag it into the light, and face it. Together.

As dawn stretched its lazy fingers across the horizon, spilling soft light into our sanctuary, the tension from the night before lingered like an unwelcome guest. I watched Nathan over breakfast, his brow furrowed in concentration as he picked at his toast. The air hummed with an energy that felt both electric and oppressive, a silent acknowledgment of the storm brewing just beneath the surface. The gentle clinking of dishes was a poor backdrop for the turmoil that stirred within us.

"You know," I said, breaking the silence, "if this were a movie, we'd be sharing a dramatic breakfast scene. The kind where a heartfelt confession suddenly changes everything." I tried to infuse some lightness into the moment, but my attempt fell flat. Nathan glanced up, a hint of a smile ghosting across his lips before the weight of reality pulled him back.

"Do you think we're the protagonists or the side characters?" he mused, the wryness in his tone almost soothing. "Because if it's the latter, I'm seriously reconsidering my life choices."

"Definitely protagonists," I shot back, leaning in conspiratorially. "And we're about to embark on an epic quest to confront our nemesis—whoever that may be. Probably with lots of witty banter along the way." I couldn't help but laugh, hoping to lighten the moment. But deep down, I knew our playful exchange was merely a facade, masking the brewing chaos just outside our window.

With our determination solidified, we decided to pay Lila Carter a visit. As we prepared to leave, the sky turned from soft pastels to a steely gray, heavy clouds promising a tempest that mirrored our own rising unease. Nathan grabbed his jacket, the fabric rough against my fingers as I helped him slip it on, my heart racing with a mixture of anticipation and dread.

"Ready?" I asked, trying to infuse some bravado into my voice.

"Not really," he admitted, his eyes darting toward the door as if it might leap forward and swallow him whole. "But we can't let fear dictate our next move."

The drive to Lila's office was an exercise in awkward silence, broken only by the low hum of the radio, which seemed far too cheerful for our current predicament. I kept glancing sideways, trying to catch glimpses of Nathan's expression, half-expecting him to crumble under the weight of his past. But he remained resolute, gripping the steering wheel as if it were a lifeline.

"Do you think she'll talk to us?" I asked, not sure what kind of reception we could expect from someone who had made a career out of dredging up other people's nightmares.

Nathan shrugged, glancing at me with a hint of mischief. "If she doesn't, we could always resort to bribery. I hear donuts work wonders."

"Or we could threaten to expose her dirty laundry," I shot back, arching an eyebrow. "But I suspect that would land us in a legal mess."

As we pulled into the parking lot, I couldn't help but notice the building's exterior: cold and imposing, a façade that matched the severity of the situation. The office was nestled between a trendy coffee shop and a quirky bookstore, the juxtaposition of warmth and familiarity amplifying the stark chill I felt as we approached the entrance.

Inside, the atmosphere buzzed with a frenetic energy, journalists and interns flitting about like moths around a flame. I could feel Nathan tense beside me, the weight of his past pressing down like a physical entity, heavy and suffocating. But I was determined to keep him grounded.

"Just remember," I whispered as we approached the reception desk, "you're more than the mistakes you made. You've grown, and that's what matters."

He nodded, though the uncertainty in his eyes lingered. A woman with a sharp bob and an equally sharp gaze looked up from her computer, her expression a mix of curiosity and annoyance.

"Can I help you?" she asked, her voice clipped as if she were far too busy to deal with interruptions.

"We'd like to speak with Lila Carter," I said, trying to sound more confident than I felt. "It's about a message she sent to Nathan."

The receptionist frowned, tapping her fingers impatiently on the desk. "You'll need to make an appointment. She's busy."

"Can't you just tell her it's urgent?" Nathan's voice cut through the tension, and I felt a flicker of pride at his resolve.

She hesitated, glancing at Nathan, her gaze assessing him like a judge weighing a defendant's fate. "Fine," she finally relented, picking up the phone with an air of reluctance. "But don't expect much. She doesn't take kindly to drop-ins."

After a brief exchange, the receptionist hung up and fixed us with a steely glare. "You can go in, but don't say I didn't warn you."

As we entered Lila's office, I immediately felt a shift in the atmosphere. The room was dimly lit, with shelves lined with awards and framed articles, each piece a testament to her relentless pursuit of truth. Lila sat behind a large mahogany desk, her dark hair falling over one shoulder like a storm cloud. She regarded us with an intensity that could strip paint from walls.

"What brings you here?" she asked, her tone sharp as a knife.

"We want to talk about the messages," Nathan said, his voice steadier than I expected. "The ones you've been sending me."

She leaned back in her chair, crossing her arms, a slight smirk playing on her lips. "Interesting. You've never struck me as the type to seek out old ghosts."

"Maybe I've decided to face my past head-on," he replied, defiance igniting in his eyes. "But I'd like to know why you're digging it up again."

Lila's gaze flicked between us, her interest piqued. "The past has a way of coming back, doesn't it? Especially when there are unanswered questions."

"Questions like why you've been watching me?" Nathan pressed, a tension crackling in the air like static. "Or threatening the people I care about?"

"I wouldn't call them threats," she replied, her tone dismissive. "Just gentle reminders that some stories don't end when you want them to. They linger, like bad dreams."

The temperature in the room dropped, the shadows lengthening as our unease deepened. Just when I thought Nathan might lose his composure, he leaned in, his expression fierce. "You're playing a dangerous game, Lila. I won't let you hurt anyone I love."

Her laughter echoed through the office, sharp and biting. "Love? That's rich coming from someone like you. But then again, maybe that's why I'm interested. The more you fight it, the more delicious the story becomes."

I exchanged a glance with Nathan, the unspoken understanding clear between us. This was more than just a conversation; it was a battle of wills, a dance between predator and prey. And I wasn't about to let Lila take the upper hand.

"Enough games," I said, my voice steadying. "We're not here for theatrics. We want answers. And we won't leave until we get them."

Lila's eyes sparkled with mischief, the thrill of the chase invigorating her. "Well then, let's see how far you're willing to go to uncover the truth. After all, the past is full of surprises."

The air thickened with tension as the stakes climbed higher, and I could feel the ground shifting beneath us, propelling us deeper into a web of secrets that threatened to ensnare us both. Whatever awaited us, we were ready to confront it, together.

The tension in the room crackled like static electricity, an invisible force pushing us all toward a reckoning. Lila Carter, her expression a mask of feigned indifference, leaned back in her chair, as if waiting for the inevitable storm to break. Nathan and I exchanged glances, a silent communication passing between us that spoke volumes of our shared resolve. This wasn't just a conversation; it was a standoff, a battle of wills where the stakes had never felt higher.

"Let's skip the theatrics, shall we?" I pressed, adopting a no-nonsense tone that felt foreign yet empowering. "You have something to say, so say it."

Lila's eyes glinted with a mix of amusement and intrigue. "Oh, sweetie, it's not about what I have to say; it's about what you're willing to uncover. Secrets are like shadows—always lurking, always waiting to be brought into the light."

"Just cut the riddles," Nathan shot back, his frustration bubbling to the surface. "What do you want from me? What's your angle?"

She tapped her fingers on the desk, a rhythmic dance that echoed the tension in the air. "You see, Nathan, people love a good story. Yours is particularly juicy, full of twists and turns. The hero-turned-villain, redemption sought but never fully attained. That's the kind of narrative that sells. And I'm in the business of selling stories."

"And scaring the hell out of people, apparently," I muttered under my breath. Nathan shot me a quick glance, a half-smile tugging at the corners of his mouth, but the gravity of the moment pressed down like a lead blanket.

"Why now, Lila?" Nathan asked, his voice steady despite the whirlwind of emotions swirling around us. "Why bring this up after all this time?"

She leaned forward, her gaze piercing. "Because the past is a fickle beast. You may have thought it buried, but it has a way of clawing its way back to the surface. And someone wants to ensure you don't forget."

I felt a shiver race down my spine. "Someone? Who? Is it the person behind the messages?"

Lila shrugged, her nonchalance unnerving. "Maybe. Or maybe it's just the ghosts of your past whispering in your ear, reminding you of your missteps. Either way, they want you unsettled. They want you afraid."

"Afraid?" Nathan echoed, disbelief coloring his tone. "I refuse to live in fear. Not anymore."

"Then why do you look so haunted?" Lila shot back, her smile razor-sharp. The corners of her mouth twitched with a glee that made my skin crawl. I could feel Nathan's resolve waver slightly, the shadows of his past flickering in his eyes.

"I'm not haunted," he said, a defiance creeping back into his voice. "I'm here to confront it. But you need to be straight with us. What do you know? Who's behind this?"

Lila leaned back again, her demeanor shifting from predator to a more contemplative state. "What if I told you it was someone close to you? Someone who knows your weaknesses?"

The words hung in the air like a bitter fog, suffocating and heavy. Nathan's face drained of color, and I felt the air thicken around us, charged with unspoken fears and unacknowledged truths.

"Close to me?" he repeated, incredulity creeping in. "What kind of twisted game are you playing?"

"Oh, Nathan, this is no game," Lila said, her tone dripping with mock sincerity. "It's simply the reality you've chosen to ignore. The past never forgets. It never lets go. Just ask anyone who's ever tried to outrun it."

"What do you want us to do?" I interjected, trying to regain control of the spiraling conversation. "Are you trying to scare us into submission, or do you actually have something useful to say?"

"Useful? That's a subjective term," she replied, her voice lilting with amusement. "But I can give you a piece of advice. If you want to confront your ghosts, you'd better be prepared for the consequences. They're not as forgiving as you might hope."

"Consequences?" Nathan echoed, his eyes narrowing. "You mean to tell me that we should just sit back and wait for whatever nightmare you're implying to come knocking? No thanks."

"Come now, Nathan," Lila chided, waving a hand dismissively. "It's more thrilling when you don't know what's lurking around the corner, don't you think?"

I shot Nathan a glance, the silent communication again passing between us. "We're not afraid of the unknown," I said, my voice gaining strength. "We're ready to face whatever comes our way."

Lila's expression morphed into something unreadable, the smirk fading as she leaned in closer, her voice dropping to a conspiratorial whisper. "Very well. But remember, once you start digging, you might unearth things you never wanted to find. People will get hurt, and you may not like what you discover."

Her words hung heavily in the air, an ominous warning wrapped in layers of ambiguity. The silence that followed was thick with unspoken fears, our collective breath held as we contemplated the implications of her statement.

"I'm not afraid of the truth," Nathan asserted, the fire in his voice rekindling. "I want to know what's happening, and I want to know who's behind those messages. It's time to end this once and for all."

Lila leaned back in her chair, amusement flickering back into her eyes. "Ah, the valiant hero ready to face the dragon. But remember, every hero has their fatal flaw. And in your case, Nathan, that flaw may just be your own heart."

"What does that mean?" I demanded, my impatience flaring.

"Love can be a powerful motivator," she replied, her voice laced with an almost musical quality. "It can also be your downfall. If you're not careful, you might just be the one who ends up hurting the people you care about most."

Nathan stiffened beside me, the tension radiating from him palpable. "You think I'd ever hurt her?"

"Wouldn't you?" Lila's eyes glinted dangerously. "Wouldn't the weight of your past crush you to the point where you lash out at the ones who matter? That's the tragedy of it all."

"Enough!" I cut in, unwilling to let Lila spin her web of uncertainty around us. "We're here to get answers, not to listen to your twisted philosophies. Just tell us what you know."

Lila sighed dramatically, as if we were the ones wasting her time. "Fine. If you're so intent on digging, then I suggest you start with the ones who haven't forgiven you. Look for the connections you think are severed."

"And then what?" Nathan pressed, his impatience boiling over.

"Then," she said, her voice a low whisper, "you'll realize just how deep this goes."

Before I could respond, the phone on her desk rang, slicing through the tension like a knife. Lila's eyes flickered with annoyance before she picked it up. "What?" she snapped, her tone all business.

I turned to Nathan, my heart pounding in rhythm with the ominous atmosphere. "What do you think she means?"

"I don't know," he replied, his brow furrowing. "But we can't let her play mind games with us."

As Lila continued her conversation, her eyes darting between us, I couldn't shake the feeling that something was off. The shadows seemed to deepen around us, cloaking our very presence. Just as she hung up, a commotion erupted outside her office door, voices rising in a cacophony that made my heart race.

Lila's expression shifted from annoyance to intrigue, a wicked smile spreading across her face. "Looks like the past has come knocking a little sooner than expected. I hope you're ready."

Before we could react, the door swung open, and a figure stormed in—someone I never expected to see again, their face a mask of fury and desperation.

"Nathan!" they shouted, and the world tilted on its axis.

I felt Nathan stiffen beside me, the air crackling with tension, as the reality of what lay ahead crashed over us like a rogue wave, threatening to pull us under into the depths of our worst fears.

Chapter 13: The Revelation

The air inside the warehouse was thick with dust and despair, every breath a reminder of the decay surrounding us. Shadows danced along the walls, shifting like phantoms in the dim light that struggled to penetrate the grime-streaked windows. My heart raced, a frantic percussion against the oppressive silence, as Nathan and I moved cautiously through the desolate space. The scent of rust and mildew clung to everything, a bitter reminder of the secrets hidden within these walls.

Nathan glanced at me, his eyes alight with a mix of fear and determination. "We have to be careful," he whispered, his voice barely above a breath. "This place has memories, and not all of them are good."

Memories. I couldn't help but wonder what ghosts haunted him here. The thought sent a shiver down my spine, and I tightened my grip on the flashlight, the beam cutting through the murkiness like a lifeline. Every step echoed, an ominous reminder of our intrusion into this forgotten world.

The last rays of daylight were swallowed by the looming structure, and I could almost hear the building groan under the weight of its own history. "Why here, Nathan? Why did you bring us to this forsaken place?" I asked, a tremor lacing my words. My curiosity was tinged with a burgeoning dread that settled deep in my bones.

He hesitated, his jaw tightening. "This was where it all started. The syndicate operated from this very spot. If we're going to find answers, we have to go back to the beginning."

The words hung heavy between us, a tether to the past that I couldn't fully grasp but could feel tangibly in the air. A chill ran through me as I took in the remnants of shattered glass and peeling paint, the echoes of laughter and cries long extinguished. "You think we'll find something here? Something that connects us?" I asked, my voice steadier than I felt.

"I have to believe it," he said, determination glinting in his eyes. "If I'm right, there's a record, something that ties our lives together in ways we haven't even begun to understand."

With every word, a part of me hoped he was wrong. I didn't want to be tangled in Nathan's past, a place shrouded in darkness and danger. Yet the undeniable pull between us was a force I couldn't resist, and the thrill of discovery ignited a fire in my veins.

As we ventured deeper, the layout of the warehouse began to reveal itself—long-abandoned machinery cast in shadows, rusting metal and splintered wood, the remnants of lives lived and lost. My eyes caught a glimpse of something shiny half-buried under debris. Curiosity piqued, I knelt, brushing away the grime to reveal a tarnished keychain, its surface etched with a familiar insignia.

"Nathan, look at this," I called, holding it up for him to see. Recognition flickered across his face, a fleeting glimpse of vulnerability.

"That's the logo of the syndicate," he breathed, taking the keychain from my trembling fingers. "This was theirs. It means we're on the right track."

Just as the weight of those words settled around us, a sudden noise shattered the stillness—a low creak followed by a sharp clatter, reverberating through the empty space. My heart lurched as I turned, the flashlight beam flickering over the jagged edges of the walls, searching for the source.

"Nathan?" I whispered, fear seeping into my bones. "Did you hear that?"

He nodded, his expression grave. "Stay close," he murmured, stepping in front of me, a protective barrier against whatever lurked in the shadows. The tension thickened, wrapping around us like a noose, tightening with every second that passed.

As we advanced, the sound came again, a rustling like the breath of a predator stalking its prey. The flashlight's beam wavered as I focused, my heart pounding a wild rhythm. I wanted to run, to escape the terror building inside me, but Nathan's presence anchored me. We were in this together, whether I liked it or not.

Suddenly, a figure darted into the light, cloaked in darkness, and instinct kicked in. Nathan pushed me behind him, his body a shield as he faced the intruder. My breath caught in my throat, an icy lump of fear that threatened to choke me. The figure paused, silhouetted against the fading light, and I could see nothing but a shadowy outline—tall, imposing, and filled with menace.

"Who are you?" Nathan's voice rang out, steady but low, like a coiled spring ready to snap.

The figure chuckled, a sound devoid of humor, echoing off the cold concrete walls. "You're in deep, Nathan. Did you really think you could come back here and not face the consequences?"

Recognition flickered in Nathan's eyes, a spark of familiarity igniting an array of emotions I couldn't decipher. I wanted to scream, to demand answers, but my voice felt lost in the whirlwind of adrenaline and uncertainty.

"Get out of here, Claire," Nathan said sharply, the urgency in his voice sharpening my focus. "This is my fight."

"No way," I shot back, the defiance igniting a spark within me. "We're in this together, remember?"

The tension hung thick in the air as the figure stepped closer, revealing a face that was hauntingly familiar, twisted with malevolence. My mind raced as the pieces began to fit together, a puzzle I was desperate to solve. The truth was lurking, just beyond reach, and I was determined to unearth it, no matter the cost.

In that moment, surrounded by shadows and secrets, I realized that the path forward was fraught with danger, yet I was irrevocably entwined in Nathan's life—and perhaps he was in mine. The revelation loomed ahead, a dark promise waiting to be unveiled, and I steeled myself for the confrontation to come, ready to face the nightmare head-on.

"Why did you come back here?" The shadowy figure's voice sliced through the tension like a knife, deep and mocking. My heart thudded in my chest, a relentless drum that drowned out the eerie stillness of the warehouse. Nathan stood his ground, muscles taut as a drawn bowstring, while I felt as though the floor had dropped out from beneath me.

"Let's cut to the chase, shall we?" Nathan replied, his voice steady despite the palpable fear that draped over us like a heavy fog. "I'm here for the records. The truth."

The figure stepped closer, allowing the beam of my flashlight to illuminate a sharp jawline and hollow cheeks—features that belonged to someone both familiar and unsettling. A chill ran through me, not from the cold, but from the sudden realization that this was not just an enemy lurking in the shadows; it was someone connected to Nathan's past.

"Truth? You think you can just waltz back in here and dig up the past like it's some old relic? You're a fool, Nathan." There was a bite to the words, a venomous disdain that filled the air between us.

"Foolishness can sometimes yield the best results," Nathan shot back, his defiance sparking a flicker of admiration in my chest. It took guts to stand against someone who seemed ready to unleash a storm.

"What do you want?" I blurted, stepping forward. I wasn't about to hide behind Nathan like a damsel in distress. My instincts screamed that this confrontation was as much about me as it was about him.

"Want?" The figure chuckled darkly, an unsettling sound that echoed against the walls. "I want to know why you're here, little girl. Playing detective in a game that's way over your head."

A surge of indignation rose within me. "I'm not just some little girl. I'm here to support Nathan, and I want to know the truth just as much as he does. So, spill it."

"Spill it?" The figure's eyes glinted with amusement, then shifted back to Nathan. "And here I thought you were smart enough to keep her out of this mess. But then again, you've always been a sucker for a pretty face."

"Enough," Nathan growled, stepping closer, anger simmering just beneath the surface. "You don't know what you're dealing with."

"Oh, but I do. I've watched you fumble through this life you've built, trying to escape a past that's clawed its way back. You think you can outrun your demons?"

The weight of those words hung heavy, swirling around us like smoke. I could see the cracks forming in Nathan's bravado, the ghosts of regret flaring in his eyes. I wanted to reach out, to anchor him, but my feet felt glued to the ground, a mix of fear and uncertainty pinning me in place.

"I'm not running," Nathan retorted, voice low and fierce. "I'm facing them."

"You think confronting ghosts will change what happened? You're wrong, Nathan." The figure stepped back, shadows pooling around him like a cloak. "There are things you can't change, no matter how hard you try. The past has a way of bleeding into the present."

"Then let it bleed," Nathan spat, a fierce resolve igniting in his eyes. "I won't let it consume me."

With that, the figure lunged forward, and the world snapped into chaotic motion. Nathan moved to intercept, but I was faster, adrenaline surging through me like wildfire. "No!" I shouted, my voice breaking the silence that had settled around us. "Get down!"

Before I could process the sudden rush of instinct, I shoved Nathan aside, catching the figure off guard as he lunged at us. We stumbled backward, crashing against a pile of debris that crumbled under our weight. The flash of metal glinted in the beam of my flashlight, a knife—no, a blade that seemed to catch the dim light and draw it in, like a hungry predator.

"Claire!" Nathan barked, scrambling to his feet and pulling me up alongside him. "Get behind me!"

"Not a chance!" I said, the defiance coursing through me igniting a spark I didn't know I had. "You're not doing this alone. We've come this far."

The figure chuckled again, dark amusement mingling with malice. "What a feisty little thing you are. But this isn't a game. You have no idea what you're up against."

"Then enlighten us!" Nathan yelled, fury mixing with fear as he took a step forward.

"You think you can just charge in here and demand answers?" The figure circled us, the shadows shifting with his movements. "You're out of your depth."

I glanced at Nathan, our eyes locking for a heartbeat. There was a shared understanding, a bond forged in the fire of fear and determination. Whatever this was, we were facing it together.

"You've been living in the shadows too long," I said, my voice steadying with each word. "But we're not afraid of the dark anymore. We want the truth, and we're not leaving until we get it."

"Bold words for someone who doesn't know the first thing about the cost of that truth," the figure sneered, the knife glinting ominously as he moved closer.

"You think you can intimidate us? Think again," Nathan shot back, confidence surging in his tone.

"Intimidation isn't the goal, Nathan," the figure said, his voice dripping with contempt. "I'm here to deliver a message. You've stirred the pot, and now the consequences are coming. You can't just leave the past behind; it will come knocking."

Suddenly, the ground beneath us shuddered, and the warehouse seemed to groan in response. My breath caught in my throat, and a frigid gust of air swept through, sending a shiver down my spine. The walls, once still and somber, seemed alive with energy, the darkness pooling and swirling like a storm ready to break.

Nathan shifted, positioning himself closer to me, his presence a steadying force. "Whatever comes, we'll face it together," he murmured, his voice low and fierce.

And then, with an unexpected rush, the figure lunged again, but this time Nathan was ready. The two collided, and the clash of bodies sent echoes through the warehouse, the sound reverberating in my chest as I felt the thrill of danger swirl around us.

In that moment, everything shifted. The battle wasn't just about Nathan's past; it was a reckoning of our shared strength, a confrontation not just with the figure before us, but with everything that lay beneath the surface. Secrets buried deep, pasts intertwined, and a future that hung in the balance like a fragile thread. The storm was brewing, and we were caught right in its eye.

The clash between Nathan and the figure erupted like a storm, all thunder and chaos as they grappled in a whirlwind of movement. My heart pounded like a war drum, urging me to act, to intervene, but the primal fear coursing through me rendered me momentarily paralyzed. Shadows flickered across the walls, morphing into grotesque shapes as I strained to comprehend the chaos unfolding before me.

"Stop!" I shouted, my voice a thin thread against the tempest. I lunged forward, desperate to reach Nathan, to pull him back from the edge of whatever precipice we were teetering on. "This isn't the way!"

"Stay back, Claire!" Nathan grunted, twisting away from the figure's grip, but I was already moving, adrenaline surging through my veins like wildfire. I couldn't let him face this alone, not when every instinct screamed that this was bigger than either of us.

"Why don't you just tell us what you want?" I pressed, inching closer, trying to distract the figure from Nathan's relentless resolve. "You're not here for a fight; you're here for something else."

The figure hesitated for a fraction of a second, and in that moment of uncertainty, I seized the opportunity. "You can't scare us into silence," I continued, my voice steadier than I felt. "Whatever this is, we'll confront it together."

The figure turned towards me, his expression shifting, and in that fleeting glimpse, I saw something human—a flicker of recognition, perhaps even regret. "You have no idea what you're stepping into," he said, his tone softer now, but still laced with menace. "This isn't just a game. You think your love can shield you from the truth? It will only bring more pain."

"Love?" Nathan spat, the word tinged with defiance. "This isn't about love; it's about survival."

"Isn't it always?" The figure smirked, regaining his composure, a shadow flitting across his face. "You think you can reclaim the past without paying the price? The syndicate won't let you walk away. Not now, not ever."

Nathan's jaw tightened, and I could feel the tension crackling between us, thick and charged. "I'm not afraid of them," he said, but there was a quiver in his voice, a hint of doubt that made my stomach twist. "Not anymore."

"Brave words for a man with so much to lose," the figure taunted, glancing at me, then back to Nathan. "You don't understand the forces at play here. You've brought her into this. You've tied her to your fate."

"Her fate is her own," Nathan countered, a fierce protectiveness boiling beneath the surface. "You think you can manipulate us with threats? You're mistaken."

With a sudden burst of movement, the figure lunged again, and this time it was Nathan who intercepted, the two of them colliding with a force that sent reverberations through the air. I watched, my heart in my throat, as Nathan grappled with the figure, their silhouettes merging and separating in a dangerous dance of power and fury.

In a desperate attempt to regain control, I reached for a nearby piece of debris—an old, rusted pipe, its jagged edge glinting ominously in the sparse light. "Get off him!" I shouted, brandishing the pipe as if it could serve as a shield against the chaos.

The figure paused, eyeing the makeshift weapon, amusement flickering across his face. "You really think that's going to stop me?"

"Maybe not," I retorted, gripping it tighter, "but I'm not going to stand by and watch you hurt him."

With a swift movement, Nathan broke free, his expression a mix of relief and surprise as he caught sight of me. "Claire, no! You don't have to—"

Before he could finish, the figure lunged again, and the world shifted into slow motion. I swung the pipe with all my strength, the metal connecting with a sickening thud against the figure's arm. He stumbled back, momentarily stunned, but I could see the fire in his eyes igniting once more.

"Why are you so determined to protect him?" he growled, shaking off the blow. "You don't know the truth about him, about what he's done."

"What's that supposed to mean?" I shot back, my voice cutting through the tension like a knife. "He's trying to make amends. He's trying to escape the past."

"Escape?" The figure scoffed, a dangerous glint in his eyes. "You think you can escape your demons? They'll always find you. They're part of you."

In a sudden burst of anger, Nathan stepped forward, his presence a beacon of defiance. "You don't know me. You don't know what I've been through to get here. I'm not the same person I was, and I refuse to let the past dictate my future."

With a snarl, the figure lunged again, but this time I was ready. I threw the pipe aside, ready to grapple with him if necessary, but Nathan interjected, stepping in front of me as if he could shield me from the storm.

"Enough!" he roared, his voice echoing off the walls, commanding the shadows to retreat. "If you want to fight, then let's settle this like men. You can't intimidate me with your threats."

In that charged moment, time seemed to stand still. The tension in the air was electric, crackling with the energy of unspoken fears and buried truths. The figure's demeanor shifted, a flicker of uncertainty crossing his face, and I seized the opportunity to press forward.

"What do you want?" I demanded, the anger in my voice rising like a tide. "If you're here to threaten us, then you're wasting your breath. We deserve answers, not intimidation. So tell us—what is it you want?"

For a heartbeat, silence enveloped us, thick and suffocating. The figure hesitated, his façade cracking just enough for me to glimpse the turmoil beneath. "You really don't understand," he murmured, almost to himself. "You're stepping into a world that doesn't play by your rules. And if you keep pushing, the truth may shatter you."

Nathan stepped closer, the fire in his eyes unwavering. "We'll take that risk. We're ready to face whatever it is you're hiding."

In an instant, the air shifted, and the figure's eyes darkened. "Then brace yourselves," he hissed, the threat palpable. "Because the truth isn't just a weapon; it's a force that will destroy everything you hold dear."

Before we could react, the ground beneath us trembled again, a deep rumble reverberating through the walls as if the very foundations of the warehouse were groaning in protest. Dust rained down from the rafters, and I stumbled back, instinctively reaching for Nathan's arm.

"Get out!" the figure shouted suddenly, urgency cutting through the tension. "You have no idea what's about to happen!"

"What do you mean?" I shouted back, panic rising in my chest as the tremors intensified.

But the figure was already retreating, disappearing into the shadows as the structure began to shudder violently. I grabbed Nathan's hand, the intensity of the moment binding us together.

"Run!" he yelled, pulling me toward the exit as the walls trembled ominously, debris falling around us like the remnants of a collapsing dream.

We sprinted through the maze of shadows, the darkness closing in like a predator. I could feel the ground shift beneath us, a sense of urgency propelling us forward, our hearts racing as we navigated the chaos.

Just as we reached the door, a deafening crack echoed through the warehouse, and the ceiling began to give way. Dust and debris rained down as we lunged for safety, the world around us spiraling into chaos.

In that fleeting moment, as we burst into the night, the figure's final words echoed in my mind—a warning and a promise, mingling with the realization that the past had come crashing into our lives, bringing a storm we were ill-prepared to face. The shadows had returned, and with them, a truth that threatened to unravel everything we knew.

And then the ground beneath us split open, a gaping chasm of uncertainty swallowing the light, plunging us into darkness as the warehouse collapsed behind us. The last thing I heard was Nathan's voice, urgent and raw, calling my name as everything fell apart.

Chapter 14: A Moment of Truth

The hotel room felt like a sanctuary, its walls adorned with soft, muted colors that dulled the lingering echoes of our earlier confrontation. I could still hear the distant clamor of the street below, a reminder of the chaos we had narrowly escaped. The air was thick with the heady scent of the lavender candles Nathan had insisted on lighting—a misguided attempt at tranquility that seemed ironically fitting, given the storm brewing inside me. I paced the small space, my heart thumping wildly, each beat a frantic reminder of the vulnerability I felt in his presence.

Nathan stood by the window, silhouetted against the fading light, his profile sharp and defined. The play of shadows danced across his face, accentuating the tension etched around his jaw. I could see the weight of the day pressing down on him, the way his shoulders had a slight slump that spoke volumes of the battle we'd just faced. I wanted to close the gap between us, to bridge the distance that felt insurmountable after everything we'd endured together. But how could I? The very fabric of our relationship had become so intricately woven with danger and distrust.

"Are you okay?" His voice cut through the silence, low and rough around the edges, pulling me back from the edge of my spiraling thoughts. I met his gaze, those dark eyes piercing through the twilight.

"Do I look okay?" I shot back, a hint of bite lacing my words. It was a defense mechanism, my way of masking the tremor in my hands, the way they longed to reach out and touch him. I wanted to be brave, but the fear clung to me like a shroud, making it difficult to breathe. "We just faced down a group of people who wanted to hurt us. I think 'okay' is a stretch."

He stepped closer, the soft glow of the candles illuminating the contours of his face, revealing the deep furrows of concern that marred his otherwise composed demeanor. "You know what I mean," he said, a teasing lilt in his voice, but the seriousness beneath it anchored us both. "I meant emotionally."

Emotionally. The word hung in the air, heavy and laden with implications. I couldn't help but laugh, a sound that felt foreign amidst the intensity of the moment. "Oh, is that all? Just a casual day of existential dread and trauma bonding?"

Nathan's lips quirked into a half-smile, and for a brief moment, the weight of our situation lifted. "That's the spirit. Humor in the face of danger is a classic survival tactic."

We exchanged a knowing look, the spark of shared experiences igniting something deeper. I felt a familiar pull towards him, a magnetic force that had been growing stronger since the day we'd met. But as quickly as it flared to life, doubts swirled around my mind like a dark storm cloud. Was this chemistry born of genuine connection, or was it merely the aftermath of adrenaline-fueled panic?

"I don't know how we got here," I admitted, my voice softer now, stripped of bravado. "It feels like we're two pieces of a puzzle that don't quite fit, but somehow, we're still trying to make it work."

"I think we fit," he said, moving closer, his presence radiating warmth. "Maybe we just need to figure out how to turn the pieces to see the full picture."

Before I could respond, he reached for my hand, his touch sending electric currents up my arm. It felt natural, like this was where I was meant to be. But with every heartbeat, the shadows of his past loomed larger, threatening to engulf us. "Nathan, what if—"

He didn't let me finish. Instead, he closed the distance between us, his hands framing my face, thumbs brushing over my cheekbones with a tenderness that took my breath away. "Stop thinking for a second," he murmured, leaning in. "Just be here with me."

And then his lips were on mine, fierce and demanding, igniting a fire that blazed through the fear and uncertainty. I melted into the kiss, losing myself in the taste of him, the warmth that enveloped us like a cocoon. It was reckless and beautiful, a moment that felt like it could shatter at any second. Every lingering doubt began to fade, replaced by a desperate need to cling to this connection, to this man who had somehow become my anchor amidst the turmoil.

But just as quickly as it had ignited, the kiss broke, reality crashing back in like a cold wave. I pulled away, breathless and trembling, the chaos of our situation flooding back with brutal clarity. "We can't, Nathan. Not like this."

His expression darkened, the vulnerability in his eyes replaced with frustration. "Why not? You felt that. I know you did."

"I did," I conceded, my heart aching at the truth of his words. "But can I really trust you? I don't know who you are beneath all of this." I gestured wildly, the emotions swirling inside me threatening to spill over. "What if you're hiding something? What if this is just... a game to you?"

"It's not a game," he said, voice firm yet softening at the edges, revealing the man beneath the bravado. "I'm not here to hurt you. I want to be here, with you."

But the shadows still lingered, whispering doubts that clawed at my mind. How could I let myself fall into this when I knew so little about the man who stood before me? My heart raced with conflicting emotions—longing, fear, desire. It was a whirlwind that threatened to consume me entirely.

"Trust isn't built in a day," I said finally, the words tasting bittersweet on my tongue. "And we've got a long way to go."

"Then let's start figuring it out," he replied, his voice a gentle challenge. "Together."

The air crackled with unspoken promises, and I couldn't shake the feeling that, despite the uncertainty, we were standing on the precipice of something extraordinary. As I stared into his eyes, I saw the flicker of hope that mirrored my own, igniting a spark that could either set us ablaze or lead us to destruction. I didn't know what the future held, but in that moment, the prospect of discovering it with him felt tantalizingly close, like the first light of dawn breaking after a long, dark night.

The aftermath of that kiss hung in the air like smoke, swirling with uncertainty and promise. I sat on the edge of the bed, trying to gather my thoughts, my heart still racing from the surge of emotions that had enveloped us moments earlier. Nathan leaned against the window, the waning light casting an amber glow over his features, making him look almost ethereal. Yet beneath that allure lay layers of complexity, shadows dancing just out of reach.

"What now?" I asked, the question slipping out before I could reconsider. It felt impossibly naive in the wake of our confrontation, yet it echoed the raw vulnerability I had just exposed.

His gaze drifted from the street below to the ceiling, as if searching for answers among the intricate patterns. "I guess that depends on what we want," he said, his voice low and contemplative. "Do we want to pretend this never happened and go back to the way things were? Or do we lean into whatever this is?"

I considered his words, feeling the weight of the choice settling like a stone in my stomach. Leaning into whatever this was—such a reckless proposition, yet it was undeniably tempting. The rush of excitement coursing through me demanded to be acknowledged, but caution tugged at my heart. "You make it sound so easy."

"It's never easy," he replied, turning to face me fully, his expression serious. "But it could be worth it. If we're on the same page."

My heart thudded uncomfortably. The idea of being on the same page felt distant, a tantalizing mirage. "And if we're not? What then?"

"Then we figure it out," he said, crossing the room with deliberate steps. He knelt in front of me, his eyes locking onto mine with an intensity that made the world around us fade. "But I'm not going anywhere. Not after everything we've been through."

The sincerity in his voice broke through my defenses, and a part of me wanted to believe him. But the shadows loomed larger, the doubts whispering in my ear. "What if your past catches up to us?" I asked, the question almost a plea. "What if it gets in the way?"

He hesitated, a flicker of pain crossing his features. "Then we face it together. I won't let anything happen to you."

There it was again—the promise, both comforting and terrifying. I wanted to wrap myself in it, to believe that we could conquer whatever storms lay ahead. "And what if you can't?" I countered, my heart aching with the weight of unspoken fears.

For a moment, he looked lost in thought, and I watched as his vulnerability bared itself, raw and unguarded. "Then I guess we'll have to find out," he said finally, his voice steadier now, as if he had resolved something within himself.

The unlikelihood of our situation settled like dust around us, swirling in the remnants of a passionate encounter and the threat of an unresolved past. "So, we just dive headfirst into the unknown, then?" I teased lightly, trying to ease the tension that clung to us like a thick fog.

He smirked, the corners of his mouth curling up. "Isn't that how most of the best stories start?"

"True," I admitted, a smile breaking through my own reservations. "But every story also has a villain lurking in the shadows. And I have a feeling yours is particularly... villainous."

His laughter echoed through the room, rich and genuine. "You might be surprised. My past isn't all doom and gloom, but it certainly has its dark chapters."

The moment hung heavy, and I felt a pang of curiosity mixed with fear. "And are you willing to share those chapters with me?" I asked, my voice barely above a whisper.

He studied me for a moment, his expression contemplative, then nodded slowly. "When the time is right. But right now, I think we should focus on this moment." He moved closer, the warmth radiating from him as he brushed his fingers against my arm, igniting a spark that made me shiver. "What do you say we get out of here? Explore the city while we still can?"

The prospect of adventure pulled at me like a siren's call. "And by 'explore,' you mean avoid running into more people who want to harm us?"

"Exactly!" His eyes danced with mischief, and I found myself laughing despite the tension still humming between us. "What's life without a little risk?"

"Maybe I prefer my risks served with a side of safety," I retorted, unable to hide my grin. But the excitement of the unknown was a drug I craved.

"Just think of it as a way to reclaim our narrative," he said, extending a hand toward me. "A little rebellion against the chaos."

I hesitated, glancing at the door that separated us from the outside world. The chaos and uncertainty lingered like shadows at the edge of my consciousness, but Nathan's unwavering gaze drew me in. I took a deep breath, letting the air fill my lungs, then placed my hand in his, feeling the warmth seep through our skin.

"Alright, let's reclaim our narrative," I said, determination simmering beneath my bravado.

Nathan's smile was infectious as he pulled me to my feet, the energy between us crackling with an undeniable tension. We slipped out of the hotel room, the hum of the city beyond beckoning us with its chaotic allure.

The streets thrummed with life—music spilled from nearby cafes, laughter echoed in the air, and the mingling scents of spices and baked goods wafted toward us like a warm embrace. I could feel my spirit lifting with each step we took away from the oppressive confines of the room.

"What's your idea of adventure?" Nathan asked, glancing sideways at me as we strolled, our fingers still intertwined.

"Hmm, let's see," I mused, pretending to think hard. "An evening of dodging danger while sampling every type of pastry we can find sounds like a solid plan."

He laughed again, a sound that sent warmth cascading through me. "I think I can manage that. But you might need to keep your wits about you. There's bound to be a sweet shop with a dark secret lurking around the corner."

"Perfect! Just what I wanted—sugar and suspense."

"Now that's a combination I can get behind."

We wandered through winding streets, our laughter mingling with the vibrant energy of the city, each moment a thread woven into the fabric of our story. I felt a shift within me, an acceptance of the uncertainty that lay ahead. Whatever shadows Nathan had in his past, whatever secrets lurked in the corners of his heart, I was willing to stand beside him as we faced them together.

"Do you think we'll look back on this as the moment it all began?" I asked, glancing up at him, a playful smile dancing on my lips.

"Or the moment we lost all semblance of sanity?" he replied, squeezing my hand.

"Touché. But I'll take a little madness if it means we get to share it."

With that, we stepped deeper into the unknown, the city enveloping us in its embrace, each step a leap of faith into a future that felt brighter and more unpredictable than ever.

The vibrant energy of the city enveloped us like a warm blanket, each footfall echoing the promise of adventure. The sun had dipped low on the horizon, splattering the sky with hues of purple and gold, casting an enchanting glow over everything. We strolled hand in hand, and every shared glance with Nathan felt like an unspoken agreement—a pact to face whatever came next, together.

"Look at that!" I exclaimed, pointing toward a small pastry shop with a charming, vintage façade. The window display showcased an array of colorful confections, each one more delectable than the last. "I bet they have the best éclairs in the city."

Nathan leaned closer to the window, a mischievous grin lighting up his face. "I can't resist a good éclair. Especially if it involves cream filling." His voice dropped playfully, a teasing glint in his eye. "You just might have to share."

"Share?" I laughed, shaking my head. "No way. You'll have to earn your bite. A pastry is a serious commitment."

"Challenge accepted," he said, feigning seriousness as he opened the door to the shop. The sweet aroma wafted out, wrapping around us like a comforting embrace. "Prepare to be dazzled."

Inside, the shop was a delightful chaos of colors and textures. Glass cases sparkled under the soft lighting, revealing pastries that looked almost too beautiful to eat. I approached the display with a sense of awe, feeling like a child in a candy store. Nathan stood beside me, the tension of the day melting away in the warmth of this shared moment.

"What's your strategy here?" he asked, eyeing the choices with a mock serious expression. "Will it be the éclairs, or will you go for something more adventurous?"

"I'm leaning toward the raspberry tart," I mused, tilting my head as I studied it closely. "But those chocolate croissants look awfully tempting. It's a tough choice."

"Life is all about balance," he said, glancing at the pastries and then back at me. "Why not both? If we're going to indulge, let's go all in."

I grinned, appreciating his enthusiasm. "Now you're speaking my language. A little indulgence never hurt anyone."

As we placed our orders, the chatter of the other patrons created a comforting backdrop. I watched as Nathan interacted with the cashier, his charm effortlessly shining through. The way he moved, the confidence in his voice, made my heart flutter. In that moment, it felt like we were two people forging a new path, untethered from the chaos that had brought us here.

With our pastries in hand, we stepped back out onto the bustling street, the evening air cool and invigorating. The sun had nearly set, and the city began to glow with the light of a thousand street lamps. I took a moment to relish the atmosphere, letting it wash over me. "This is what I needed," I said, taking a bite of the éclair. The cream burst forth, rich and sweet, and I closed my eyes, savoring the moment.

"Good, right?" Nathan watched me, amusement dancing in his eyes. "You look like you've just discovered the meaning of life."

"It's definitely a contender," I said, wiping a stray bit of cream from my mouth, and his laughter bubbled up again, wrapping around us like a favorite song.

We wandered through the streets, finding ourselves at a small park where the sounds of laughter and music drifted from nearby festivities. A local band was playing, and the atmosphere was infectious. People danced, their movements fluid and joyful under the glow of string lights that hung overhead, creating a canopy of twinkling stars.

"Let's dance!" Nathan suggested, his enthusiasm palpable.

"Are you serious? I can't just—"

"Why not?" He grabbed my hand, pulling me into the crowd. "This is our moment! No one knows us here. We can be whoever we want."

His eagerness was contagious, and before I could argue, he twirled me into the fray. I stumbled slightly, laughter bubbling out of me, and he grinned, his eyes sparkling with delight. We moved together, the music wrapping us in its rhythm, our bodies swaying in sync as if they had been doing it forever.

"See? You've got this!" he encouraged, his voice rising above the music. "Just let go!"

With each beat, I felt the walls I had built begin to crumble. The fear and uncertainty that had shadowed me all day faded with each turn and sway, replaced by a sense of liberation. I lost myself in the moment, our laughter blending with the melody, the world around us blurring into a kaleidoscope of colors and sounds.

As the song shifted to something slower, Nathan pulled me closer, our bodies pressed together in a way that felt intimate and electrifying. The shift in tempo caused the crowd to become more fluid, twirling and spinning as couples found their groove. I melted into him, my head resting against his shoulder, breathing in the warmth of his presence.

"This," I said softly, my heart racing, "this feels perfect."

"Just wait," he replied, his voice low and husky, sending shivers down my spine. "It gets better."

Before I could respond, he leaned back slightly, a glint of mischief in his eyes. "Close your eyes."

"What?" I asked, tilting my head back to look at him.

"Trust me."

I hesitated but eventually nodded, closing my eyes and allowing him to guide me. I could feel his warmth radiating, the steady thrum of his heart matching my own. He shifted us slightly, and I could hear the distant laughter and music fading into a gentle hum, replaced by the sound of rustling leaves and the soft whisper of the evening breeze.

Then, in an unexpected turn, I felt him lift me slightly, spinning me gently, and laughter erupted from my lips, uncontrollable and joyous. "Okay, okay! I'm going to fall!" I exclaimed, my heart racing with exhilaration.

"Never," he promised, his grip secure. "I've got you."

As he set me down, the world shifted once more. I opened my eyes to find myself facing him, the laughter fading into a charged silence. His gaze locked onto mine, and for a heartbeat, everything else fell away.

But just as I began to lean into that intoxicating moment, a commotion erupted from the edge of the park. My heart lurched as I turned to see a group of people moving toward us, their expressions fierce and determined. The jovial atmosphere shattered around us, replaced by tension as I instinctively stepped closer to Nathan, my pulse quickening.

"What's going on?" I asked, anxiety creeping into my voice.

He frowned, his body tensing beside me. "I don't know, but we should—"

Suddenly, a shout pierced the air, cutting through the music and laughter like a knife. "There they are!"

Panic gripped me as I recognized the urgency in the shouts, the chaotic energy coiling tighter around us. Nathan grasped my hand firmly, pulling me away from the crowd as I felt my breath hitch in my throat. "We need to move, now!"

My heart raced with dread as we pushed through the throng of people, the reality of our situation crashing down like an avalanche. Shadows from Nathan's past were no longer lurking—they were closing in, and the safety we had momentarily found felt precariously thin.

Just as we neared the park's exit, I felt a sharp tug at my arm, and I whipped around to see a figure emerging from the crowd, their face obscured but their intent unmistakable. "You can't run from this!" the voice called out, low and menacing, cutting through the chaos like a knife.

In that moment, as Nathan turned to face the threat, the world shifted again, plunging us into a darkness that promised no easy escape. My heart raced with uncertainty, and I realized that the battle wasn't just with external forces—it was also with the trust I had begun to build, now teetering on the edge of the unknown.

Chapter 15: The Confrontation

The flickering lights of the abandoned subway station cast eerie shadows across the crumbling tiles, their once-bright colors now muted and grimy. The air was thick with the smell of damp concrete and rust, a scent that reminded me too much of the past. As I stepped cautiously through the cavernous space, my heart thrummed with a rhythm that felt both exhilarating and terrifying. Each footfall echoed in the vast emptiness, a stark reminder that I wasn't just here to explore the remnants of a forgotten era; I was here to confront the specter of Nathan's past, a shadow that loomed larger than the dim illumination around me.

Nathan had always been the brave one, the protector. He wore his strength like armor, and yet I had seen the cracks beneath that facade, the vulnerability he tried so hard to hide. His nightmares, those restless nights where he tossed and turned, muttering names I didn't recognize, had drawn us to this forsaken place. I had decided then that I would not remain a bystander, waiting for him to fight his battles alone. This time, I would stand alongside him, shoulder to shoulder, ready to face whatever darkness awaited.

As I moved deeper into the station, the distant sound of dripping water punctuated the silence, each drop a countdown to the confrontation I had steeled myself for. Nathan's former associates were not just out for revenge; they were desperate men, cornered animals who would do anything to protect their secrets. I couldn't let fear dictate my actions. Instead, I allowed my resolve to blossom, fueled by the strength of our bond and the knowledge that I had something to protect—our future, a future that flickered like the lights above, fragile yet full of potential.

A shuffling sound from the shadows caught my attention, a low murmur that twisted in the stale air. I paused, my pulse quickening, straining to hear over the cacophony of my thoughts. "Nathan?" I whispered, though I knew he wouldn't respond; we had agreed on silence. The element of surprise was our ally tonight. We were the intruders in this derelict domain, not the frightened victims we had once been.

And then I saw him—a silhouette emerging from the darkness, tall and imposing. My breath caught in my throat. This was it. The man who had haunted Nathan's dreams had finally come to life, stepping into the pale glow like a ghost from the past. He was everything I had imagined, and yet, nothing at all. The sharp angles of his face were obscured by shadows, but his eyes shone with a predatory gleam, calculating and cold.

"Look who's decided to join the party," he drawled, his voice smooth as silk yet laced with an undercurrent of menace.

"Not here for a celebration," I shot back, my voice steadier than I felt. "I'm here to end this."

His laugh echoed through the hollow space, a sound devoid of humor, more like the cawing of a raven than any sort of joy. "End this? You think you have any power here? You're just a pawn in Nathan's little game."

A flicker of anger surged through me, igniting a fire I didn't know I possessed. "Maybe, but pawns can become queens, you know. You should have done your homework."

The man stepped forward, and I could finally see the twisted smile on his lips. He leaned casually against a rusty pillar, a picture of arrogance. "You're bold, I'll give you that. But boldness doesn't equate to survival, darling."

"Neither does hiding behind your thugs," I retorted, forcing myself to stay calm. This wasn't just about Nathan anymore; this was about reclaiming my power, asserting my place in this tangled web of danger. "If you think I'm going to let you walk away unscathed, you've miscalculated."

Just then, a familiar figure emerged from the shadows—Nathan. Relief washed over me, but it was quickly swallowed by the tension that electrified the air. "You shouldn't have come here," he warned, his voice low, roughened by concern.

"And let you face this alone? Not a chance," I replied, my gaze never wavering from the enemy before us.

"Ah, the lovebirds unite," the man mocked, clearly reveling in our dynamic. "How quaint. But love won't save you here. I'm a professional, sweetheart. You're nothing but a distraction."

"We're not the ones who should be worried," Nathan said, stepping closer to me, his protective instincts flaring to life. "You underestimated her. She's stronger than you think."

With that, the atmosphere shifted, an undercurrent of tension thickening as the man straightened, a hint of irritation flickering across his features. "You think this is about her? This is personal, Nathan. You made a choice to betray your own, and now you'll pay for it."

"I didn't betray anyone," Nathan countered, his voice steady, yet I could sense the storm brewing just beneath the surface. "You're the one who's lost your way, blinded by greed and vengeance."

"Enough with the pleasantries!" he barked, and suddenly the atmosphere was charged with danger, the weight of the moment pressing down like a thick fog. I felt the world narrow, time stretching as I braced myself for the inevitable clash.

This was it. My heart raced, but not with fear; it was fueled by a fierce determination. I turned to Nathan, my eyes locking with his. "We can do this together."

With a nod, he positioned himself beside me, a united front against the looming threat. The confrontation had begun, and there was no turning back. In that moment, I understood something profound: our love wasn't a shield; it was our sword, forged in the fires of adversity, sharp enough to cut through the darkness that threatened to consume us.

In the dim light of the abandoned subway station, the air hung heavy with dust and unspoken fears. Graffiti-streaked walls loomed like watchful sentinels, and the echo of our footsteps reverberated through the hollow tunnels, each step a reminder of the peril we faced. Nathan's hand brushed against mine, a silent promise of support, though I could feel the tension radiating off him like heat from a fire. His gaze, normally filled with warmth, was now hardened with the weight of his past. It was time to confront the specter that had haunted him for far too long.

"Are you ready?" he asked, his voice low and steady, as if we were preparing for an art exhibit rather than an impending showdown.

I chuckled softly, a mix of nerves and bravado bubbling to the surface. "Ready as I'll ever be to meet your worst nightmare. How do you think he'll greet us? With a hug, or perhaps a lovely bouquet of regret?" My attempt at levity hung in the air, but Nathan merely shook his head, a small smile breaking through his apprehension.

As we descended deeper into the depths of the station, the flickering lights cast eerie shadows that danced along the walls, painting a surreal picture of our surroundings. The faint sound of dripping water echoed in the background, a haunting melody that underscored the gravity of our mission. I could feel the heartbeat of the city pulsating above us, a stark contrast to the stillness enveloping this forgotten place. Every instinct in me screamed that we were being watched, that we were stepping into a trap meticulously laid out by Nathan's former associates. Yet, I wouldn't falter.

"We need to split up," Nathan said suddenly, his eyes narrowing with determination. "I'll draw him out. You stay hidden until I signal you."

"Not a chance," I replied, my voice rising with indignation. "This isn't just your fight, Nathan. I'm not sitting on the sidelines while you play the hero."

He opened his mouth to protest, but I cut him off. "This is about both of us. You've kept me in the dark long enough. I deserve to stand beside you, not behind you."

For a moment, he looked as if he might argue, but then something shifted in his expression—an acceptance, perhaps even admiration. "Fine. But stay alert. If things go south, I need you to run."

I nodded, my heart pounding with a mix of fear and resolve. With that, we moved deeper into the shadows, knowing that the confrontation awaited us just ahead.

Suddenly, a figure emerged from the darkness, sharp and angular, with an unsettling confidence that set my instincts on high alert. It was the man Nathan had dreaded, the one whose name had hung over our lives like a dark cloud. His presence was overwhelming, and I felt the air grow thick with danger as he stepped into the flickering light, a sinister grin spreading across his face.

"Well, well, if it isn't Nathan and his little sidekick," he drawled, his voice dripping with condescension. "I almost didn't think you'd have the guts to show up. Did you really believe you could run from your past forever?"

Nathan stepped forward, his posture rigid, fists clenched. "You don't scare me anymore," he spat, his voice steady, though I could sense the underlying tremor of fear.

"Oh, but I should," the man replied, his tone mocking. "You think you've escaped my grasp? You're still tangled in the web I spun, and I'm here to ensure you never break free."

Before I could process his words, I saw Nathan's face transform from determination to something akin to fury. "You're wrong. I'm not the same man you once knew. I'm not afraid of you."

I took a step closer to Nathan, my heart racing. "And I'm not afraid of you either," I interjected, my voice stronger than I felt. "You've threatened him long enough. This ends here."

The man's laughter echoed through the cavernous space, a cold, hollow sound. "Cute, really. You think you can stand up to me? You're just a distraction, a fleeting moment in his story. And when the dust settles, it will be me who walks away."

"Dust settles, huh?" I replied, my voice dripping with sarcasm. "I'd wager it'll be you eating that dust instead. You see, we've come prepared."

The smirk on his face faltered for a fraction of a second, and I seized the opportunity. "Nathan, now!"

In an instant, Nathan lunged forward, his movements fluid and determined, as if he had shed years of burden in that one motion. The confrontation erupted into chaos, and I joined him, adrenaline surging through my veins as I faced the man who had haunted our lives.

The struggle was visceral, a wild dance of defiance and fear, where each punch thrown felt like reclaiming a piece of our story. I didn't hold back; my resolve crystallized into strength as I fought not just for Nathan but for my own right to exist without the shadows of our past looming over us.

"Is this all you've got?" I taunted, dodging a punch and retaliating with a swift kick that sent him stumbling back.

"Fighting back with style now, are we?" Nathan quipped, catching his breath as he delivered a powerful blow to our adversary's midsection.

As the struggle intensified, I could see the desperation in our opponent's eyes, the realization that he was no longer in control. And for the first time, it dawned on me that this confrontation was not merely about Nathan's past; it was about us, about forging our own narrative in the face of adversity.

With one final push, Nathan and I combined our strengths, and together, we forced him against the cold, unforgiving wall of the subway station. The air crackled with tension, and for a moment, it felt as if time stood still, all the weight of our fears hanging in the balance.

"You think you can take everything from us?" I breathed, my voice steady, as I stared into the eyes of the man who had once sought to control our lives. "You have no power here. This is our story now."

With that declaration, a new chapter began, one we would write together, free from the constraints of the past. The darkness around us began to recede, and with it, the shadows that had once threatened to consume us.

The air was thick with a sense of foreboding as Nathan and I made our way through the forgotten tunnels of the abandoned subway station. The distant echo of dripping water was the only sound that accompanied our footsteps, creating an eerie rhythm that underscored the gravity of our situation. Shadows danced along the crumbling walls, the flickering light from Nathan's flashlight revealing graffiti that spoke of lives once lived in this underground world. Each step drew us closer to a confrontation that would change everything—yet I couldn't shake the nagging feeling that we were being watched.

"Nathan," I said, my voice breaking the oppressive silence, "are you sure this is the right place? It feels... too quiet."

He glanced at me, his expression a mix of determination and worry. "It's where they said he'd be. We can't back down now. Not when we're so close."

With a nod, I tried to match his resolve, though doubt curled around my heart like a creeping vine. The stakes had never been higher, and yet, there was something exhilarating about standing at the edge of danger. Together, we had pieced together Nathan's fragmented memories, uncovering a web of deceit spun by the very people he once called friends. As we descended further into the station's depths, the urgency of our quest pressed down on me, urging me forward.

Suddenly, a sound echoed through the tunnel—an unmistakable shuffle of feet, followed by a low, menacing laugh that sent a shiver down my spine. My heart raced as Nathan's grip on my hand tightened, the warmth of his touch grounding me amidst the growing tension.

"Stay close," he whispered, his breath warm against my ear, igniting a flicker of hope even in this darkness.

We pressed on, determined to confront the specter of Nathan's past, a man who had orchestrated his nightmares. As we rounded a bend, the beam of Nathan's flashlight illuminated a figure leaning casually against a rusty pillar. His presence was as chilling as the damp air that surrounded us, and the grin that stretched across his face was all too familiar.

"Well, well, if it isn't the prodigal son and his fearless companion," the man drawled, his voice oozing with disdain. "You really shouldn't have come here. This is a place for ghosts, not living fools."

I felt a surge of indignation rise within me, stoking the embers of my courage. "We're not afraid of you," I shot back, my voice steady despite the trembling in my knees. "You can't keep hiding behind shadows and intimidation. It's time to face the truth."

Nathan's jaw clenched, and for a moment, the walls of the subway seemed to close in around us. The man—Daniel, Nathan's former partner in crime—stepped forward, his confidence a stark contrast to our resolve. "Ah, the brave little sparrow has found her voice. But you have no idea what you're up against."

"Maybe not," I replied, feeling a rush of adrenaline. "But I do know that Nathan deserves a chance to move on. You can't keep dragging him back into your darkness."

Daniel's expression flickered, irritation flashing in his eyes. "You think you can save him? He's tangled in a web far beyond your understanding. And now, you're tangled in it too."

Nathan moved protectively in front of me, his body tense. "I won't let you use me anymore, Daniel. Not as your pawn, not as your victim."

The tension in the air crackled as Daniel laughed, a sound that echoed through the empty station. "You really think it's that simple? You're in my territory now, Nathan. I've already made my arrangements, and trust me, they won't end well for you or your little girlfriend."

His words hung heavy in the air, and I felt a wave of dread wash over me. The mention of my safety triggered something deep within me—a fierce need to protect not just Nathan but also myself. "You're wrong," I declared, stepping out from behind Nathan's protective shield. "You've underestimated us. We're not here to play your games. This is about reclaiming our lives."

Daniel's eyes narrowed, the laughter fading as he sized me up. "Is that so? Maybe I should take you down a notch, show you just how misplaced your bravado is."

In that moment, I saw an opening, a flicker of uncertainty beneath his bravado. "You think you can intimidate us? You're nothing without your threats."

"Watch your mouth," he warned, but there was a crack in his demeanor—a hint of doubt that suggested he might not be as in control as he wanted us to believe.

Nathan, emboldened by my words, stepped closer. "You don't scare us anymore. This is our fight, and we'll take you down together."

The atmosphere shifted, charged with defiance. I could sense the impending clash, the collision of old fears and newfound strength. As Daniel's smile faded, a feral intensity took its place. "You really think you can change the outcome? It's adorable, but you're playing a dangerous game."

Before we could respond, a rumble echoed from the far end of the tunnel. Dust fell from the ceiling, and the ground beneath us trembled. "This isn't over, Nathan," Daniel spat, his eyes narrowing with malice. "You've opened a door you can't close."

Then, as quickly as he had come, he turned and disappeared into the shadows, leaving us in stunned silence. The air was thick with unspoken words, the threat lingering like a storm cloud overhead.

"What just happened?" I breathed, my heart racing as the echoes of Daniel's laughter faded into the darkness.

Nathan's expression hardened as he looked down the tunnel. "He's right. This isn't over. Not by a long shot."

Just then, the rumbling intensified, and without warning, the ground beneath us cracked open, sending a shockwave through the station. Instinctively, I grabbed Nathan's arm, and together we stumbled back, our eyes wide with fear.

As the darkness began to engulf us, a piercing scream erupted from the shadows, a sound that would haunt me long after the dust had settled. The last thing I saw was the flicker of movement—a figure emerging from the collapsing tunnel—before everything went black.

Chapter 16: Aftermath and Awakening

The air hung thick with the scent of damp earth and remnants of smoke, a lingering testament to the chaos that had unfolded just hours before. I stood at the edge of the clearing, watching as Nathan knelt beside the smoldering remnants of what had once been our sanctuary. The sun peeked through the heavy canopy of trees, casting fragmented rays that danced across his tousled hair, giving him an almost ethereal glow. Yet, even in that moment, the world felt heavy with the weight of unspoken truths and lingering fears.

"Do you think it's really over?" His voice, gravelly yet tender, sliced through the silence, pulling me back from the edge of my thoughts. I turned to him, the rawness of his expression stirring something deep within me—a mix of worry and warmth that I couldn't quite put my finger on.

"I want to believe it is," I replied, my gaze drifting back to the wreckage. The flames had consumed everything so quickly, leaving behind charred remains that mirrored the turmoil swirling inside me. "But there's a nagging feeling, like we've only just scratched the surface of whatever this is."

Nathan stood, brushing ash from his jeans, his determination palpable even in the face of uncertainty. He stepped closer, the intensity of his gaze piercing through the lingering shadows of doubt. "We've come this far. We can't let whatever is left out there dictate our lives."

As the last vestiges of sunlight began to wane, the air chilled, wrapping around us like a shroud. The forest felt alive, every rustle and creak echoing the tension that gripped my heart. I took a breath, the coolness stinging my lungs, and I looked into Nathan's eyes, searching for a spark of reassurance. What I found instead was a flicker of vulnerability, a reflection of my own.

"I've never felt this way about anyone before," I admitted, the words slipping out before I could second-guess them. "It's terrifying."

"Terrifying and exhilarating." He stepped closer, bridging the space between us. "That's how you know it's real."

His words hung in the air, an invitation wrapped in a challenge. I wanted to reach for him, to close the distance that had somehow grown during our time apart, yet the weight of our situation held me back. I could feel the remnants of fear gnawing at the edges of my resolve, whispering caution even as my heart raced at the thought of what could be.

"What if we're just fooling ourselves?" I whispered, my voice barely above the rustle of the leaves. "What if the danger isn't over?"

"Then we fight." Nathan's tone was firm, unwavering. "Together. We've faced darkness before. We can do it again."

His conviction sparked something inside me, a fire that pushed back against the fear coiling in my stomach. I stepped forward, a brave move fueled by the sheer force of my growing feelings for him. "Together," I echoed, the word tasting sweeter on my tongue.

Just as our eyes locked, a distant rustling shattered the fragile peace surrounding us. My heart stuttered, the warm glow of connection doused by the cold wave of fear that washed over me. Nathan's posture shifted, alert and tense, as we both instinctively turned toward the sound.

"Did you hear that?" he asked, his voice low and urgent.

"Yeah, I did," I replied, the breath catching in my throat. The forest, once so alive with its vibrant hues, felt suddenly menacing, the shadows stretching like dark fingers toward us. My pulse raced as I peered into the thickening gloom, the trees standing sentinel, guarding secrets I wasn't ready to uncover.

We stood in silence, tension coiling tighter around us as the noise intensified. It sounded like movement, but there was no telling whether it was the wind or something far more sinister. I reached for

Nathan's hand, the warmth of his palm grounding me in the face of uncertainty.

"Let's investigate," he suggested, his eyes narrowing in determination.

"Are you sure?" I hesitated, torn between the thrill of adventure and the instinctual urge to run.

He met my gaze, his grip tightening reassuringly. "If there's something out there, we need to know. We can't let fear hold us back."

With a slow, deep breath, I nodded. Together, we stepped forward, the darkness of the trees looming like a wall around us. Each footfall seemed to echo, a reminder that we were not just fighting for our lives but for a chance at something more—something we'd both discovered amid the chaos.

As we ventured deeper, the underbrush crackled beneath our feet, the forest a labyrinth of shadows and whispers. My senses heightened, every flicker of movement drawing my attention, the adrenaline coursing through me like wildfire. Nathan was a steady presence beside me, his focus unwavering as we navigated the unfamiliar terrain.

Suddenly, a figure darted between the trees, and I stifled a gasp, adrenaline flooding my system. Nathan squeezed my hand, signaling me to stay close. "What was that?" I whispered, my voice trembling.

"Stay behind me," he instructed, his tone laced with protective urgency. We moved cautiously, following the sound of rustling leaves and twigs snapping underfoot. Each step felt like a dance on the edge of danger, the thrill of the unknown igniting a fire within me.

The clearing ahead opened up, revealing a scene that stole my breath away. A group of figures emerged from the shadows, their faces illuminated by the pale moonlight filtering through the treetops. They appeared almost spectral, moving with an otherworldly grace. I could see the glimmer of something metallic in their hands—tools or weapons, perhaps.

"Who are they?" I murmured, barely able to keep my voice steady.

"I don't know, but we need to be careful," Nathan replied, his eyes scanning the group with an intensity that made my heart race. The air crackled with anticipation, a strange energy humming around us as we watched the scene unfold, our hearts in sync, both wary and hopeful as we prepared for whatever was to come.

The figures in the clearing moved like shadows, fluid and purposeful, a blend of curiosity and caution swirling in the air around them. My heart raced as I felt Nathan's fingers tighten around mine, grounding me even as my mind reeled with possibilities. What were they doing out here in the middle of the night? The silver moonlight cast an eerie glow, illuminating the tension that seemed to wrap around us like a thick fog.

"Are they... friends or foes?" I asked, my voice barely a whisper. I could feel the thrum of energy in the air, a mixture of fear and anticipation weaving a delicate tapestry of suspense. The figures paused, glancing in our direction, their faces obscured by the darkness, but their intent was unmistakable. They were here for a reason.

"Let's not stick around to find out," Nathan replied, his voice steady but low, a mix of authority and concern. I nodded, but a part of me burned with curiosity. This could be the answer to the unanswered questions that had haunted us since the confrontation—the catalyst for a new beginning, or perhaps the harbinger of more danger.

Just as we turned to retreat, one of the figures stepped forward, breaking the spell that held us captive. A woman with wild hair that tumbled around her shoulders like a waterfall of night, her eyes gleaming with an intensity that rivaled the moon's brightness, locked onto mine.

"Wait!" she called, her voice strong yet melodic, cutting through the cool night air. "We mean you no harm!"

Nathan's grip on my hand tightened, and I felt the muscles in his arm tense. "What do you want?" he asked, his tone firm, protective instincts on high alert.

The woman took another step closer, raising her hands as if to show she held no weapons. "We're here to help," she said, her eyes darting between Nathan and me, gauging our reaction. "There's much you don't understand, and time is running out."

"Help?" I echoed, skepticism dripping from the word. "And how exactly do you propose to do that?"

"Let's just say we have information that could change everything," she replied, her gaze steady and unwavering. "But we need your trust first."

Trust. That word echoed in my mind, a reminder of how tenuous our situation had become. I exchanged a glance with Nathan, searching for a flicker of assurance in his blue eyes. I found it there, but it was marred by uncertainty. He nodded slightly, a silent agreement to hear her out.

"Alright," Nathan said slowly, "we're listening. But if you try anything—"

"Then we'll be the ones in trouble," the woman interrupted with a sly smile, a glint of mischief playing at the corners of her mouth. "I promise, we're not the enemy here. My name is Lira, and my friends and I are looking for a way to stop what's coming."

"What's coming?" I asked, the question slipping from my lips, curiosity overriding my caution. The air felt charged, as if the very trees were leaning in to listen.

Lira glanced around, her expression shifting from playful to serious in an instant. "There's a darkness spreading, and it's targeting those like you—those who have faced the chaos and lived to tell the tale. You've unwittingly become part of something much bigger than yourselves."

"Bigger than us?" I scoffed, my skepticism bubbling back to the surface. "What do you mean? We're just trying to figure out our own lives here, not become heroes or something."

"That's the beauty of it," she replied, a hint of a grin still lingering on her lips. "Sometimes, the universe doesn't give you a choice. It thrusts you into a role you never asked for. You and Nathan—your connection, it's powerful. It's part of what makes you a target."

I felt the weight of her words settle over me, heavy and suffocating. The thought of being hunted sent a chill racing down my spine. "Why us? What do we have that makes us so special?"

"It's not just about you two," she explained, her voice softening. "There's a network of people like you, individuals who have faced their own battles, who possess gifts that can influence the outcome of what's to come. You're part of that, even if you don't realize it yet."

"Gifts?" Nathan echoed, his skepticism evident. "What gifts?"

"Gifts that connect to the fabric of this world," Lira said, her tone serious now. "Emotional energy, resilience, love—it creates ripples that can alter the course of events. But if we don't act, those ripples could turn into tidal waves of destruction."

My mind raced, grappling with her words. Love? Resilience? I had never thought of my feelings for Nathan as a weapon or a tool for change, but the way she spoke hinted at a deeper connection—a truth that pulsed just beneath the surface of our reality.

"What's the first step?" Nathan asked, his gaze shifting from me to Lira, determination replacing hesitation.

"We need to gather others, people like you," she replied. "There's a meeting point—an old barn just outside the city. It's where we can strategize, understand how we can combat this threat together."

The urgency in her voice resonated within me, and I could feel the edges of my fear begin to dissolve, replaced by a flicker of hope. "And what if we don't agree to this? What if we walk away right now?"

Lira's smile faded, replaced by a solemnity that chilled me. "Then you risk facing it alone. But know this: whatever is coming, it's not something you can handle by hiding. It will find you, and it will take everything you hold dear."

The gravity of her words hung heavy in the air, filling the silence that enveloped us. Nathan and I exchanged a look that spoke volumes. I could see the wheels turning in his mind, the determination mixed with an unmistakable hint of fear.

"Alright," he finally said, his voice steady. "We'll go. But if we find out you're leading us into a trap—"

"You'll have to trust us," Lira interjected, a spark of challenge lighting her eyes. "Trust isn't given lightly, and I understand your hesitance. But together, we have a chance to turn the tide. Alone, you're just running toward a storm."

As we stood there, the uncertainty hung in the air, but something shifted within me. The path ahead might be fraught with danger, but the thrill of the unknown beckoned. With a deep breath, I squeezed Nathan's hand, my heart racing as I realized that whatever lay ahead, I was ready to face it—with him. Together, we stepped into the darkened woods, a step closer to unraveling the mystery of our connection and the challenges that awaited us.

The moon hung low in the sky, a silent sentinel illuminating our path as we ventured deeper into the forest, following Lira through the tangled underbrush. Each step felt like a precarious leap into the unknown, the tension crackling in the air around us. The urgency of our situation pulsed in my veins, a reminder that we were no longer mere participants in our own lives; we had become players in a larger, darker game.

"Do you think this barn of yours is safe?" I asked, breaking the silence as we navigated a narrow path. The sound of rustling leaves seemed to echo my apprehension, a chorus of nature weighing in on our decision. "I mean, we have no idea who else will be there."

Lira glanced back, her expression unreadable, a mix of mischief and seriousness dancing in her eyes. "Safe? That's a loaded question in our world. It's as safe as we can make it." Her tone was light, but her words held an undercurrent of warning. "But sometimes you need to walk into danger to find the truth."

"Great pep talk," Nathan quipped, casting a sidelong glance at me. "We might be dealing with a doom-and-gloom situation here, but I still appreciate the motivational speech."

I chuckled, grateful for the way his humor could slice through the tension. "Maybe we can start a self-help series for heroes in peril," I suggested, my heart lighter for a moment. "How to maintain your sanity while the world collapses around you."

"Step one: Don't trust anyone named Lira." He winked, but his smile faded as he turned his gaze back to the path ahead, his brow furrowing in thought.

The laughter faded, leaving an uncomfortable silence hanging between us as we continued onward. The trees loomed closer, their branches arching overhead like skeletal fingers. The shadows danced around us, and the air thickened, almost tangibly, as if holding its breath in anticipation of what lay ahead.

Finally, we reached a clearing, and in the distance, the outline of the barn emerged against the twilight. It stood defiantly, weathered and ancient, a monument to secrets long kept. The moonlight bathed it in silver, illuminating the rough-hewn timbers and the broken windows that stared out like weary eyes.

"Here we are," Lira announced, her voice a blend of excitement and apprehension. "This is it. Welcome to our makeshift headquarters."

"Headquarters? More like a haunted house," I murmured, glancing at Nathan, who nodded in agreement, a wry smile tugging at his lips.

"Haunted or not, we should check it out," he said, his adventurous spirit igniting again. We stepped forward, the crunch of gravel beneath our feet breaking the stillness of the night. As we approached, the barn loomed larger, the shadows playing tricks on my mind, distorting the familiar into something menacing.

Pushing the door open, it creaked in protest, the sound echoing within the cavernous space. Dust motes danced in the pale light, swirling like tiny galaxies caught in a forgotten moment. The interior was dim but alive with the promise of activity. Flickering lanterns cast soft glows, revealing a group of people huddled together, their faces shadowed but their energy palpable.

"Everyone, this is Nathan and our friend..." Lira paused, a teasing glint in her eyes. "What's your name again?"

"Just call me trouble," I replied with a smirk, stepping forward as if to make my presence known. "I seem to attract it."

The group erupted into laughter, the tension momentarily dissolving in a sea of camaraderie. It was a welcomed relief, yet the underlying seriousness of our purpose loomed heavy in the air.

Lira began introducing us, but I found myself drawn to a man standing slightly apart from the rest. His features were sharp, with dark hair that fell over his forehead in an unruly fashion, giving him a roguish charm. He caught my gaze and held it, his eyes a striking shade of green, glimmering with a mix of curiosity and something deeper.

"Who's the charming one over there?" Nathan whispered, nudging my side. I felt heat rise in my cheeks as I turned to him, feigning innocence.

"That's just the light," I retorted, trying to mask the sudden flutter of my heart. "It's very flattering."

"Right," Nathan replied, skepticism coloring his tone. "If that's the case, I should start charging for my lighting services."

Lira finished the introductions, and the group settled into a circle, the atmosphere shifting as the gravity of our situation returned. "We don't have much time," she began, her voice steady and serious. "We've pieced together some information about the threat we're facing. It's more insidious than we thought."

"What exactly are we up against?" Nathan asked, his brow furrowed, the momentary lightness evaporating.

"A cult of sorts," Lira replied, her gaze unwavering. "They seek to harness the energy of people like you—those who have faced trials and come out stronger. They believe it grants them power. They're coming for you."

A chill swept through me at her words, and the room fell into a heavy silence, each of us grappling with the enormity of what she had revealed. "What do we do?" I asked, my voice steadier than I felt.

"First, we prepare," Lira said. "But we can't do it alone. We need to gather more allies, reach out to others who have experienced similar awakenings. They're out there, and they'll be crucial in facing what's coming."

"But what if they're not ready?" I pressed, the weight of our situation pressing down. "What if they're just ordinary people like us?"

"Ordinary people can do extraordinary things when pushed," she replied, her tone fierce. "Trust me. We've seen it happen before."

The group began to strategize, their voices blending into a whirlwind of plans and possibilities. I found myself lost in thought, my mind racing as I tried to process everything. I was a regular person thrust into a world I barely understood, yet here I was, discussing battles and alliances. The notion felt surreal.

Suddenly, a loud crash reverberated outside the barn, shaking the wooden walls and snapping me out of my thoughts. We all froze, the air thick with shock. I exchanged worried glances with Nathan, who moved closer, a protective instinct radiating from him.

"What was that?" he murmured, his voice low.

Before I could respond, the door burst open, and a figure rushed inside, breathless and wide-eyed. "They're coming! We need to go now!"

Panic erupted in the room as everyone sprang into action, the sudden urgency a stark reminder of the danger we were facing. My heart pounded in my chest, and I caught Nathan's eye, a silent agreement passing between us. Whatever was out there was closer than we had anticipated, and our fight was only just beginning.

As chaos unfolded around us, I felt a thrill of fear mixed with resolve. I was no longer just a bystander in my own life; I was stepping into the fray. But as we readied ourselves to face whatever storm awaited us, I couldn't shake the feeling that we were racing against time—and that some battles would come at a cost we weren't prepared to pay. The air crackled with tension, and I couldn't help but wonder: would we emerge stronger, or would this be the moment that unraveled everything we had fought to protect?

Chapter 17: The Edge of Darkness

A chill raced down my spine as I bent to retrieve the note, its edges crisp and the ink still slightly wet, as if hastily penned by a trembling hand. The porch beneath my feet felt less like home and more like a stage where shadows lurked, waiting to pounce. My heart thudded against my ribcage, a frantic drumbeat urging me to read the message that bore the weight of uncertainty. "Beware the light you seek; it draws the darkness closer." I read the words aloud, my voice wavering like a candle flame in a draft, and I couldn't shake the feeling that I was being watched. The world outside seemed too still, as if nature itself was holding its breath, waiting for my next move.

I tucked the note into my pocket, but it felt as heavy as a stone, a reminder that the peace we had fought so hard to establish was as fragile as glass. I turned to the kitchen, where the scent of cinnamon and apples still lingered, remnants of the pie I'd baked that morning. I poured myself a cup of coffee, hoping the warmth would chase away the chill settling in my bones. But my mind was far from the comforting aroma; it spiraled back to Nathan and the wild unpredictability of our recent days.

The door swung open just as I took my first sip, and there he was—Nathan, with his tousled hair and that lopsided grin that had a knack for igniting butterflies in my stomach. But today, there was something darker in his gaze, a shadow lurking behind his warm brown eyes. "Hey," he said, stepping inside, his presence a welcome distraction. "I thought I'd find you here, lost in your thoughts."

"More like lost in a warning," I replied, holding out the note. "Someone wants to remind me that our troubles are far from over."

He took the paper, his brow furrowing as he read the words. The warmth of his hand brushed against mine, sending a flicker of comfort through me despite the tension hanging in the air. "This is... cryptic. But I wouldn't let it get to you. We've faced worse together."

"Have we?" I challenged, folding my arms. "This feels different, Nathan. Like we're standing at the edge of something dark, and it's beckoning us to take a step closer."

He met my gaze, a storm brewing in his eyes. "Or it's a trick, meant to scare us into retreat. We've fought too hard to let fear dictate our choices."

His words struck a chord within me. I had been on the brink of retreating into the shadows, of letting anxiety swallow me whole, but Nathan's determination sparked a fire of resilience within. "So what do we do? Sit here and wait for whatever's lurking to show itself?"

"Not a chance," he replied, his voice steady and sure. "We confront it. Together."

We spent the afternoon plotting our next steps, turning the dining table into a makeshift strategy board littered with old notes, a map of the town, and a timeline of the bizarre occurrences that had plagued us. Nathan had a way of organizing chaos, his methodical nature balancing my frenzied thoughts. With each detail we uncovered, I felt the grip of fear loosening, replaced by a shared sense of purpose.

"I'll talk to Mrs. Collins," I suggested, referencing the town's unofficial historian, a woman whose endless supply of gossip often danced around kernels of truth. "If anyone knows about the shadows hanging over this place, it's her."

"Good idea," Nathan replied, tracing a finger over the map. "And I'll check in with the local police. There's been enough weirdness lately that they might have something useful."

As the sun dipped below the horizon, painting the sky in shades of amber and violet, our resolve solidified into something unbreakable. We wouldn't be mere victims in our story; we were the authors, ready to take control of the narrative.

With a renewed sense of purpose, we set out into the crisp evening air. The town, usually vibrant with life, felt eerily quiet. As we walked through the familiar streets, my heart raced—not with fear, but with a rush of adrenaline. Every corner seemed to hold its breath, and the shadows cast by the streetlights stretched like fingers, urging us to turn back.

"Hey, look," Nathan pointed towards the old library, its facade looming ominously in the twilight. "Maybe we should start there. Books can hold secrets, too."

The library stood like a fortress of knowledge, its ancient stone walls whispering tales of yesteryears. The scent of old paper and leather greeted us as we pushed open the heavy doors, the creak echoing like a ghostly sigh. We navigated through the maze of shelves, and I marveled at how each volume seemed to pulse with life, stories waiting to be unearthed.

As Nathan scanned the titles, I found myself drawn to a dusty section tucked away in the corner. The books here were neglected, their spines cracked and faded, but I sensed something significant lurking among them. My fingers brushed over the titles, each a relic of forgotten lore. Then, one in particular caught my eye—a leather-bound tome, its cover embossed with an intricate symbol. I pulled it from the shelf, the dust clouding the air as I opened it, revealing pages filled with handwriting that appeared to be centuries old.

"Look at this," I said, excitement thrumming in my veins. "It's a diary of sorts, detailing the history of our town. Maybe it has something about the shadows we've been seeing."

Nathan joined me, peering over my shoulder as I began to decipher the faded ink. The entries told of an ancient pact, one that had been forged to keep a darkness at bay, a darkness that threatened to resurface. Each word I read sent ripples of dread and fascination through me. The ink revealed stories of struggles and sacrifices made by those who came before us, and I could almost hear their whispers echoing through the pages.

"This is it," I breathed, my pulse quickening. "We need to dig deeper. This could be the key to understanding what's happening now."

Nathan nodded, his expression resolute. "Then let's keep looking. Whatever shadows are gathering, we'll face them head-on."

As we delved into the pages, I felt the weight of our journey pressing down on us, a blend of fear and determination coiling within. The thrill of discovery danced in the air, igniting the courage that had flickered to life earlier. Together, we would shine a light into the darkness, our hands clasped tightly as we dared to confront the unknown.

As we pored over the ancient diary, the dim light from the overhead lamp cast flickering shadows on the pages, creating an ambiance both eerie and exhilarating. The library had grown quieter, as if the walls themselves were straining to eavesdrop on our discoveries. The writing spoke of a time when the town had been a sanctuary, protected by an agreement forged in secrecy and upheld by generations. The deeper we dove into the text, the more I felt an inexplicable connection to those who had come before us—echoes of their courage reverberating in my chest.

"This," I said, tapping a finger against a particularly detailed passage, "this speaks of a ritual, something that was done to bind the darkness. But look here," I continued, flipping a few pages forward. "It also mentions that the binding is not permanent. It can weaken over time."

Nathan leaned closer, his breath warm against my ear as he read. "So, you're saying our quaint little town might have been under some sort of spell, and now it's unraveling?"

"Exactly," I replied, a thrill running through me. "And it sounds like someone—or something—has been trying to break that spell."

His expression shifted, a mixture of concern and curiosity etched across his features. "You think the note was a warning from whoever is trying to exploit this? Like, 'Hey, we're coming for you'?"

"It fits," I mused, unable to shake the feeling of being pulled into a plot far more complex than I'd anticipated. "But it also suggests that we might not be the only ones trying to figure this out. What if others are looking for the same answers?"

"Then we have to be quicker," Nathan said, the determination in his voice cutting through the tension. "We can't let them get to it first. Let's split up tomorrow and gather more information. You hit up Mrs. Collins while I check in with the police. We can meet back here after."

The plan was formed, but beneath the excitement bubbled an undercurrent of unease. I couldn't help but worry about the unknown—what if the shadows were already in motion, preparing to strike before we could even understand their game? "Be careful, alright? I don't want to lose you in this mess," I warned, my voice barely above a whisper.

He turned to face me, his gaze steady and intense. "You won't. I promise."

The next morning dawned with an almost unnatural stillness, the sun's rays piercing through the haze of clouds like a searchlight. I dressed in layers, partly for the chill that lingered in the air, but mostly as armor against the anxiety tightening in my chest. My first stop was Mrs. Collins' house, a quaint cottage adorned with climbing roses that seemed to cling to the very essence of nostalgia. The familiar sight calmed me, a reminder that some things in our world remained untouched by darkness.

I rapped lightly on the door, the sound echoing in the quiet morning. Mrs. Collins opened it almost immediately, her gray hair piled on top of her head like a soft cloud, and a knowing smile lighting up her face. "Ah, dear, come in! I was just about to make tea. You must tell me all about your latest adventures."

"Adventures might be a strong word," I replied, stepping inside, the warmth enveloping me like a hug. "But I could really use your insight on some... unusual occurrences around town."

We settled in her cozy living room, filled with shelves of books and mementos from a life well-lived. The aroma of fresh tea wafted through the air as I explained the note and the diary. Mrs. Collins listened intently, her sharp blue eyes gleaming with intrigue.

"You're right to be cautious, dear," she said, setting her cup down with a soft clink. "This town has always held secrets. Secrets that some would prefer remain buried."

"Do you think there's a connection to the old pact?" I asked, hoping for clarity amidst the murky waters of the past.

She leaned back, her fingers steepled under her chin as she contemplated. "There are tales, of course. Legends passed down through whispers. The original settlers believed they made a bargain to protect their home from evil forces. But as time went on, the details became muddled, and those who sought to revive the old ways were often shunned."

A shiver ran down my spine. "And what if those details are coming back to haunt us?"

"Then you'd best be ready to defend what's yours," she said, a spark igniting in her voice. "But it's not just about knowledge; it's about heart and courage. You must be willing to stand firm against whatever dark forces are at play."

I left her home feeling invigorated, her words ringing in my ears as I stepped back into the crisp air. There was power in knowledge, but there was also danger in awakening the past. I could only hope Nathan was faring just as well.

When I met up with him later that afternoon, the weight of the day was heavy on his shoulders. "I didn't find much," he admitted, rubbing the back of his neck in frustration. "Just more bureaucracy and a lot of vague references to disturbances. But—" he paused, gauging my expression. "There's been an uptick in reports about strange sightings near the woods. Shadows that seem to move on their own."

"Great," I muttered, a knot forming in my stomach. "Just what we need. More shadows."

"Maybe it's time we go into those woods ourselves," he suggested, the challenge lighting a fire in his eyes. "If something is stirring, we need to confront it before it confronts us."

"Are you suggesting we go camping?" I teased, trying to mask my apprehension with humor. "I'd like to think of myself as more of a 'coffee and comfy blankets' kind of gal."

"C'mon, it'll be fun!" Nathan insisted, his enthusiasm infectious. "We'll bring flashlights, snacks—how can you say no to snacks?"

"Snacks are a strong argument," I conceded, biting back a grin. "But I can't shake the feeling that we're poking a sleeping bear. What if it doesn't just want a snack?"

"Then we'll show it what we're made of," he replied, a determined glint in his eyes that sent a surge of adrenaline through me. "We'll face whatever it is, together."

His unwavering confidence bolstered my resolve, and I found myself nodding, even as a flicker of fear danced in my chest. Together, we would navigate the shadows, exploring not just the depths of the woods, but the uncharted territories of our own hearts. The risks were monumental, but so were the stakes, and we were ready to embrace the adventure ahead—whatever it might bring.

The woods loomed before us like a threshold to another world, the trees standing tall and silent, their gnarled branches reaching out as if to warn us against trespassing. I adjusted the straps of my backpack, my heart pounding with a mix of excitement and apprehension. The late afternoon sun filtered through the leaves, casting dappled shadows on the ground, but an unsettling chill hung in the air, whispering secrets I wasn't sure I wanted to hear.

"Ready for an adventure?" Nathan asked, his tone teasing, yet I could see the seriousness in his eyes. The bravado he wore like a second skin couldn't completely mask the tension threading through him.

"More like an expedition into the unknown," I replied, shooting him a playful glare. "You do know that 'adventure' implies there's some level of fun involved, right?"

"Fun is subjective," he countered, winking at me. "But I'll make you a deal: if we encounter a bear, I'll take the lead, and you can be my brave sidekick."

"Brave? More like panicked." I rolled my eyes, but a smile tugged at my lips. With Nathan at my side, I felt a surge of courage that was hard to deny. He had this uncanny ability to turn my fears into jokes, and in the dim light of the approaching twilight, that spark of humor was a welcome reprieve.

We pressed on into the thickening woods, the path beneath our feet crunching with the fallen leaves, each step echoing with uncertainty. The sunlight ebbed, and the shadows deepened, transforming the landscape into a patchwork of light and dark. Every rustle of leaves or snap of twigs heightened my senses, and I could feel the air grow heavier with unspoken tension.

"I can't shake the feeling that we're being watched," I murmured, casting furtive glances over my shoulder.

"Just the trees," Nathan said, though his smile faltered as he took in the gloom that enveloped us. "Or maybe a squirrel plotting its next nut heist."

I chuckled but couldn't entirely shake the unease. As we ventured deeper, the world seemed to shift around us, the sounds of the forest muting into an eerie stillness. It was as if nature itself had paused to witness our approach.

"Let's check the area near the creek," Nathan suggested, pulling out a flashlight as the last remnants of daylight slipped away. "The diary mentioned it as a gathering place."

We trudged through the underbrush until we reached a clearing where the creek meandered, its water shimmering under the beams of our flashlights. The gentle sound of flowing water brought a sense of calm, momentarily dulling the edge of our anxiety.

"Look!" I pointed toward the opposite bank, where the ground was disturbed, leaves scattered as though something had recently crossed. "Do you think this could be from whatever is causing the trouble?"

Nathan knelt to examine the tracks. "It's possible. They look too big to be from any ordinary animal, and it's not just the disruption. There's an odd smell in the air, almost like... sulfur?"

"Sulfur? As in 'demonic presence' sulfur?" I raised an eyebrow, half-laughing and half-serious.

"Or maybe just a really angry skunk," he said, trying to lighten the mood, but I could see the unease creeping back into his expression.

Suddenly, a sound shattered the night's stillness—a low growl emanating from the shadows of the trees. My heart raced as the noise grew louder, the darkness shifting in a way that felt distinctly alive. "What was that?" I hissed, instinctively inching closer to Nathan.

"I don't know, but we should probably—"

Before he could finish, a large shape burst from the underbrush, moving faster than I could comprehend. We both froze as a figure emerged, silhouetted against the pale moonlight. It was a person, but not just any person—clad in tattered clothing, their face obscured by a hood, eyes glinting like shards of glass.

"Who are you?" Nathan called out, his voice steady despite the sudden panic in the pit of my stomach.

The figure stepped forward, a wicked grin splitting their face, sharp teeth glimmering. "You've come looking for answers, haven't you?" Their voice was smooth, dripping with an unsettling mix of amusement and menace.

"Answers to what?" I shot back, feigning bravado even as my pulse quickened.

"Answers to questions best left buried," they replied, the growl from earlier morphing into a dark chuckle. "But perhaps it's too late for that now."

My heart raced, and instinctively, I took a step back, only to feel Nathan's hand on my arm, steadying me. "We're not afraid of you," he said, his voice a protective barrier against the tension crackling in the air.

"Fear is a delicious flavor," the figure mused, their gaze sweeping over us with unsettling intensity. "It sharpens the senses. But trust me, it's not fear you should be worried about."

A chill ran through me as they stepped even closer, their presence swallowing the light around us. "What do you want?" Nathan demanded, his voice rising with tension.

"Ah, but it's not about what I want," the figure replied, tilting their head in a way that made the hair on my arms stand on end. "It's about what you're willing to sacrifice to uncover the truth."

I exchanged a quick glance with Nathan, the silent communication between us crystal clear—we needed to escape this madness. "We're not sacrificing anything," I declared, trying to infuse my words with a confidence I didn't entirely feel. "Just tell us what we need to know."

The figure laughed, a sound that echoed through the trees like a bell tolling in the distance. "And here I thought you'd be more entertaining! But you're right; it's time for a little revelation."

The ground beneath us trembled slightly, as if responding to their words, and my heart lurched as a chill wind rustled the leaves.

"You think this is just a game?" I shot back, fear clawing at my insides.

"Oh, darling," the figure whispered, a predatory gleam in their eyes, "it's much more than a game. This is just the beginning."

Before I could react, they raised a hand, and the shadows around us twisted and writhed, coiling like living tendrils, creeping closer as the world around us began to darken. I felt Nathan's grip tighten on my arm, his presence anchoring me even as panic surged within.

"Run!" he shouted, pulling me back toward the path we'd come from.

But the shadows surged forward, blocking our escape, their forms shifting into monstrous shapes that promised nightmares. Just as I thought we were cornered, a blinding light burst forth, illuminating the darkness in a wave of brilliant energy. I squinted against the brilliance, trying to make sense of what was happening as the figure recoiled, their expression twisting in rage.

"Not yet!" they screeched, but their voice faded as the light swallowed the night.

Nathan and I stumbled back, adrenaline fueling our movements as the light pulsated around us, pushing against the encroaching darkness.

"What is happening?" I gasped, bewildered, my senses overwhelmed.

"I don't know," Nathan breathed, pulling me closer as we stood at the precipice of an unfathomable reality. "But we need to get out of here—now!"

With the shadows recoiling and the mysterious figure momentarily distracted, we turned to flee, but as we dashed toward the light, a chilling laugh echoed behind us, resonating with a promise that the shadows would not relent, and the darkness was only just beginning to unfurl its tendrils around our lives.

Chapter 18: The Gathering Storm

The air inside the bar was thick with the scent of spilled beer and something I could only describe as unwashed despair. Shadows danced along the walls, cast by flickering candles that struggled to maintain their flicker against the onslaught of dismal overhead lights. I slid into a booth in the far corner, the leather cracked and worn, a testament to years of secrets whispered over half-finished drinks. This was a haven for the lost and the damned, a perfect rendezvous point for those of us teetering on the edge of something much bigger than ourselves.

Nathan arrived just moments later, his figure cloaked in a heavy, dark coat that seemed more like a shield than a garment. As he approached, his usual air of confidence was replaced by an edge of unease. His eyes, usually warm and inviting, held the weight of uncertainty. "You look like you've seen a ghost," I remarked, raising an eyebrow as he slid into the seat across from me.

"More like a few too many bad decisions," he replied, attempting a grin that faltered at the edges. "But we have to keep moving. I called in a few favors, and they're on their way."

"Favors? Who exactly are we waiting for?" I couldn't hide the skepticism in my tone. This whole situation felt precarious. The walls of the bar seemed to close in, the dim lighting emphasizing the tension that clung to us like a second skin.

Nathan leaned forward, his voice low. "Some of my old colleagues from the department. They're willing to help, but we need to be careful. If word gets out..." He let the sentence hang ominously in the air, the implications swirling like smoke from the dwindling candle on our table.

The bar's door swung open, admitting a gust of chilly air along with two figures, both of whom looked like they'd just stepped out of a noir film. They wore trench coats that flared slightly with every movement, and their eyes, sharp and discerning, scanned the room before landing on us.

I nudged Nathan. "Are they going to order drinks or get us killed?"

"Let's hope for the former," he muttered, a hint of humor breaking through the tension.

The newcomers approached with a purpose, and as they settled into the booth next to ours, I could feel the palpable shift in energy. One of them, a woman with a striking auburn bob and a piercing gaze, extended her hand. "I'm Riley, and this is Max. We heard you were looking for some information."

Max, with a face that could've been chiseled from stone, nodded curtly. "We don't have much time. Let's get straight to it."

"What do you know?" Nathan asked, leaning in. I admired his determination, even as the stakes escalated.

Riley pulled out a small notepad, flipping it open with deft fingers. "There's been a pattern—odd occurrences, strange sightings. It all ties back to a group that's been operating in the shadows, and they seem to have an interest in you, Nathan."

I felt my heart quicken. "In him? Why?"

"Your past is a bit more tangled than you let on," Max interjected, his voice a low growl. "They think you have something they want. Something valuable."

I shifted, suddenly aware of how exposed we were in this dimly lit sanctuary. "And how do we know we can trust you?"

"Trust is a luxury in our line of work," Riley replied, her eyes sharp. "But we're here because we don't like what they're doing. And if you're going to take them down, we want in."

Nathan's expression hardened, the resolve in his voice steady. "Then let's talk about what we need to do."

The conversation flowed like a well-choreographed dance, words mixing with the lingering scent of alcohol and the muted clinking of glasses around us. As the pieces of the puzzle began to fit together, I felt a surge of adrenaline—a heady mix of fear and exhilaration. Each revelation pushed us deeper into a tangled web of deceit and intrigue.

But just as we began to forge a plan, a familiar figure caught my eye from across the bar. My breath hitched as I recognized him. A ghost from my past, someone I never expected to see here. Carter, my former partner in more ways than one, leaned against the bar, nursing a whiskey as he watched us.

"Is that who I think it is?" I whispered, glancing back at Nathan and Riley, who both followed my gaze.

"Do you trust him?" Nathan asked, his tone serious.

"I don't know," I admitted, feeling a pang of betrayal wash over me. The trust we were trying to build was fragile, and now it felt like it was about to shatter. Carter had left me once before, and the wounds from that abandonment were still fresh.

"Then we keep him at a distance," Nathan decided, a protective edge to his voice. "We can't afford any surprises."

But as the night wore on, our plans unraveled in ways I never anticipated. Each revelation only led to more questions, and the weight of uncertainty settled heavily on my shoulders. I could feel the atmosphere shifting, the camaraderie we had briefly fostered crackling with tension.

Suddenly, a figure loomed in the shadows near the entrance, watching us intently. My instincts kicked in, and I instinctively leaned closer to Nathan, our shoulders brushing. "I think we're being watched."

"Keep your cool," he murmured, but I could see the tension in his jaw, the way his fingers clenched around the table edge.

The door swung open again, a chill creeping in, but this time it wasn't just the cold air. It was something darker, something that made my skin prickle.

In that moment, as the bar blurred around us and the shadows deepened, I understood: trust would be a luxury, but survival? That would depend on making the right choices—and quickly. The storm was gathering, and we were right in its path.

The room vibrated with a tension that was almost palpable, as if the very air had thickened with unsaid words and unmade choices. I could feel the eyes upon us, darting between the shadows and the bar's flickering light, weaving through the murky atmosphere that had settled like a shroud. Nathan's gaze locked onto mine, a silent communication passing between us, something electric and dangerous.

"Maybe we should move this conversation somewhere more private," Riley suggested, her eyes scanning the bar with the precision of a hawk. "We're drawing too much attention."

"Good idea," I agreed, feeling the weight of my instincts. "The last thing we need is a scene."

We slipped out of the booth, the soft leather groaning in protest as we left. Nathan motioned for me to follow him toward the back of the bar, where a narrow hallway led to a dimly lit area that felt like a forgotten memory of what once might have been a storied backroom. The walls were lined with peeling wallpaper, its pattern long faded, and the flickering bulb overhead buzzed ominously, casting strange shadows that danced like specters.

Max ushered us into a small, sparsely furnished room that was little more than a closet with a table. He closed the door behind us, blocking out the raucous laughter and clinking glasses from the bar. The muffled sounds only heightened my sense of urgency.

"Alright, spill it," Nathan said, leaning over the table, his expression fierce. "What do you know about this group?"

Riley exchanged a glance with Max before answering. "They're called The Syndicate. A collection of rogue agents and unsavory characters who have managed to slip through the cracks of law enforcement. They're resourceful, ruthless, and they're playing a long game."

"Playing a long game for what?" I interjected, the worry threading through my voice.

"Power, influence," Max replied, his tone grim. "They've been operating under the radar for years, gathering intel, manipulating events. And you, Nathan, seem to be at the center of their plans."

"Why me?" Nathan asked, his voice edged with frustration.

"They think you have access to something they need," Riley explained, her brows knitting together in concern. "Something that could give them an edge."

The weight of her words settled over me like a dense fog, and I glanced at Nathan, who looked pensive, a storm brewing behind his eyes. "What kind of access?"

Riley hesitated. "Files, intel on ongoing operations. You were involved in something big, something that rattled a lot of cages."

"Yeah, well, I didn't exactly plan on being the center of attention for a group of sociopaths," Nathan shot back, running a hand through his hair in exasperation.

As we debated the implications, the room felt increasingly constricting, the air thick with the weight of impending doom. Just then, I felt a shiver skitter down my spine as I caught a glimpse of movement outside the cracked door. I could see a figure lurking in the hallway, their face obscured by the shadows.

"Someone's here," I whispered urgently, my heart racing.

Max tensed, moving to the door. "We need to see who it is."

He eased it open a crack, and in an instant, everything changed. The figure outside slipped inside with the confidence of someone who knew the lay of the land. It was Carter, and the relief flooding through me was quickly overshadowed by a wave of wariness.

"Fancy seeing you here," he said, his tone light, but his eyes were as serious as ever. "I heard about the meeting. Thought I'd drop in."

Nathan's expression hardened. "And just how did you find out?"

Carter's smile faltered, but he maintained his cool demeanor. "Let's just say old contacts have a way of finding each other. I'm here to help. I can get you information."

"Information or trouble?" Nathan countered, crossing his arms.

Carter shrugged, a nonchalant gesture that felt more like a cover for something deeper. "Depends on how you play it. But if you want to go after The Syndicate, you'll need all the help you can get."

"Why should we trust you?" I blurted out, the question hanging heavy in the air.

Carter looked at me, his eyes momentarily softening. "Because I'm not the enemy. Not anymore. The stakes are too high for old grudges. We need to focus."

There was something in his voice, a vulnerability beneath the bravado that made me hesitate. I exchanged glances with Nathan, who seemed equally torn between the past and the urgency of our present circumstances.

"Fine," Nathan relented after a moment, his voice laced with wariness. "But if you so much as step out of line—"

"I get it," Carter interrupted, holding up his hands in surrender. "You'll shove me right back out the door."

Riley, watching the exchange with keen interest, broke the silence. "If he has contacts, then we should listen. We can't afford to be picky."

The uneasy truce solidified with the weight of necessity, and together we began to lay out our plan, each suggestion punctuated by sharp glances and whispered thoughts. Carter stepped forward with a sense of authority that surprised me, outlining a way to infiltrate The Syndicate's operations.

"First, we need to gather intel on their upcoming meeting," he explained, pacing slightly as he spoke. "They're planning something big, and if we can get in, we might be able to find out what they're really after."

Nathan nodded, his focus sharpening. "Where do we start?"

Carter smirked, the familiar glimmer of his old charm returning. "I have a few leads, but it involves going into the lion's den."

"Fantastic," I quipped, crossing my arms. "I always wanted to be a meal for a pack of sociopaths."

The tension in the room eased slightly as a ripple of laughter broke through the seriousness. But beneath the banter, the stakes remained high, and every lighthearted quip felt like a fragile facade.

With plans unfolding before us, I couldn't shake the feeling that we were standing on the edge of a precipice, the abyss lurking just beyond our sight. Trust was a currency we could hardly afford, and betrayal loomed like a dark cloud overhead. As we prepared to move forward, I couldn't help but wonder who would emerge from the shadows unscathed—and who would get left behind in the storm.

The plan had morphed from a vague idea into a well-structured mission, though the execution remained an uneasy prospect. Our small group was a patchwork of old loyalties and fragile alliances, stitched together by a common enemy and the faint hope of survival. Carter leaned against the wall, arms crossed, a casual air about him that belied the tension crackling in the air.

"Alright, we need to move quickly," he said, his voice low and steady, like the rumble of thunder in the distance. "The Syndicate has a meeting tonight, and we can't miss our chance to get intel. I have a friend who can get us inside."

"Who's your friend?" Nathan asked, skepticism etched on his face.

"Let's just say she knows how to blend in with the crowd," Carter replied, a flicker of something indecipherable passing through his eyes. "Her name is Sasha. She used to work undercover."

I arched an eyebrow. "An undercover agent? And she's just willing to help us?"

"More or less," Carter replied with a wry smile. "Though I'm sure her motives aren't purely altruistic."

"Great," I said, rolling my eyes. "Nothing like a little ambiguity to lighten the mood."

Riley pushed off the table, her expression serious. "Ambiguity or not, if she can get us in, we need to take that chance. It's now or never."

As we finalized our plans, adrenaline coursed through me. This felt like a scene straight out of a spy novel, except we were the ones caught in the plot, and the stakes were dangerously real. I could almost hear the ominous soundtrack playing in my head, heightening the anticipation of what was to come.

The bar's ambiance faded as we slipped back into the main area, the din of chatter and clinking glasses momentarily overwhelming. The world outside was an unscripted chaos, and as we stepped into the street, I felt the weight of the night press against my skin like a heavy blanket. The sky above was a dark canvas speckled with stars, a distant reminder of normalcy amidst the impending storm.

We hopped into a nondescript car, its muted colors blending seamlessly with the city's nighttime palette. Carter took the wheel, a hint of mischief dancing in his eyes. "Buckle up, folks. This is going to be a wild ride."

"Don't worry; I can handle it," I shot back, unable to resist the opportunity for a little banter, despite the tension coiling in my stomach.

As we sped through the streets of Queens, my mind whirled with thoughts of what lay ahead. The Syndicate was not just any criminal organization; they were cunning, resourceful, and had a talent for disappearing without a trace. Each passing block felt like an unspoken countdown, the reality of our mission looming larger with every heartbeat.

"You ready for this?" Nathan's voice broke through my thoughts, pulling my gaze to his. His eyes were dark, reflecting both concern and determination, the kind that demanded answers.

"I've never been more ready for anything in my life," I replied, trying to inject a confidence I didn't entirely feel. "What's the worst that could happen? We get caught and end up in a villain's lair?"

"Don't tempt fate," Riley cautioned, her voice steady but edged with apprehension. "This is serious."

"I know," I said, meeting her gaze. "But if we're going to stop this, we have to take the plunge."

Carter drove us to a dilapidated warehouse that loomed in the distance like a sleeping beast. Its windows were dark, and the air around it hummed with an energy that felt ominous. "This is the place," he said, parking the car behind an old delivery truck. "Sasha should be waiting for us inside."

As we stepped out into the night, I could feel the weight of the moment settling on my shoulders. The darkness seemed to whisper secrets, each rustle of leaves and flicker of distant streetlights amplifying my anxiety. I glanced at Nathan, who met my gaze with a reassuring nod, a silent promise that we were in this together.

We crept toward the entrance, the echo of our footsteps swallowed by the surrounding silence. Carter pushed open the door, revealing an interior cloaked in shadow. The air was musty, carrying with it the scent of dust and something metallic that set my teeth on edge.

"Sasha?" Carter called, his voice cutting through the stillness.

From the shadows emerged a figure, her silhouette striking against the dim light. "You must be Carter," she said, her voice smooth yet commanding. "And these must be your friends."

She stepped into the light, and I took a moment to take her in. Sasha was tall, with striking features that held an air of authority, her dark hair framing her face like a halo of midnight. She wore a leather jacket that hugged her frame and jeans that looked as though they had seen a hundred adventures.

"We need to move fast," she said, cutting through the pleasantries. "They're not known for their patience."

"What's the plan?" Nathan asked, his posture tense, eyes flicking toward the back of the warehouse as if sensing an unseen threat.

"We go in as a group. I'll introduce you as new recruits," Sasha replied, a glint of mischief in her eyes. "And if things get dicey, stick close to me."

"Sounds like a plan," I said, my voice steady, though inside I felt like a bundle of nerves ready to unravel.

As we entered deeper into the warehouse, the atmosphere shifted, and the sound of muffled voices drifted through the air, growing louder with each step. The dim light illuminated a gathering of shadowy figures, their conversations a mixture of laughter and heated discussions.

"Remember, keep your cool," Sasha warned, her tone dropping to a whisper. "And whatever you do, don't blow your cover."

The tension crackled like static in the air as we moved closer, and my heart raced in tandem with the rising stakes. Just as we approached the circle of gathered individuals, a figure broke away from the throng and turned toward us.

"Carter," he said, his voice low and menacing, the smirk on his face chilling. "I didn't think you'd come back. You really should know better than to associate with the likes of them."

The room seemed to dim as the realization sank in; he was someone I recognized. A name that had crossed my path in whispers and warnings. A member of The Syndicate.

Panic gripped me, but before I could react, the atmosphere shifted. The air turned electric, and the playful banter faded, replaced by a palpable tension. I looked at Nathan, and we shared a silent understanding—whatever came next would test our resolve, our trust, and our very lives.

The man's eyes gleamed with something sinister as he stepped closer, the weight of the moment thickening. "Welcome to the real party, kids," he sneered, his smile widening as the darkness around us deepened.

In that instant, I knew we were in far deeper than any of us had anticipated, and the night was only just beginning.

Chapter 19: The Web Tightens

I had never truly understood the fragility of life until the walls began to close in around me, a slow, suffocating tightening of the noose that threatened to strangle the remnants of my peace. It began with a notification, a ping on my phone that shattered the mundane tranquility of my morning coffee. I had settled into a sunbeam on our small apartment balcony, the aroma of fresh espresso swirling in the air as I scrolled through social media. But there it was, a link shared by an acquaintance that sent chills racing down my spine. "Look at this!" it exclaimed, along with a video showing Nathan and me strolling hand in hand down Main Street, oblivious to the storm brewing just beneath the surface.

The screen flickered to life, and my heart sank. The footage, grainy yet unmistakably invasive, depicted our every move over the past month: laughing at our favorite café, window-shopping for the perfect plant to liven our apartment, and those stolen moments of intimacy when we thought we were alone in our little bubble. But that bubble had burst, and the shards were digging into my skin, a reminder of how exposed we were to the very world we thought we could hide from.

"What the hell is this?" I whispered, half to myself and half to Nathan, who had just stepped outside with his own steaming mug, blissfully unaware of the tempest gathering in my heart. He glanced at my phone, his brow furrowing as he took in the sight.

"This is... unsettling." His voice was a low rumble, laced with the seriousness that had become a hallmark of our recent exchanges. "Who would do this?"

I could only shake my head, a lump forming in my throat. It felt as though the very air around us had thickened, heavy with the weight of suspicion and dread. The walls of our sanctuary, once adorned with laughter and shared dreams, now felt like a prison, trapping us in a web woven by unseen hands.

Nathan moved closer, his hand brushing against mine, a silent promise of solidarity amidst the chaos. "We need to figure out who's behind this," he said, determination flickering in his eyes. There was something fierce about him in that moment, a flame that flickered defiantly in the face of impending darkness. "We can't let them win."

But how could we fight against an enemy cloaked in shadows, one that knew our every move? As I leaned into him, seeking solace in his warmth, I felt the gnawing anxiety clawing at the edges of my mind. We had been so careful, so diligent in our attempts to remain under the radar, yet here we were, thrust into the glaring spotlight of public scrutiny.

"Do you think it's the same person?" I asked, my voice barely above a whisper. Memories of our previous encounters with danger danced in my mind, the way it had loomed like a predator, waiting for the right moment to strike. The thought that we might be dealing with a repeat offender made my skin crawl.

"I don't know, but we can't dismiss the possibility," Nathan replied, his voice steady despite the storm brewing inside us. "If it is, then we're running out of time. We need to expose whoever's pulling the strings before they come for us again."

The fire in his words ignited something within me, a spark of resolve that flickered to life amid my trepidation. I couldn't allow fear to paralyze us; I needed to harness it, channel it into action. "What's the plan?" I asked, my tone shifting from one of despair to defiance.

Nathan leaned back against the railing, his eyes narrowing in thought as he strategized. "First, we gather intel. We can't go after shadows. Let's track down whoever posted that video. If we can find them, maybe we can unearth the source of this madness."

I nodded, already feeling the rush of adrenaline coursing through my veins. The thought of stepping back into the fray was daunting, yet exhilarating. Together, we were a force to be reckoned with, and as Nathan squeezed my hand, I could feel the power of our bond, a tether that would guide us through the darkness.

"Okay, we start with the video," I said, my voice gaining strength. "We'll follow the digital breadcrumbs."

The plan was set, and though a sense of dread lingered at the back of my mind, I felt a new resolve solidifying in my chest. This was no longer just about survival; it was about reclaiming our lives from the clutches of a lurking threat. But as we moved through our apartment, gathering our tools—laptops, phones, notes—I couldn't shake the feeling that eyes were upon us. Every shadow seemed to stretch longer, every creak of the floorboards echoed like a warning.

"Are you ready?" Nathan asked, and his steady gaze grounded me, dispelling the rising tide of anxiety that threatened to pull me under.

"More than ready," I replied, forcing a smile that I hoped would mask my underlying fears.

We dove into our investigation, the soft click of keyboards echoing like a heartbeat in the silent apartment. Hours melted away as we scoured social media, tracing the digital footprints that led to our unwelcome fame. With every click, I felt the walls around us close tighter, the web of manipulation tightening its grip. We were no longer merely hunting for answers; we were battling a faceless enemy that had turned our lives into a game of cat and mouse.

And as night crept in, cloaking the world in shadows, I couldn't shake the unease coiling in my stomach. There was a palpable tension in the air, a feeling that our every move was being monitored, recorded, twisted into something sinister. Each ping of my phone became a jolt of fear, each notification a reminder that we were being watched. I caught Nathan's eye, and in that shared glance, I saw the same resolve, the same underlying fear that threatened to unravel everything we held dear.

Whatever game was being played, we were now players in a high-stakes drama, and the thrill of the chase was intoxicating, even as the stakes rose higher than we could have ever imagined.

The glow from the computer screen illuminated our faces, creating an eerie halo around us as we delved deeper into the digital labyrinth. Nathan and I were enveloped in the warm cocoon of our living room, but outside, the world had turned dark and foreboding. It felt like we were both seeking comfort and courting danger, the fine line between security and vulnerability growing ever thinner.

"I can't believe this," I muttered, scrolling through the comments beneath the video. The reactions ranged from shock to bizarre conspiracy theories, each one more ludicrous than the last. "Some people think we're part of a reality show. Do they really think our lives are so fascinating that we'd sign up for this kind of nightmare?"

Nathan chuckled, but there was a nervous edge to his laughter. "If this were a reality show, we'd definitely win for the most absurd plot twist. 'Surveillance and Coffee: A Modern Love Story.'" He grinned, but I could see the tension lining his jaw.

"Let's not give them any more ideas," I said, trying to sound light-hearted, but it didn't quite reach my eyes. "They might just cast us in a spinoff about our impending doom."

"Maybe we can pitch it to the producers," he replied, raising an eyebrow. "At least we'd have a chance to confront the mastermind behind this circus."

As the banter hung in the air, I felt the weight of unease settle back in. We were at a crossroads; every keystroke propelled us further into a chasm of uncertainty, and I could feel the edges of my reality fraying. Nathan's resolve had become a balm against my fears, but even his fierce determination couldn't shield us from the looming shadows.

"Let's focus," I said, clearing my throat as I sat up straight, steeling myself for what lay ahead. "We need to track down the source of that video. If we can find out who posted it, we might discover how deep this goes."

Nathan nodded, his demeanor shifting to that of a strategist. "I'll take social media; you handle the comments section. Let's see if we can unearth anything useful."

Our fingers flew across the keyboards, the clicks echoing like distant gunfire in the tense silence. Hours blurred into a haze of information, each revelation a small thread we could tug at to unravel the larger tapestry of deception surrounding us.

Just as fatigue began to creep in, a notification popped up on my screen—a direct message from an unknown account. My heart raced as I hesitated, the instinct to delete it battling with curiosity. Nathan leaned over, glancing at my screen.

"Open it. What do you have to lose?"

With a deep breath, I clicked. The message was short and cryptic: "I know who's watching you. Meet me at the old bridge at midnight."

My pulse quickened. "What the hell? Who is this?"

Nathan's eyes narrowed. "Could be a trap. Or it could be our ticket to the truth."

"Or it could just be someone with a flair for the dramatic," I countered, my voice tinged with skepticism. "What makes us think this isn't just another layer of the game?"

"Because we have to take risks if we want to get ahead of this. If this person knows something, we can't just ignore it." Nathan's tone brooked no argument. His fierce determination was contagious, and a flicker of hope ignited within me.

I chewed my lip, weighing the options. "Fine. But if we're going, we're going armed with the knowledge that it could be a setup."

"Always," Nathan replied, a glint of mischief in his eye that momentarily eased my apprehension. "Let's not go in unprepared."

As the clock inched closer to midnight, we gathered our essentials: flashlights, a couple of snacks—because even in the face of danger, a girl needed her granola bars—and my trusty pepper spray, which I clutched like a lifeline. There was something both thrilling and terrifying about this spontaneous mission, an adrenaline rush that sent our hearts racing.

Stepping out into the night, the cool air wrapped around us like a damp shroud, the world outside our apartment transformed into a labyrinth of shadows. The streets, usually buzzing with life, felt eerily quiet. Each rustle of leaves and distant siren echoed ominously, as if the universe were conspiring to keep us in suspense.

As we approached the bridge, the moonlight danced on the surface of the water below, casting a silvery sheen that belied the darkness lurking beneath. I shivered involuntarily, more from the chill in the air than the creeping sense of danger that loomed.

"This is insane," I muttered, looking around. "What are we even doing here?"

"Searching for answers," Nathan said, his voice steady. "And maybe a little bit of closure."

"Or an ambush," I retorted, trying to keep the mood light despite the growing tension coiling in my stomach.

"Better to confront it head-on than to let it fester," he replied, a hint of a smile playing on his lips. "Besides, if we make it out of this, we'll have a hell of a story to tell."

We reached the bridge, its rusted beams creaking softly in the breeze. The sense of isolation was palpable, and every fiber of my being screamed to turn back. But Nathan stood firm, eyes scanning the dark for any sign of life.

"I'll go first," he said, stepping cautiously onto the bridge. "Just stay close."

"I'll be right behind you, but don't get any bright ideas about heroics," I called after him, the sarcasm dripping from my words, but underneath it was genuine concern.

As we made our way across, the air thickened with anticipation. The sound of water lapping at the banks below mirrored the uncertainty swelling in my chest. Just as we reached the midpoint, a figure emerged from the shadows, cloaked in darkness but unmistakably human.

"Are you the ones looking for answers?" the figure asked, their voice a whisper that danced on the breeze, sending chills down my spine.

I exchanged a glance with Nathan, who nodded, taking a step forward. "Who are you?"

The figure stepped into the moonlight, revealing a familiar face—someone I hadn't expected to see, someone whose very presence was a jolt to the system. "I know everything. And if you want to protect yourselves, you need to listen."

The words hung in the air, heavy with unspoken promises and looming threats, setting the stage for the revelations that would unfold. It felt like a doorway opening into a hidden chamber of secrets, each heartbeat resonating with the urgency of our precarious situation. We had stepped into the unknown, but there was no turning back now.

The figure stepped into the moonlight, and the recognition hit me like a punch to the gut. Chloe. She had been a ghost from Nathan's past, someone he had spoken of only in hushed tones, a shadow looming over our present. I could see the tension in Nathan's shoulders stiffen as her presence brought a rush of memories, both good and haunting.

"What are you doing here?" Nathan's voice was sharp, a blade slicing through the charged air between us. I could feel the weight of their shared history pressing down, threatening to crush whatever fragile calm we had managed to muster.

"I'm here to help," Chloe replied, her eyes darting nervously between us. "I didn't expect you to show up, but it seems fate has a twisted sense of humor." Her lips curled into a smirk that didn't quite reach her eyes.

"Help?" I echoed, incredulous. "You have a funny way of showing it." The sharpness of my words surprised even me, but the notion that she could swoop in now, after everything, stirred a protective instinct in my gut.

"Look, I know you're both scared, but you have to listen to me," Chloe insisted, her tone shifting from playful to urgent. "There's a reason you're being targeted, and it's not just Nathan's past. There's something much bigger at play here."

I glanced at Nathan, who was still processing her presence, his expression a mix of disbelief and concern. "What do you mean bigger? What are you talking about?"

Chloe took a step closer, lowering her voice to a conspiratorial whisper. "There's a group—one that monitors people like us. They dig into your life, your past, and they won't stop until they have what they want. Nathan, they think you have something they need."

My heart raced at the implications. "What could they possibly want from you? What did you get yourself into?"

Nathan's silence was deafening, but it was his eyes that spoke volumes, revealing shadows of regret and choices he had never shared with me. "You don't understand," he said finally, his voice strained. "I thought I could leave that behind, but it seems I was wrong."

"Fantastic," I muttered, feeling the world tilt beneath me. "So, what? We're just supposed to sit here and let them pick us off one by one?"

"No," Chloe replied sharply, her voice rising. "We fight back. But you have to trust me, both of you. This isn't just about Nathan; it's about all of us."

Trust was a fragile commodity, especially now, with Chloe's sudden appearance stirring up the murky waters of Nathan's past. "Why should we trust you?" I shot back, crossing my arms defensively. "You just waltz back in and expect us to believe you have our best interests at heart?"

"I can help you," she insisted, a hint of desperation creeping into her voice. "I have information that could turn the tables. I've been tracking them ever since I found out they were after you."

"Wait," Nathan interjected, stepping closer to her. "How do you know about all of this? What have you been doing?"

"I have my sources," Chloe replied cryptically, her gaze darting around the dimly lit surroundings as if she were expecting someone to leap from the shadows. "But I need your help too. They're not just watching you; they're watching me, and I'm running out of time."

"What do you mean running out of time?" I asked, my heart pounding in my chest. "What's going to happen?"

Before she could answer, a sound shattered the night—a rustling from the bushes nearby. Instinctively, Nathan and I moved closer together, the protective barrier forming between us as we scanned the darkness. "Did you hear that?" I whispered, my voice barely above a breath.

Chloe nodded, her eyes widening. "We need to get out of here. Now."

Nathan grabbed my hand, and we began to back away from the bridge, our senses heightened, ready to react to any threat. Just as we turned, the shadow of a figure emerged from the darkness, silhouetted against the moonlight. My breath caught in my throat as the reality of our situation crashed down on me.

"Who the hell are you?" Nathan demanded, stepping in front of me, ready to defend.

The figure stepped forward, revealing a face I recognized but hadn't seen in years—Julian, a former associate of Nathan's from that murky world he had tried so hard to escape. My stomach twisted at the sight of him, a man whose very existence seemed to reek of trouble.

"I thought you might be interested in a reunion," Julian said, a predatory smile spreading across his face. "I see you've been busy, Nathan. I hope you're not planning on running away from your old friends."

"Get lost, Julian," Nathan growled, his voice low and threatening.

"Ah, but it's not that simple, is it?" Julian continued, his eyes glinting with amusement. "You see, I'm here to help you both. There's a game at play, and you're all just pawns. I can offer you a way out. Or I can ensure you never leave this place."

The air grew thick with tension, and I felt the weight of his words settling over us like a suffocating blanket. "What do you want?" I asked, my voice steady even as panic threatened to break through.

Julian shrugged, feigning nonchalance. "Just a little information exchange. You see, I know who's watching you, and I can tell you how to get them off your backs. But it's going to cost you."

"Why should we trust anything you say?" Nathan spat, his jaw clenched.

"Because, my dear Nathan," Julian said, his voice dripping with sarcasm, "your precious little world is about to crumble. And I happen to know how to keep it from happening—if you're willing to play nice."

Chloe shifted nervously beside me, and I could feel the weight of uncertainty pressing down. The balance of power had shifted, and we were now caught in a precarious web of alliances and betrayals.

"Don't listen to him," Chloe urged, stepping forward. "He's just using you to settle his own scores."

Julian chuckled, a cold, humorless sound. "You should really mind your own business, Chloe. You're in over your head."

The standoff felt electric, the air crackling with unspoken threats. Nathan's eyes were locked on Julian, a storm brewing within him, and I could feel the pulse of fear, anger, and determination swirling around us.

"What's it going to be, Nathan?" Julian pressed, taking a step closer, his presence looming like a dark cloud. "Are you going to play this game, or do I need to remind you of the consequences of your past?"

Just as Nathan opened his mouth to respond, a piercing sound shattered the night—an unmistakable crack followed by a flash of light. My heart plummeted as the realization hit. Someone had just fired a shot, and we were all caught in the crossfire.

In that instant, time slowed, and every instinct screamed at me to run. We were no longer just players in this twisted game; we had become targets, and the stakes had never been higher. As the world around us spiraled into chaos, I grabbed Nathan's arm, pulling him close as the darkness threatened to swallow us whole.

Chapter 20: Confrontation at Dusk

The warehouse loomed ahead, a hulking shadow against the fiery sky as the sun dipped below the horizon, casting long, skeletal fingers of darkness across the pavement. I felt the weight of the air, thick with the promise of confrontation, pressing down on my chest. Each step toward the entrance sent a jolt of electricity through my veins, mingling with the swirling emotions that danced just beneath the surface. I had come to know the churning turmoil within Nathan, the man whose past now felt as tangible as the rusted metal that surrounded us. Tonight, we would face the demons that had haunted him, and I would stand by his side, come what may.

As we approached the creaking doors, Nathan's hand brushed against mine, his fingers trembling slightly, a rare moment of vulnerability breaking through the tough exterior he wore like armor. I caught his gaze, those warm, deep eyes now shadowed with uncertainty. The tension was palpable, thick enough to cut with a knife. "You ready?" I asked, my voice steady despite the chaos swirling in my mind.

"Not even close," he replied, a sardonic twist to his lips that barely masked the fear beneath. "But I guess we don't get to choose our battles, do we?"

I offered him a reassuring smile, though inside I felt like a tightly wound spring, ready to snap. This place, with its peeling paint and broken windows, felt like a relic of old wounds and unresolved grievances. The air was heavy with the scent of rust and decay, the kind of smell that made you acutely aware of the passage of time and the ghosts that lingered in its wake. I wanted to believe we were here to find closure, but a gnawing sense of dread told me otherwise.

Stepping inside, the dim light cast eerie shadows that danced across the concrete floor, creating an unsettling atmosphere that only heightened my apprehension. The faint sound of dripping water echoed in the vast space, an unsettling rhythm that felt like a countdown to some inevitable climax. My heart raced as we moved further into the belly of the beast, each echoing footfall a reminder of the confrontation that lay ahead.

"Nathan," I said, lowering my voice to a whisper, "what if he's here? What if he's waiting for us?"

"He will be," Nathan replied, his tone suddenly grave, all traces of sarcasm stripped away. "He's always waiting. He knows how to play this game."

We paused, standing side by side, our breath mingling in the chill of the warehouse. I could see the muscles in Nathan's jaw clench, the tension radiating off him like a heat wave. This was more than a simple confrontation; it was a reckoning. I squeezed his hand tighter, grounding both of us in that moment, reminding him that he was not alone in this fight.

The flickering fluorescent lights overhead buzzed ominously, and just then, a sound sliced through the stillness—a low, mocking laugh that echoed off the walls like an unwelcome ghost. My stomach lurched as I recognized the voice, a sinister melody that played in the back of Nathan's mind like a bad memory.

"Ah, the lovebirds have finally arrived." The voice dripped with contempt, each word a dagger aimed at our hearts. From the shadows emerged a figure cloaked in darkness, a man whose presence twisted the atmosphere, amplifying every fear I had about this encounter. Nathan's past materialized before us, and with it, a rush of adrenaline surged through me.

"Derek," Nathan hissed, his voice barely above a growl. The name hung in the air like a bad omen, and I could see the storm brewing in Nathan's eyes, a mix of anger and something more vulnerable, something I couldn't quite put my finger on.

"Did you really think you could escape me? After all this time?" Derek's smile was a shark's grin, sharp and predatory. "I've waited for this moment, Nathan. I've waited for you to come crawling back."

A chill swept through me, tinged with disbelief. "You're not going to intimidate us, Derek," I shot back, my voice stronger than I felt. "We're not afraid of you."

He turned his attention toward me, eyes narrowing, as if suddenly realizing I was an unexpected variable in his twisted game. "And who might you be? The new toy? A distraction for Nathan's pathetic existence?"

I felt Nathan tense beside me, his body rigid, and I could almost see the gears turning in his mind, weighing the options of how to handle this confrontation. "Leave her out of this, Derek," he said, his voice low but steady, like a river that ran deep and unyielding. "This is between you and me."

Derek laughed again, a sound that grated against my nerves. "Oh, but she's the crux of it, isn't she? The reason you've let your guard down. The reason you think you can reclaim a life you've long forfeited. But you're still the same weakling I always knew."

My heart raced, not just from fear but from a deep-seated fury rising within me. I had witnessed Nathan's strength, the layers of resilience he had built over the years, and I refused to let Derek strip that away. "Weakness isn't defined by who you fight against, but by who you choose to stand with," I said, meeting Derek's gaze head-on. "And Nathan stands with me."

The silence that followed felt electric, crackling with tension. Nathan's gaze softened briefly, a flicker of surprise that told me I had struck a chord. For a heartbeat, it felt like the world had paused, the chaotic dance of shadows and light frozen in time. But Derek's laughter shattered the moment, dark and menacing, reminding us that we were far from safe.

"Such sweet sentiment," he mocked, taking a step closer. "But love doesn't win battles, darling. It only blinds you to the reality of the fight ahead."

The atmosphere shifted, thickening with the promise of violence. I could sense Nathan's resolve hardening beside me, the flicker of vulnerability giving way to a fierce determination. The lines had been drawn, and there was no turning back now. In that moment, I knew that whatever happened next, we would face it together, united against the storm that was about to break.

Derek's laughter echoed through the warehouse like an unwanted guest at a party no one wanted to attend. The noise ricocheted off the rusted beams, a dissonant melody that reminded me of shattered glass. My pulse quickened, the adrenaline surging through my veins, urging me to push back against the palpable menace in the room. I could feel Nathan's energy shifting beside me, a quiet storm brewing just beneath the surface, but I refused to let fear paralyze me.

"Love blinds? That's rich coming from you," I retorted, crossing my arms defiantly. "You've clearly never experienced it. Maybe that's why you're lurking in the shadows like a bad sequel." The words were out before I could second-guess myself, and the slight smirk on Nathan's face told me I'd hit a nerve.

Derek's expression darkened, his bravado faltering for a fraction of a second. "You think this is a game?" He stepped forward, invading my personal space, and I stood my ground, my heart pounding like a war drum in my chest. "You don't know what you're getting into, sweetheart. This is a fight for survival, not just some melodrama between lovers."

"Survival?" I scoffed, matching his intensity. "You wouldn't know survival if it knocked on your door and asked for a cup of sugar. You're living in the past, Derek. Clinging to your petty grudges like a child who refuses to let go of a broken toy."

Nathan shot me an incredulous look, half-amused and half-worried. "That was... bold."

"Someone has to be," I replied, shrugging off the tension. "Besides, what's the worst he can do? Hurt my feelings?" I turned my attention back to Derek, who was momentarily taken aback by my defiance. "I've survived worse than your empty threats."

His eyes flared with a mix of rage and admiration, and I could sense the shifting dynamics in the room. "You really think you can stand between us? Between me and what's rightfully mine?" He gestured grandly, as if we were in a theater and he was the leading man in this tragic farce. "Nathan betrayed me. He deserves everything coming to him."

"I don't think you're the one to decide what he deserves," I shot back, my voice firm. "You've spent your life twisting love into a weapon. It's pathetic, really."

The tension hung heavy in the air, thick like the humidity before a summer storm. Nathan's body radiated a heat that matched my own, and I could see the flickers of past anguish wrestling within him. The boy I had come to know, the one who wore his heart on his sleeve and shared his dreams with me, stood poised to confront the man who had once shattered his world.

"Enough!" Nathan's voice thundered, cutting through the charged atmosphere. "This isn't about you, Derek. It never was. It's about moving forward, about breaking free from the chains you've tried to wrap around me." The fierceness in his tone sent a thrill of pride racing through me. There was a warrior inside him, a man ready to reclaim what had been stolen.

Derek's smirk returned, cruel and self-satisfied. "Is that what you think? That you can just walk away? I've spent years building this moment. You'll regret turning your back on me."

"You've wasted those years." Nathan stepped closer, the air thickening with a new kind of energy—one of resolve and determination. "You're living in a fantasy, clinging to a past that has long since rotted away. I'm not your puppet anymore."

"Is that so?" Derek's voice dripped with sarcasm, yet I could sense the chink in his armor. The veneer of control he wielded was beginning to crack. "What makes you think you can fight me? You're nothing without your little friend here. She's your anchor, Nathan, and without her, you'll drown."

The moment his words sank in, I felt a flicker of doubt, an unwelcome intrusion that threatened to unravel my composure. But Nathan's hand tightened around mine, grounding me. "I'm not drowning. Not now, not ever."

With that declaration, the atmosphere shifted, an electric pulse racing through us, igniting something primal. I felt the air vibrate with the tension of unsaid words, and in that moment, I knew that this confrontation was about more than just Nathan's past; it was about our future. The stakes had never been clearer.

Derek's eyes narrowed, a predator assessing its prey. "You think your love can save you? You're both fools. This ends tonight." He lunged forward, a sudden movement that sent adrenaline coursing through me. I instinctively stepped back, pulling Nathan with me, but there was nowhere to hide in this cavernous space.

As if summoned by the chaos, the fluorescent lights flickered ominously, casting erratic shadows that danced like specters around us. "You want a fight, Derek?" I challenged, heart racing. "Then let's see what you've got."

"Sweetheart, you're in way over your head," he taunted, closing the distance between us.

I locked eyes with Nathan, and in that shared glance, I felt an unspoken understanding pass between us. Whatever darkness lay ahead, we would face it together. The world outside had always seemed daunting, but this confrontation felt like a catalyst for change—a chance to strip away the shadows that had clouded Nathan's past.

In a flash, Nathan surged forward, his movements fluid and fierce, surprising Derek as he sidestepped a strike meant to incapacitate. "You want to take me down? You'll have to do better than that!" The determination in Nathan's voice ignited something inside me, fueling my resolve. I stepped back, not out of fear, but to give him space, to let him fight his own battle.

Derek stumbled, momentarily thrown off balance, and I seized the opportunity. "Maybe you've underestimated what love can do, Derek!" I shouted, my voice echoing off the walls. "It's not just a crutch; it's a weapon, and it's going to cut you down!"

In that moment, as the confrontation escalated, I felt the weight of our intertwined fates. The past was rising up to meet us, but I refused to let it define who we were. With every pulse of adrenaline coursing through my veins, I prepared to stand by Nathan, ready to fight not just for our present, but for a future untainted by the shadows of old grudges.

Derek roared in frustration, and as his fury filled the air, I realized that this was not just a battle of strength—it was a reckoning for everything we had faced together. We would emerge from this stronger, or we wouldn't emerge at all. And I would fight tooth and nail for our chance at happiness, no matter the cost.

The warehouse loomed like a dark sentinel against the dimming sky, its rusted exterior whispering secrets of forgotten days. The scent of impending rain hung in the air, mixing with the industrial grit that clung to the concrete. I could feel the pulse of adrenaline thrumming in my veins, a rhythm that matched the urgency of our task. Nathan stood beside me, his jaw clenched, eyes scanning the shadows for a figure I could only assume was the specter of his past—the one who had vowed revenge. The weight of our choices pressed heavily on us, each decision reverberating with consequences.

As the last rays of sunlight dipped below the horizon, the world seemed to hold its breath. I turned to Nathan, taking a moment to study him. His dark hair, tousled by the evening breeze, framed his face, casting him in a mix of vulnerability and strength. "Are you ready for this?" I asked, my voice barely more than a whisper, thick with both fear and resolve.

"Ready or not, we don't have a choice." His response was laced with an intensity that both comforted and unnerved me. "I can't let him hurt you, not again."

Before I could respond, a flicker of movement caught my eye from the corner of the warehouse. My heart sank. A figure emerged from the shadows, tall and imposing, with a smirk that spoke volumes of the darkness lurking within. It was Liam, Nathan's former associate, whose twisted sense of betrayal had turned him into a relentless adversary. The streetlight cast an eerie glow around him, transforming his features into something almost grotesque.

"Well, well, look who we have here," Liam drawled, the sarcasm dripping from his words like venom. "The prodigal son returned, hand in hand with his new toy." His gaze shifted to me, filled with malice. "I was wondering when you'd come back to play."

Nathan stepped forward, an unyielding barrier between Liam and me. "This isn't a game, Liam. You need to leave us alone."

Liam laughed, a sound that chilled me to the bone. "Oh, but it is a game, Nathan. A very dangerous one. And you've set the stakes higher than you could've imagined." He leaned casually against a rusted pillar, the picture of nonchalance despite the storm brewing around us. "You really think you can walk away from this? From me?"

"I'm not walking away from anything," Nathan replied, his voice steady but the tension in his shoulders was evident. "You're the one who made this personal."

With a swift movement, Liam pulled a knife from his belt, its blade glinting ominously in the faint light. "Let's cut to the chase, shall we? You can either hand over what's rightfully mine, or I can make this a lot more... interesting."

I held my breath, the implications of his words sinking in like lead. "What are you talking about?" I asked, my voice steady despite the fear coursing through me.

"Oh, didn't Nathan tell you?" Liam's eyes sparkled with malicious delight. "I'm after something he's been hiding—something that belongs to me. A little piece of treasure that he took without permission."

Nathan shot me a glance, an unspoken warning etched across his face. "You don't want to know, Anna. Just trust me."

But curiosity was a beast, and it was rearing its head. "What treasure?" I pressed, unable to shake the feeling that understanding the depth of this confrontation might be our only chance at survival.

Liam's grin widened, revealing a hint of madness behind it. "Let's just say Nathan's past isn't as clean as he'd like you to believe. He's got a little secret buried in that charming smile of his." He turned his gaze back to Nathan, the animosity simmering between them palpable. "And I intend to dig it up."

"Enough!" Nathan's voice thundered through the tension. "You think you can intimidate us into submission? You're wrong."

But the certainty in his words felt fragile, as if the weight of Liam's revelations could shatter it at any moment. The air crackled with tension, the looming threat of violence hanging thick like fog. I could see the resolve in Nathan's eyes, but it flickered with uncertainty. He was facing not just a foe but the ghosts of his past—a tangled web of choices and consequences that had brought us to this precarious moment.

"Let's make this easy," Liam taunted, twirling the knife with a nonchalance that made my stomach churn. "You give me what

I want, and maybe, just maybe, I'll let her walk away unharmed. Otherwise..." He let the threat linger in the air, a chilling promise.

My heart raced, the implications weighing heavily on me. "Nathan, don't—" I started, but he cut me off.

"Stay back, Anna," he said, his voice fierce but tinged with desperation. "This is between me and him."

"Of course, I wouldn't dream of involving the delicate flower," Liam mocked, his eyes glinting with sadistic amusement. "But we both know she's your weakness. And weaknesses... well, they're just opportunities waiting to be exploited."

I felt the cold fear clutch at my chest, a deep-seated dread that twisted my insides. "You don't have to do this, Nathan," I urged, stepping forward despite his protests. "We can figure this out together."

But Liam's laughter echoed in the dimly lit space, cutting through my words like a knife. "You think you can solve this with pretty words? This is a world where trust is a commodity, and betrayal is the currency. You'll learn that soon enough."

Suddenly, the atmosphere shifted. The tension coiled tighter, and I could see Nathan's resolve begin to fracture, the ghost of his past looming ever larger. Just then, the sound of sirens pierced the night, a distant wail that brought a flicker of hope amidst the chaos.

Liam's demeanor shifted, a glimmer of panic flashing in his eyes. "We don't have time for this," he snarled, glancing over his shoulder as if the approaching lights were the harbinger of his doom.

But Nathan was already moving, a fierce determination igniting in his eyes. "You're not getting away this time, Liam."

Before I could process what was happening, Nathan lunged forward, and chaos erupted. The knife flashed as Liam reacted, and I found myself standing at the precipice of a storm, the fate of our future teetering on the edge of a knife. In that moment, as the world around us spiraled into darkness, I realized I was about to face a decision that would alter everything.

And then, just as quickly, the lights of the police cars illuminated the warehouse, bathing the scene in blue and red. But what awaited us beyond that door? What secrets lay buried in Nathan's past that could either save us or condemn us to a fate we couldn't foresee?

Chapter 21: The Fractured Bond

The silence that enveloped the room was almost deafening, punctuated only by the rhythmic ticking of the clock on the wall. I found myself staring at its steady march, each second a reminder of the turmoil swirling in my chest. The air felt thick, laden with the remnants of our confrontation. Nathan sat across from me, his jaw set, eyes a stormy gray that matched the clouds gathering outside the window. The storm was no longer just in the sky; it had seeped into our very lives.

My mind flickered back to the moments before everything unraveled. The fierce intensity of our argument, each word a dagger, had left scars deeper than any physical wound. Nathan's past had clawed its way into our present, unveiling secrets I had been blissfully unaware of, secrets that now hovered between us like a specter, taunting me with unanswered questions.

"What were you thinking?" I finally broke the silence, my voice barely above a whisper, laced with frustration. "You can't just keep things from me, Nathan. You think you're protecting me, but you're only building a wall."

He flinched at my words, his fingers curling into fists on the table. "I was trying to keep you safe, Lily. You don't understand what I'm dealing with."

"Safe? Or sheltered? There's a difference, you know." I leaned forward, needing him to see the truth in my eyes. "I can't stand here pretending everything is okay while you're drowning in your past. I deserve to know the whole story."

He exhaled slowly, the tension in his shoulders visible. "And what if knowing changes everything? What if it tears us apart?" The vulnerability in his voice shattered something within me. The bravado was gone, replaced by a raw honesty that drew me closer, yet pushed me away.

"Maybe it's already tearing us apart," I countered, my heart pounding. "How can we move forward if you're holding back pieces of yourself? I can't love a shadow, Nathan. I need the man, flaws and all."

He looked down, the weight of my words anchoring him to the chair. I could see the turmoil behind his facade, the fear that gnawed at him like a relentless tide. "I thought if I just kept it buried, it wouldn't matter. But now..." He trailed off, the confession hanging in the air like a fragile thread.

"Now it matters more than ever," I insisted, leaning closer, desperate to bridge the widening gap. "We can't heal unless we're both all in. You have to trust me with your darkness, Nathan. I'm not going anywhere."

He finally met my gaze, and for a moment, the storm within him calmed. "You're the last person I wanted to hurt." His voice cracked, the weight of his confession making the air feel charged. "I thought I was protecting you."

"From what? From knowing you?" The bitterness of that statement surprised me, yet it lingered in the room like a ghost, begging for acknowledgment. "You think I can't handle it? You think I'm some fragile flower that can't see the thorns?"

A flicker of amusement danced in his eyes, and for a moment, I could almost believe everything was fine. "You're far from fragile, Lily. But what I've faced... it's not something I ever wanted to drag you into."

I paused, the air crackling with the unsaid. "Then let me decide, Nathan. Let me choose if I want to wade into those waters. It's my right to know."

He ran a hand through his hair, frustration and resignation warring on his features. "You're right, but it's not just my story to tell. It involves people who—"

"Who what? Who you're trying to protect? Nathan, you don't get to decide who I can handle or not. I love you, and that means sharing the burdens, however heavy." My heart raced, a mixture of anxiety and determination fueling my words.

He was silent for a long moment, and as the shadows deepened in the room, I felt the weight of unspoken thoughts pressing down. The storm outside rumbled, a low growl that mirrored the tension between us. "Okay," he finally said, his voice steadying as if he had made a decision. "I'll tell you everything. But I need you to promise me something."

"Anything," I replied, my heart pounding in anticipation.

"Promise me you won't run. Promise me that whatever I say, you'll still be here when it's done."

His gaze held mine, a mix of hope and fear swirling in the depths. I swallowed hard, knowing that this was a moment I would either cherish or regret. "I promise," I said, my voice firm, though the tremor in my chest betrayed my resolve.

He took a deep breath, and I could see the storm within him shift, clouds parting just enough to let some light through. "Alright. But be prepared. It's a lot."

I nodded, steeling myself for the truths that were about to unfold. The very foundations of our relationship felt shaky beneath my feet, but I refused to let fear dictate my path. If love was about embracing the chaos and the beauty, then I was ready.

As Nathan began to speak, his words became a tapestry of revelations, each thread woven with pain and resilience. I listened intently, my heart aching for the boy he had been and the man he had become. With every secret he laid bare, I could feel the distance between us narrowing, each truth a step closer to healing.

And though the storm raged on outside, inside, I could sense the potential for something new—a bond tempered in fire, forged in the depths of our vulnerabilities. I was ready to face whatever darkness lingered in his past, ready to embrace the shadows that shaped him, because I knew that in the end, it was those very shadows that made him whole.

Nathan's voice had barely left the air when the weight of his revelations hung between us like a fog, thick and suffocating. I leaned back in my chair, feeling the sharp edges of reality cut deeper than the jagged truths he had laid bare. His past was a jigsaw puzzle with pieces missing, and I was starting to see the jagged outlines that would never quite fit into the picture of the man I loved. "I thought I was the only one with secrets," I muttered, my fingers tracing the rim of my glass absentmindedly.

"You're not," he replied, his gaze unwavering, as if he could see straight through to my soul. "We all have things we'd rather keep buried." There was an ache in his voice, an unspoken admission that resonated within me. Secrets were like shadows, lurking just beyond the light, waiting for the perfect moment to pounce.

"Like that night at the bar?" I asked, my voice dipping low. "The one where you got that scar on your cheek?"

He winced, as if I had struck a nerve. "You know about that?"

I nodded, recalling the whispers I'd overheard, the sidelong glances exchanged between his friends. "I'm not blind. You can't throw a punch like that without someone noticing."

His lips curved into a half-smile, though it didn't reach his eyes. "You're right. That was a different time. A different me."

"What happened, Nathan?" My heart raced, urging me to pry deeper, desperate to peel away the layers of his guarded exterior. "What made you into the man sitting in front of me?"

He leaned forward, resting his elbows on the table, the tension crackling like electricity in the air. "It's a long story," he said slowly, measuring each word as if he were laying down bricks in a fragile wall. "But it's not pretty."

"Since when have I been afraid of a little ugly?" I quipped, attempting to lighten the moment. "I mean, look at my life. I have a knack for finding trouble."

He chuckled softly, the sound rich and warm, easing some of the tension between us. "You've certainly found it with me."

"Touché." I smirked, enjoying the fleeting normalcy that flickered through the haze of our conversation. "So, what's the 'ugly' part? Did you rob a bank or something?"

He hesitated, the smile fading as shadows crept back into his expression. "Not quite. But there was a fight—a big one. And it wasn't just about throwing punches." His voice dropped to a whisper, as if confessing a sin. "It was about survival."

I felt my breath hitch. "Survival?" The word hung in the air, heavy with implications. "What do you mean?"

"There were debts to settle, people to protect. I was caught up in a world that demanded loyalty in the worst ways. I did things I'm not proud of," he admitted, each word dripping with regret. "But it's not just that. I lost people—people who meant everything to me. I made choices that haunt me to this day."

I studied him, watching the shadows of his past play across his features. This was a man forged in fire, shaped by choices that weighed on his conscience like chains. "And you think telling me this will make me run away?"

"It's possible," he replied, his gaze flitting away, searching for something beyond the walls of the room. "I've seen what happens when people learn the truth. I've lost friends, family... love. I can't bear to see that happen with you."

I took a deep breath, steadying myself against the waves of emotion crashing inside. "Nathan, I'm not going anywhere. I might trip over my own feet occasionally, but I'm not leaving you."

His eyes flickered back to mine, a hint of hope breaking through the storm. "You really mean that?"

"Of course. Unless you're harboring a second family or something." I tried to keep my tone light, but I could see the way he tensed. "I'm joking! Sort of."

A ghost of a smile appeared on his lips, but it quickly faded as the weight of his past pulled him back. "You shouldn't joke about that. It's not far from the truth."

"Okay, maybe not the best joke." I sighed, feeling the moment slip through my fingers. "But seriously, Nathan. You have to trust me. Whatever this is—whatever darkness you think is lurking—let me face it with you. You don't have to carry it all alone."

He hesitated, and in that pause, I saw the battle waging in his mind. Finally, he nodded, albeit reluctantly. "Alright. I'll tell you everything. But if it gets too much, you promise me you'll walk away."

"Deal," I said, a mix of anticipation and dread swirling in my stomach. "Now, spill."

He leaned back, his expression turning pensive. "It all started with a friend—a brother, really. His name was Daniel. We grew up together, and when we got older, we fell into a crowd that was... less than savory." He swallowed hard, the memories etched in his brow. "I thought I could handle it. I was invincible, or so I thought."

His gaze shifted to the window, as if searching for solace in the gray clouds outside. "Daniel was the type of guy who would do anything for his family. And when his brother got mixed up with the wrong people, I followed him into that mess, thinking I could help."

"Help how?" I pressed, my curiosity piqued despite the darkness of the tale.

"We thought we could resolve it—just a few fists thrown, a few threats made. But things escalated. We got caught up in a turf war. One night, everything went wrong. I lost Daniel that night."

The words hung in the air like a weight, suffocating and raw. "You lost him?" I whispered, feeling the gravity of his loss settle over us.

"He took the fall for me. Tried to protect me, and it cost him everything." The pain etched in his voice was unmistakable, a gaping wound that refused to heal. "Ever since then, I've been trying to live with that guilt. I thought I could bury it, but it's like trying to outrun a shadow."

My heart ached for him, the depth of his sorrow resonating with my own hidden struggles. "You're not that person anymore, Nathan. You survived, and you've changed."

"Have I?" His gaze bore into mine, a mix of hope and skepticism. "Or am I just pretending? Maybe I'm still that scared kid trying to fight the world on my own."

"You're not alone anymore," I insisted, feeling the weight of his past pressing down like a heavy shroud. "You have me. Let me be your light in that darkness."

He fell silent, the storm of emotions swirling between us as he contemplated my words. The air grew charged, and I sensed the fragile threads of our connection tightening, pulling us closer together.

But just as the moment felt poised to shift, the door swung open, interrupting the weighty atmosphere. Sarah, my friend, bounded in, her energy a stark contrast to the gravity of our conversation. "Hey, lovebirds! You'll never guess what I just heard!"

As she blurted out the latest gossip, the tension in the room broke like glass, scattering pieces of our intense moment across the floor. But beneath the surface, I felt the unresolved currents still tugging at our connection. The shadows loomed, ready to descend again, and I knew that as much as we wanted to breathe easy, the fight for our relationship was far from over.

The moment Sarah burst into the room, a whirlwind of energy and excitement, the delicate thread of intimacy Nathan and I had been weaving snapped. She was a beacon of light, and while her presence was usually a welcome distraction, right now it felt like a well-timed interruption—like someone suddenly turning on a bright lamp in a darkened room.

"What are you two doing in here?" she asked, her eyes flickering between us with a knowing gleam. "Having a heart-to-heart or just brooding?"

"Definitely not brooding," Nathan replied, his voice dripping with sarcasm as he pushed back in his chair, attempting to reclaim some sense of normalcy. "We were just discussing the merits of emotional vulnerability. You know, typical first-date stuff."

"Right, because every couple starts their relationship by unpacking traumatic childhood memories." Sarah raised an eyebrow, crossing her arms with a teasing grin. "Good luck with that one, buddy. You're going to need it."

"Thanks for the encouragement," Nathan shot back, his tone playful but with an undercurrent of weariness.

I couldn't help but laugh, the tension dissipating just a fraction. "Just trying to keep things interesting," I said, leaning back in my chair and relishing the banter. "After all, who needs Netflix when you have real-life drama?"

Sarah's smile widened, but as she glanced back at Nathan, the laughter faded from her eyes. "Are you okay? You look like you've just fought a bear and lost."

"It was more of a metaphorical bear," Nathan replied, raking a hand through his hair, his expression softening as he met Sarah's concerned gaze. "But I'll survive."

"Survive is good," she said, her voice dropping an octave, seriousness seeping into the lightheartedness of earlier. "But are you actually okay? I mean, you both look like you've been through the wringer."

As if on cue, a wave of fatigue washed over me. I could feel the remnants of our earlier conversation clinging to the edges of my consciousness, a weight that refused to lift. "Just a little rough patch," I admitted, shooting a glance at Nathan. "But we're working through it."

"Or at least attempting to," Nathan interjected, the corner of his mouth quirking up again. "I think I've successfully confused her with my past."

Sarah rolled her eyes, lightening the moment again. "Well, as long as you're not planning a sequel to that horror story, we should be fine."

"Speaking of horror stories," I said, my voice turning serious, "did you hear about that thing at the old Millwood place?"

"What thing?" Sarah leaned closer, intrigued. "I heard rumors, but they've been getting crazier by the day."

"Crazy is an understatement," Nathan said, his attention piqued. "What did you hear?"

I glanced between them, then lowered my voice conspiratorially. "Apparently, a few nights ago, someone spotted lights flickering in the windows. Then there was screaming. They think it might be haunted or something."

"Great, so we're living in a real-life horror movie?" Sarah chuckled, but there was a hint of unease in her eyes. "I always knew that place was sketchy, but this is next level."

"Are we really discussing ghost stories when I just laid bare my soul?" Nathan teased, though the seriousness in his voice told me he was trying to mask his own discomfort.

"Hey, this is the perfect distraction," I replied, the corners of my mouth twitching. "Plus, ghost stories are far less traumatic than discussing lost friends and the weight of guilt."

"Touché," Nathan replied, a grin breaking through. "But I'm still up for discussing my deep emotional scars if it means we can avoid the ghosts."

"Deep emotional scars it is," Sarah said, her laughter bubbling again. "But seriously, if you two ever need to escape from all the drama, I vote for a ghost hunt at Millwood. Nothing like an adventure to clear the air."

"I don't think that's a great idea," Nathan said, frowning slightly. "If it's haunted, who knows what we'd be walking into?"

"Haunted or not, it's still better than the monster of our own making," I shot back, the undercurrent of seriousness returning. "Right?"

Nathan's expression shifted slightly, the glimmer of humor fading. "You're right, but maybe not the kind of adventure we need right now."

As the conversation ebbed and flowed, the sunlight filtering through the window began to dim, casting elongated shadows across the floor. The weight of unspoken truths lingered in the corners, and I could feel it creeping back in, threatening to blanket us again. I glanced at Nathan, hoping for some glimmer of reassurance, but he seemed lost in thought, his brow furrowed as he stared out the window.

"Hey," I said, reaching out to touch his hand gently, "whatever you're thinking about, don't let it take you away from us."

He turned to me, his expression softening as our hands connected, grounding him in the moment. "I'm trying. It's just... there are parts of me that I'm not sure will ever be okay."

"Not okay is our middle name right now," I replied, attempting to inject levity back into the conversation. "Let's take this one step at a time. We can't rush healing, and we definitely can't rush ghost hunts."

Nathan chuckled, the warmth of his laughter wrapping around us. "True. But if we ever do go ghost hunting, you're in charge of the flashlight."

"I'm in charge of the snacks," Sarah chimed in. "And if I hear one ghostly whisper, I'm out. I don't have time for that nonsense."

"Deal," I said, squeezing Nathan's hand. "But I expect you both to be brave, right?"

As the air lightened momentarily, the distant rumble of thunder outside reminded us that the storm wasn't done with us yet. It loomed just beyond the horizon, a reminder of the darkness still waiting to unfold.

A sudden crash of thunder made me jump, and in the same breath, my phone buzzed loudly on the table, slicing through the atmosphere. I glanced down to see a message from an unknown number, my heart racing as I opened it.

"Lily," it read, the words simple yet jarring, "you need to meet me. Now. It's about Nathan."

I felt the color drain from my face as I locked eyes with Nathan, who was still gripping my hand. "What is it?" he asked, the humor vanishing from his tone.

"I... I don't know," I stammered, the gravity of the message weighing heavily on me. "But it sounds serious."

"Who sent it?"

"I don't know," I replied, shaking my head. "Just some unknown number."

"Maybe it's a prank," Sarah suggested, her brow furrowed with concern. "Or someone trying to scare you."

But I could see Nathan's expression hardening, a flicker of something darker dancing behind his eyes. "No," he said, his voice firm. "It's not a prank. We need to go."

"What? Go where?" I asked, my heart thumping loudly in my chest.

"Wherever that message leads," Nathan replied, standing abruptly, determination flooding his features. "I won't let anyone threaten what we've built."

With that, the shadows deepened around us, the storm of uncertainty closing in, and I knew that this was just the beginning. I could feel it in my bones—the calm before another storm was brewing, and it was going to be anything but quiet.

Chapter 22: In the Wake of Chaos

The sun poured through the kitchen window, splattering golden light across the worn oak table where I sat, nursing a steaming mug of chamomile tea. The rich scent enveloped me like a soft blanket, but the warmth couldn't chase away the chill that clung to my heart. Outside, the world bustled in its usual rhythm—children's laughter floated from the playground, and the familiar chirp of the morning birds provided a symphony of normalcy that felt achingly distant. I could see it all, yet I was tethered to a past that refused to fade, each echo a reminder of the chaos we had endured.

Nathan's shadow loomed large in my thoughts, a figure etched in both my dreams and nightmares. His laugh, once a melody I craved, now twisted like a thorn in my chest. I could almost hear his voice, the easy banter that had filled our evenings with warmth and light. But now, it was a ghost, a cruel reminder of the love I had let slip through my fingers. I thought about the guilt that haunted him—how it draped over him like a thick fog, clouding his once-bright spirit. I longed to reach out, to bridge the chasm that had grown between us, but the fear of abandonment loomed larger than any hope of reconciliation.

As the days turned into weeks, I found refuge in the company of friends. They were my lifeline, a colorful tapestry woven from laughter, support, and late-night ice cream binges. Each gathering was a reminder that life, in all its messy chaos, still held moments of joy. Sarah, with her unyielding optimism and penchant for oversized sweaters, was the first to notice the cracks in my facade. She watched me, her bright blue eyes piercing through my attempts at normalcy. "You're not fooling anyone, you know," she teased one evening, nudging me with her elbow as we lounged on my couch, surrounded by the remains of our pizza feast.

"Fooling? Who, me?" I replied, forcing a laugh that felt foreign on my lips. "I'm just peachy, thanks." The sarcasm dripped like honey, and I felt the edges of my smile crack.

She raised an eyebrow, her expression softening. "You don't have to put on a show for me, you know. I'm here for the messy bits, too."

That was Sarah—ever the realist, always ready to peel back the layers I so desperately tried to keep intact. Her presence was a balm, and as we talked late into the night, sharing secrets and dreams, I felt the tension within me start to ease, if only slightly.

But as the sun dipped below the horizon, casting a warm blush across the sky, I could feel Nathan's name hovering in the air between us, an unspoken word. The next morning, the call came when I least expected it, shattering my fragile sense of calm. The sound of my phone buzzing against the table jolted me from my thoughts. I looked down, my heart racing as I recognized his name on the screen. For a moment, the world paused, and all I could hear was the frantic thrum of my heartbeat.

"Hello?" I answered, my voice steadier than I felt.

"Hey, it's me." His voice was rough, like gravel underfoot, and the familiarity of it sent a rush of memories flooding back—moments spent in the kitchen, laughter mixing with the scent of fresh coffee. "Can we talk?"

A million questions raced through my mind. What could we possibly say to each other after everything? But the hesitation in his voice urged me to respond. "Sure," I said, my own resolve surprising me. "Where?"

He hesitated, and I imagined him pacing, running a hand through his hair, a nervous habit I'd always found endearing. "How about that little café on Oak Street? You know, the one with the terrible Wi-Fi but amazing pastries?"

It was a place that held memories of shared smiles and whispered secrets, a sanctuary before chaos had come crashing down. I nodded, even though he couldn't see me, and managed to mumble an agreement.

The moment I walked into the café, the familiar warmth enveloped me, the smell of freshly baked croissants wafting through the air. I spotted Nathan at a small table in the corner, his posture hunched as he stared into his coffee like it held the answers to life's most complex questions. My breath caught in my throat, a mix of excitement and anxiety swirling within me as I approached.

"Nathan," I said softly, taking a seat across from him. The silence stretched between us, heavy and charged, filled with unspoken words and tangled emotions.

He looked up, and for a moment, the world faded away, leaving just the two of us. "I've missed you," he said, his voice low, tinged with something that felt like regret. I wanted to reach across the table, to bridge that distance, but the fear of what lay on the other side held me back.

"I've missed you too," I admitted, the truth slipping out before I could catch it. My heart ached with the honesty of it.

Nathan ran a hand through his hair, the familiar gesture sending a shiver down my spine. "I know things have been... complicated. I just wanted to say I'm sorry for everything. I've been a fool."

His words wrapped around me, softening the edges of my anger, but they also ignited a spark of vulnerability I hadn't expected. "It's not just you," I replied, the bitterness creeping into my tone despite my best efforts. "We both made choices."

"Can we start over?" he asked, his eyes pleading, a rawness in his gaze that pierced through my defenses. The question hung in the air, suspended in time, as I wrestled with the weight of my own heart.

In that moment, the café buzzed around us, life carrying on while we stood at a crossroads, the past and future colliding in a way that felt both exhilarating and terrifying. I could sense the hope in his voice, a fragile thing, and I wanted to cradle it, to nurture the possibility of what could be. But the scars of our shared chaos were still fresh, and the fear of falling again loomed large. I took a breath, the tension coiling tighter, and in that delicate balance of hope and fear, I realized I had a choice to make.

The tension in the café seemed to vibrate with each heartbeat, a palpable energy thickening the air between Nathan and me. I focused on the steam rising from his coffee, the swirling patterns momentarily distracting me from the whirlwind of emotions that threatened to overwhelm. There was a familiar ache in my chest, a bittersweet pull that urged me to lean in, to embrace the possibility of rekindling what had once felt so right. But the jagged edges of our shared history were still fresh, like a wound that had yet to scab over.

"I know it sounds ridiculous, but I think about that rainy afternoon at the bookstore," he said suddenly, his voice almost a whisper. "You remember? You convinced me to buy that old leather-bound novel, insisting it was the key to understanding the universe."

I chuckled, the sound surprising me, slicing through the tension. "It was a terrible book! Full of pretentious prose and absolutely no plot."

"Exactly! But you sold it like it was the next great American classic," he shot back, a flicker of that playful spark igniting in his eyes. I couldn't help but smile; it was that wit, that teasing banter that had once drawn me to him like a moth to a flame. "I still have it," he added, a hint of pride in his tone.

"Why am I not surprised?" I said, shaking my head with mock disapproval. "You should really let go of that sentimental hoarding. It's not good for your mental health."

Nathan laughed, the sound warm and genuine, and for a fleeting moment, the shadows receded, revealing a glimpse of the connection we had shared. But just as quickly, the weight of reality crashed back in, drowning the warmth in cold uncertainty.

"Things were different then," I said, my tone shifting. "We were different."

He leaned in, his gaze steady and sincere. "I want to be that person again. The one who could make you laugh, the one you could rely on. I want to fix this, whatever 'this' is between us."

I wanted to believe him; I truly did. But the voice of caution whispered reminders of the chaos that had unraveled us, the pain that had etched lines on our hearts. "You can't just say those things and expect everything to be fine. I can't be the only one trying to make this work," I said, my voice a little sharper than I intended.

"I know," he replied, the weight of his admission hanging heavily between us. "I've been doing a lot of thinking. About us, about everything. I want to be better—better for you, better for me. I just need a chance to prove it."

"Prove it?" I echoed, my heart fluttering with a mix of hope and skepticism. "And how do you plan to do that, exactly? We can't just hit the reset button on everything we've been through."

"Why not?" He leaned back, a playful smirk creeping onto his face, a slight spark of mischief dancing in his eyes. "I mean, if I can convince you to trust me again, maybe we can both forget that time I tried to impress you with my culinary skills and nearly set the kitchen on fire. I could hardly even boil water."

"Oh, you mean the infamous 'pasta incident'? How could I forget? I think I'm still finding bits of burnt garlic in my kitchen." I couldn't suppress a laugh, the memory bringing a much-needed lightness to the conversation.

"You see? That's the spirit! We can rebuild on laughter," he said, and for a heartbeat, I could almost believe it could be that simple. But I knew that rebuilding required more than shared laughter—it demanded vulnerability, and that was where I felt the walls close in around me.

The conversation flowed, a dance of memories and laughter that spun out like a comforting blanket, but my heart remained guarded. The truth was, every playful jab masked a lingering fear. Could we really step back into the light, or were we merely clinging to the shadows of what once was?

As I pondered, the café door swung open with a jingle, and a rush of chilly autumn air swept through, bringing with it the scent of cinnamon and something sharper—a hint of change. A woman with bright red hair and a camera slung around her neck strode in, her vibrant energy lighting up the space. She took a seat at a nearby table, setting her eyes on Nathan and me, curiosity piqued. It was impossible not to notice her keen gaze, as if she sensed the tension simmering just below the surface.

"Looks like we have an audience," Nathan remarked, tilting his head toward her, a sly grin on his lips.

"Great, just what we need—social media fodder," I said, rolling my eyes in mock exasperation.

"Relax, it's not like we're the only two people in a café having a conversation. It could be worse. We could be having a dramatic breakup or something." His laugh was infectious, but beneath it, I felt a knot tighten in my stomach.

"Ah, yes. Because nothing screams 'healthy relationship' like being observed while hashing out your emotional baggage."

"I think they're more interested in the pastries." He nodded toward the woman, who was now snapping photos of the assorted baked goods. "But I appreciate the vote of confidence."

Just as I was about to respond, the woman approached our table, her camera slung casually over her shoulder. "Sorry to interrupt, but I couldn't help but overhear. You two have such chemistry! Are you actors or something?"

I glanced at Nathan, who raised an eyebrow, the corner of his mouth twitching in amusement. "Only if you count our roles in this messy production of life," he said, a playful twinkle in his eye.

"Not actors, just a couple of people trying to figure things out," I added, half-joking but also half-wondering if we were anything more than that—just two lost souls wandering through the debris of our past.

"Oh, come on! You're both way too good-looking to not be on stage. I mean, you've got that whole 'will-they-won't-they' vibe going on," she insisted, leaning on the edge of our table, her enthusiasm palpable.

"Trust me, it's more of a 'should-they-or-shouldn't-they' situation," I said, unable to suppress my smile despite the undercurrent of tension.

"I'm Harper," she said, extending a hand, her bright smile infectious. "And I'm pretty sure this café would be a fantastic set for a romantic comedy. Imagine the montage! There's laughter, tension, and all that good stuff."

Nathan chuckled, his eyes glinting with a mix of mischief and charm. "And here we thought we were just trying to enjoy our coffee."

"Ah, but every good coffee deserves a great story, right?" she said, her tone earnest. "You never know who might be watching. So, are you going to write your own script, or are you going to let someone else tell it for you?"

Her words hit me with unexpected force. Could I really allow our narrative to be penned by anyone other than ourselves? I glanced at Nathan, the unspoken question hanging heavily between us. Would we take charge of our story, or would we let fear and guilt dictate the ending?

"Maybe we're just at the part where we're figuring out the plot twist," I finally said, my heart pounding with the realization that this was our story to write, and no one else's.

As the laughter echoed around us, I felt a surge of determination. Maybe the path forward wasn't clear, but in that moment, it felt like a flicker of hope had ignited, illuminating the way through the shadows that had haunted us.

Harper's infectious energy filled the café, creating a bubble of lightness that momentarily dulled the edges of our heavy conversation. I found myself drawn into her exuberance, the way she wore her passion like a vibrant scarf wrapped around her neck. "You two have a story worth telling!" she insisted, her gaze darting between Nathan and me as if she could physically pluck our emotions from the air and weave them into a narrative tapestry.

"Believe me, it's not as romantic as it sounds," I said, biting back a smile. "More like a cautionary tale at this point."

Nathan shrugged, his easy confidence returning like an old friend. "Every great story has its bumps, right? A little chaos only makes it more interesting." His tone was playful, but I could see the flicker of sincerity in his eyes.

Harper leaned closer, her curiosity insatiable. "So, tell me, how do you two navigate the chaos? Is it like one of those rom-coms where you inevitably end up at the same party and realize you can't live without each other?"

"Let's hope it's a little less predictable than that," I retorted, half-laughing. The absurdity of our situation didn't escape me. "But if that's the case, then someone's definitely going to trip over their own feet in the process."

"Well, there's your setup," Harper replied, beaming. "You can't have a romance without a little slapstick!"

Nathan chuckled, and I felt the tension between us ease, replaced by the lighthearted banter that had always been our lifeline. Harper's presence was refreshing, an unexpected balm that softened the harsh edges of my reality. She became a catalyst, urging us to confront the complexities of our relationship with a touch of humor and a willingness to embrace the messiness of life.

The conversation flowed easily, punctuated by laughter and glances that felt charged with meaning. As I watched Nathan lean back in his chair, his face relaxed and open, I could feel the walls I had carefully constructed begin to tremble. Maybe there was a path forward that didn't require complete abandonment of my heart's desires, a way to blend vulnerability with strength. But just as I started to entertain the idea, the café door swung open again, and a gust of wind swept through, causing a few napkins to flutter off the table.

The newcomer was a tall man with dark hair, his expression serious as he scanned the room. He looked vaguely familiar, but I couldn't place him. With purpose in his stride, he made his way toward us, his presence shifting the atmosphere in an instant. My heart skipped a beat, unease creeping back in.

"Excuse me," he said, his voice low and steady as he approached. "Are you Nathan?"

"Yeah, that's me," Nathan replied, glancing at me with a flicker of concern in his eyes.

"I need to talk to you. It's urgent," the man said, his gaze unwavering.

The shift was immediate; the lighthearted atmosphere evaporated as if a dark cloud had suddenly rolled in. "What's this about?" Nathan asked, his demeanor shifting from playful to guarded.

"I can't discuss it here. It's... complicated," the stranger said, his eyes darting around the café, as if searching for eavesdroppers.

"What could be so urgent that it can't be said in public?" I interjected, crossing my arms defensively. Instinctively, I felt the need to protect Nathan, to shield him from whatever storm was brewing.

The man hesitated, his gaze flicking back to me, and then to Nathan. "It's about the accident," he finally said, his voice low enough that I had to strain to hear him.

The words hit like a punch to the gut, and I could see the color drain from Nathan's face. "What do you know about it?" Nathan asked, his tone suddenly icy.

"I can't explain everything here," the man replied, his expression taut with urgency. "But there are things you don't know. Things that could change everything."

I felt a chill wash over me, the warmth of the café fading as the gravity of the situation settled around us like a heavy blanket. I glanced at Nathan, who was now fully engaged, his eyes narrowing in determination. "I don't like the sound of that. You need to tell me what you're talking about, and you need to do it now."

"Fine. Can we talk outside?" the man urged, his voice barely above a whisper, as if the walls themselves could eavesdrop.

"Absolutely not!" I exclaimed, feeling my protective instincts surge. "Whatever you have to say, you can say it right here. I'm not letting you drag him into a back alley for some secretive confession."

Nathan looked between us, a mixture of frustration and concern crossing his face. "I want to hear what he has to say, okay? If it's about the accident, I have to know."

Before I could respond, Harper chimed in, her bright demeanor dimmed by the tension. "I think we should all hear this, then. Whatever it is, it sounds like it needs to be said."

Reluctantly, I nodded, feeling the weight of the moment settle on my shoulders. "Fine. Then spill it."

The man took a deep breath, clearly weighing his words. "There are elements surrounding the accident that haven't been addressed. Things that the police didn't find—things that are being hidden."

Nathan leaned in, his face a mask of intensity. "What do you mean? Hidden by whom?"

"By someone close to you," the stranger replied, his voice steady but laced with gravity. "And if you don't act quickly, you could find yourself in deeper trouble than you realize."

I felt a knot tighten in my stomach as I glanced at Nathan. His expression shifted, shadows dancing across his features as the implications of the man's words settled in. "What kind of trouble?" he asked, his voice barely above a whisper.

The man took a step closer, lowering his voice further. "I can't say too much here, but trust me when I tell you that this isn't over. You need to be prepared for what's coming."

The weight of his words pressed down on us, and I could feel the tension thickening the air. The café, with its cheerful ambiance, seemed a million miles away. Suddenly, a warm cup of coffee felt as fragile as glass, teetering on the edge of chaos.

"What do you want from me?" Nathan's voice was low and steady, but I could see the flicker of fear in his eyes.

"I want to help," the man replied, his expression earnest. "But you need to be ready to hear the truth."

A silence enveloped us, a suffocating blanket of uncertainty that clung to my skin. I could sense the turning point; the moment where everything we had tried to rebuild might come crashing down once more.

"Let's go outside," Nathan finally said, standing and moving toward the exit with a determination that pulled at my heart. I didn't want to let him go, but I knew that whatever was to come would be crucial. As we stepped outside into the crisp air, I felt a chill that had nothing to do with the season.

The stranger glanced around before lowering his voice. "You need to understand the stakes involved. This is bigger than just you, Nathan. This could involve others, and you need to prepare yourself for what you might learn."

As the shadows deepened and the streetlights flickered to life, a sense of impending doom settled around us. Just as I opened my mouth to ask another question, the ground beneath us rumbled slightly, a low, ominous sound that echoed in the distance.

I turned to Nathan, whose eyes were wide, brimming with a mix of fear and determination. "What do you mean by 'others'?" he asked, his voice barely above a whisper.

But before the man could respond, the sky darkened, a strange heaviness pressing down as a distant siren wailed. It grew louder, a sound that seemed to resonate with the anxiety swirling within me. My heart raced as I scanned the horizon, suddenly aware that whatever was about to unfold would change everything.

And in that moment, standing on the precipice of revelation and chaos, I realized that our world was about to be turned upside down once again.

Chapter 23: A Love Rekindled

The aroma of freshly brewed coffee wrapped around me like a warm embrace as I stepped into the quaint little café on the corner of Maple and 4th. Sunlight streamed through the large windows, illuminating the scattered tables adorned with mismatched chairs, each telling its own story of weary patrons and joyful reunions. I paused for a moment, the bustling world outside fading away as I inhaled the rich scent, allowing it to ground me in the present. This was my refuge—a place where time seemed to slow down, and the chaotic rhythm of life softened into a gentle lullaby.

As I stood in line, my gaze drifted to the chalkboard menu, hand-painted in vibrant colors that contrasted beautifully with the rustic wooden panels. Each drink offered was a little adventure in itself, but today, I craved the familiar comfort of a caramel macchiato. The barista, a cheerful young woman with a radiant smile and an ever-ready quip, seemed to know the regulars by heart. As I placed my order, her light-hearted banter pulled a genuine smile from me, a rarity these days.

But then, just as the warmth of my coffee cup seeped into my palms, a familiar figure caught my eye from the corner of the café. There he was, Noah, seated at a table in the far right corner, his head bent over a sketchpad, pencil dancing furiously across the pages. The world around him faded into the background, but my heart quickened, every beat a reminder of the history we shared—of laughter and heartache, of whispered dreams and unfulfilled promises.

Noah had been my first love, the one who understood the unspoken parts of me, who saw beyond the surface into the depths of my soul. But life, with all its unpredictable twists, had pulled us apart, leaving a gaping hole in both our hearts. We had danced around our feelings, skirting the edges of vulnerability, but the burdens we carried had weighed heavier than our love, casting shadows on what could have been.

A sudden burst of laughter drew my attention back to him, and I caught a glimpse of the smile that had once set my heart ablaze. It was tinged with a hint of melancholy, a reflection of the man he had become—more complex and layered, yet still undeniably Noah. The edges of his once-boyish charm were softened by the years, but his essence remained intact. My heart fluttered, caught in a web of nostalgia and longing.

The moment hung between us, suspended like a delicate thread, and I felt an irresistible pull. I couldn't simply turn away; the universe had conspired to bring us back together, however unexpectedly. Gathering my courage, I approached his table, heart pounding in my chest like a drum echoing in the quiet of the café.

"Mind if I join you?" I asked, trying to keep my voice steady, though it trembled slightly like the leaves outside in the autumn breeze.

He looked up, surprise flickering in his blue eyes, quickly replaced by recognition. "I... sure," he stammered, his smile hesitant yet warm. "I was just working on some sketches."

The thought of him, deeply engrossed in his art, pulled at my heart. Noah had always had a way of seeing the world differently, transforming the mundane into something magical through his drawings. "You haven't lost your touch, I see," I remarked, glancing at the intricate lines etched on the paper. "What are you working on?"

He hesitated, a shadow crossing his face before he turned the sketchpad toward me. The image was hauntingly beautiful—a landscape that seemed to merge reality with fantasy, a reflection of the turmoil in his heart. "Just a little something," he said, but his eyes told a different story. They were windows into his soul, revealing the burdens he carried, the weight of unspoken fears.

We fell into conversation as easily as slipping into a favorite pair of shoes. Words flowed like the coffee that filled our cups, and I was surprised at how quickly the tension melted away. We spoke of the past, reminiscing about the carefree days when love felt like an endless summer, punctuated by laughter and stolen kisses. The café buzzed around us, but in our little bubble, the world outside faded into a pleasant hum.

"Do you remember that time we got caught in the rain?" I teased, a laugh escaping my lips. "You insisted we run through the park instead of taking cover."

"Of course! And you got so mad when I splashed you with puddles," he chuckled, his laughter a balm to my soul. "You were furious, but I thought you looked like a wildflower dancing in the storm."

"More like a drenched cat!" I shot back, feigning indignation, but the warmth of shared memories flooded my heart. "I almost didn't speak to you for a week."

His expression shifted, a flicker of vulnerability glimmering in his eyes. "I missed you, you know. Even then, I knew you were special."

A charged silence settled between us, the air thick with unspoken words. I could feel the weight of our shared history, the moments we had lost, and the potential for what could be. In that instant, something shifted, a silent understanding blossoming like wildflowers in spring. Maybe it was time to confront the past, to peel back the layers of hurt and begin anew.

In a moment of courage that surprised even me, I reached across the table and took his hand. It was a simple gesture, but it felt monumental, a silent promise to face whatever lay ahead together. His hand was warm, calloused from years of work, yet it felt like home. "I've missed you," I confessed, my voice barely above a whisper, but the weight of those words hung between us, heavy yet liberating.

The corners of his mouth lifted into a smile that lit up his entire face, igniting a spark of hope within me. "Maybe it's time we stop running from what we feel. We both deserve a chance to heal, don't you think?"

A thrill coursed through me, a daring hope ignited in the wake of his words. Yes, we had our scars, our burdens, but perhaps love was not merely a fleeting feeling but a journey worth taking, even through the dark.

The sun continued its slow descent, casting a golden hue across the café, making the moments feel suspended in time, almost cinematic. Noah's hand, warm against mine, pulsed with a familiar energy that sparked dormant feelings within me, as if we were two puzzle pieces that had been searching for each other through the years. The initial awkwardness melted away, replaced by a comforting sense of intimacy, a cocoon woven from threads of shared history and unspoken promises.

"Did you ever finish that mural you were working on?" I asked, unable to contain my curiosity about his artistry. It had always been a window into his soul, a glimpse of his dreams and demons. He had poured so much of himself into those vibrant strokes, often losing track of time as he painted.

Noah's smile faded slightly, replaced by a flicker of uncertainty. "I tried," he admitted, his voice barely above a whisper. "But I lost my way, you know? Sometimes it feels like I'm just drawing in circles." He looked down, tracing invisible lines on the table with his finger, an artist caught in a moment of self-doubt.

I leaned forward, intrigued by the shadows lingering in his eyes. "You know, art isn't always about the end result. It's the process that matters. Sometimes, it's okay to make mistakes or even leave things unfinished. It's part of the journey."

He met my gaze, a spark igniting as our eyes locked. "You've always had a way of seeing things differently. That's why I..." He paused, inhaling deeply as if to steady himself. "That's why I was drawn to you in the first place."

A pleasant shiver raced down my spine at his words. It was an acknowledgment, a tether to the emotions we had shared and the reasons we had fallen apart. "And yet here we are, at the same table," I mused, glancing around the café, feeling the weight of the world outside pressing against the windows. "Maybe we both needed a little detour to find our way back."

He chuckled, a soft sound that filled the space between us. "If this is a detour, I'll take it. Just don't ask me to navigate; I'm notoriously bad with directions." His eyes sparkled with mischief, a glimmer of the boy I had loved long ago, the one who could make even the dullest moments feel alive with laughter.

"Trust me, I'll keep the map handy," I replied, grinning back at him. "And you can provide the snacks. I hear they're essential for long journeys." The banter felt natural, a comfortable rhythm that lifted my spirits, and I could see his walls slowly crumbling, brick by brick.

As the evening progressed, our conversation deepened, peeling back the layers of our lives like the pages of an old book. He spoke of his struggles as an artist, the pressure to create something worthwhile, while I shared my own battles—how I had dived into work to escape the emptiness left in the wake of our separation. Each revelation was a thread, weaving us closer, binding our stories together with a shared understanding of loneliness and the pursuit of meaning.

But beneath the surface, I sensed an undercurrent of hesitation. There was something Noah wasn't saying, a shadow lurking just out of sight. I studied his face, the way his brow furrowed slightly whenever the conversation strayed too close to vulnerability.

"What's holding you back?" I asked gently, my voice barely above a whisper. "You don't have to carry that weight alone anymore."

He looked away, staring into the depths of his coffee cup as if seeking answers in the dark liquid. "It's just... it's complicated. I don't want to drag you into my mess. You deserve more than that." His honesty stung, a reminder of the scars we both carried.

"And you don't think I've faced my own share of chaos?" I replied, frustration threading through my words. "We both have our demons, Noah. It's what makes us human. But maybe... just maybe, we can figure it out together."

He lifted his gaze, and I saw a flicker of something akin to hope mixed with fear. "I don't want to hurt you again," he murmured, the weight of his past hanging heavily between us. "I never meant to let you down."

"Then don't." The words fell from my lips with surprising conviction. "Let's face this together. I'm not the girl you once knew, and you're not the boy who left. We've changed, and that means we have a chance to build something new—if you're willing to try."

The café felt alive around us, the clatter of dishes and laughter of patrons swirling like a comforting backdrop to our intimate exchange. For a fleeting moment, the noise faded as he processed my words, his expression softening. "You really mean that?"

"Of course. Life is too short to dwell on the past. I'd rather navigate the chaos with you by my side than pretend everything is fine alone." I squeezed his hand, feeling a pulse of warmth, a reminder that we were both still here, willing to fight for what mattered.

He held my gaze, the flicker of hope in his eyes growing into a flame. "Okay, then. Let's do it. But we need to take it slow. One step at a time."

"Agreed," I said, my heart racing at the thought of us starting anew. "Just promise me one thing."

"What's that?"

"Whenever you feel like you're about to retreat into that sketchbook of yours instead of sharing with me, just say the word. I'll be your light, however dim it may be."

His smile returned, a genuine brightness that warmed me from the inside out. "I promise. But in return, you have to let me in too, even when it's messy. I don't want to be the only one trying to figure this out."

"Deal," I replied, feeling a rush of exhilaration wash over me. In that moment, it was as if the universe had aligned, pulling us together once more. We had both been lost, but now, perhaps, we could be found.

As we sat there, our hands intertwined, the world outside moved forward, oblivious to the small revolution taking place at our table. Hope lingered in the air, a heady fragrance that danced like the last rays of sunlight before dusk settled in. I knew the road ahead would be fraught with challenges and uncertainty, but for the first time in a long while, I felt ready to embrace it, hand in hand with the man who had once captured my heart and was beginning to do so again.

The glow of the café wrapped around us like a cozy blanket as Noah and I delved deeper into conversation, each word pulling us closer together. The warmth from our intertwined hands felt electric, a tangible reminder that the barriers we had built around our hearts were beginning to crumble. With every shared laugh, I sensed the flickering flame of our connection reigniting, brighter and more vibrant than before.

"Tell me," I said, leaning forward, my curiosity piqued. "What's the most ridiculous thing you've ever done for art? I want to hear about the wild side of Noah."

He chuckled, the sound light and infectious, and I felt a flutter of excitement in my chest. "Oh, you have no idea. There was this one time I spent a whole night in a haunted house to get inspiration for a piece. I thought it would help me capture the essence of fear or something profound."

I raised an eyebrow, fighting back a smile. "A haunted house? Seriously? And how did that go?"

"Not great, to be honest," he admitted, scratching the back of his neck sheepishly. "I ended up hiding in a corner after hearing the floorboards creak. Turns out, I'm not as brave as I like to think."

"Cowardice can be a fine artistic choice," I teased. "But did you at least get anything good out of it?"

"No, just a few sketches of shadows and a lot of panic." He shook his head, laughter dancing in his eyes. "It's hard to channel creativity when you're trying to convince yourself that the ghosts aren't real."

"Perhaps you just need a co-conspirator," I suggested playfully. "Next time, take me along. I promise to bring snacks and bad jokes to lighten the mood."

"Deal," he replied, a hint of mischief flashing across his face. "But you might have to sleep with one eye open. I'm known for my midnight ghost impressions."

"Oh, I can handle that," I said, my confidence bolstered by the way his laughter intertwined with mine. "Just don't expect me to bail you out when the real ghosts start haunting!"

As the evening wore on, the conversations shifted from lighthearted banter to deeper reflections. We spoke about our dreams, the aspirations that had shifted and morphed during our time apart. I revealed my longing to find balance between my work and personal life, the relentless push for success often overshadowing my happiness. He listened, his eyes softening with understanding, as if each word was a thread binding us tighter together.

"And what about you?" I asked, my curiosity taking hold again. "What's your dream now?"

Noah hesitated, his gaze drifting out the window to the street beyond, where shadows stretched long in the gathering dusk.

"Honestly, I just want to create something that means something. I feel like I've lost my voice, and it scares me. I don't want to be just another artist with a mediocre portfolio."

"Isn't that a bit dramatic?" I leaned back, crossing my arms playfully. "Your work is amazing! You're not mediocre. You just need a spark, a little inspiration. We can find it together."

His eyes lit up at my suggestion, and for a moment, it felt like we were standing on the precipice of a grand adventure, just waiting to leap. "What if we had a challenge?" he proposed, his excitement palpable. "Let's each create something inspired by the other—something raw and honest."

"That sounds terrifying!" I exclaimed, a mix of delight and anxiety dancing in my stomach. "But also... intriguing. It could be a disaster, or it could be the best thing we've ever made."

"I'll take my chances if you will," he replied, a grin spreading across his face, his earlier hesitations momentarily forgotten. "Let's push each other to be brave, to be true to ourselves."

Just then, the café door swung open, the chime announcing the arrival of a new patron. I turned instinctively to see who it was, but my heart sank when I spotted a familiar figure—a tall, dark-haired man with a confidence that radiated like the sun. Mark. My ex. The one who had walked away when I needed him most.

"Seriously?" I muttered under my breath, my heart pounding with a mixture of dread and disbelief. Why now? Why here?

Noah followed my gaze, his expression shifting to one of concern. "Do you know him?"

"Yeah, that's Mark. My ex." I swallowed hard, feeling the tension tighten around us like a noose. "This is... unexpected."

"Do you want me to—?" he began, but I shook my head, the last thing I wanted was to drag Noah into the past I was desperately trying to escape.

"No. I'll handle this," I replied, forcing a smile, though my insides twisted with uncertainty. I didn't want my past to overshadow this moment, but the sight of Mark dredged up emotions I thought I had buried long ago.

Mark spotted me, his face breaking into a smile that felt both genuine and unsettling. "Hey! Fancy seeing you here," he called out, striding over as if he owned the place. The air thickened, the atmosphere shifting as the reality of the moment settled in.

"Yeah, just catching up with an old friend," I said, my voice even, despite the flutter of anxiety thrumming beneath the surface. I gestured to Noah, whose expression was a mix of curiosity and protectiveness. "This is Noah."

"Nice to meet you, Noah," Mark said, extending a hand, his eyes narrowing slightly as they darted between us. "So, you're the one who got her out of hiding."

"I didn't realize I was hiding," I shot back, my bravado igniting in the face of my ex's smugness.

"Guess it's all relative," Mark replied, a smirk playing on his lips. "You always had a knack for retreating into your little world. But hey, if it takes someone else to pull you out, that's great."

I felt Noah tense beside me, the air thick with unspoken tension. "We were just talking about art," Noah interjected, attempting to steer the conversation away from the undercurrents swirling around us.

"Art?" Mark's tone turned dismissive. "More like playing with crayons, if you ask me. You know what's really worth pursuing? Stability. A real future."

The words cut deeper than I expected, igniting a fire of indignation within me. "And what exactly does that mean?" I asked, unable to keep the sharpness out of my voice. "A life devoid of passion?"

Before he could respond, Noah interjected. "What you might call 'stability,' I see as settling for mediocrity." His tone was calm yet firm, the tension between them palpable. "Sometimes it takes a little chaos to find true inspiration."

Mark's eyes narrowed, assessing Noah with a mixture of contempt and surprise. "Good luck with that, buddy. You might just get burned."

"Maybe," Noah replied, unfazed. "But at least I'm willing to take the risk."

The atmosphere thickened, each word a blow in the unspoken battle of wills. I felt like a spectator in my own life, watching as old wounds reopened and new ones threatened to surface. My heart raced, caught between the weight of my past and the spark of hope in the present.

As Mark opened his mouth to respond, the café door swung open again, and a figure stepped inside, cloaked in shadows. The clatter of coffee cups fell silent, and for a moment, the world held its breath. My pulse quickened as the stranger turned, revealing a face that sent a chill racing down my spine—a face I had never thought I would see again.

"Is this a bad time?" she asked, a smirk dancing across her lips as she locked eyes with me.

Every instinct screamed at me to flee, to run from the chaotic whirlwind now consuming the café, but my feet felt like they were rooted to the ground, the air thick with tension and unspoken truths.

Chapter 24: The Dawn of Tomorrow

The air shimmered with a coolness that danced against my skin, a whisper of promise carried on the breeze as I stood on the balcony of my small, cluttered apartment, surveying the city that sprawled like a living, breathing entity below me. The skyline, jagged and bold, rose into a violet sky streaked with the last remnants of daylight, each building a testament to resilience, much like the journey I had traversed to stand here today. It was a view I had cherished, one that often offered solace, but tonight it felt different. Tonight, it pulsed with a kind of energy that thrummed through my veins, urging me to take that leap into the unknown.

Beside me stood Jonah, his silhouette stark against the twilight, hands tucked deep into the pockets of his worn leather jacket. He was my constant, the anchor amidst the chaos, yet even he seemed to radiate a nervous energy, his gaze darting toward the horizon as if searching for the words that would set us both free. The past had a way of creeping back into our lives, uninvited and relentless, and we both carried our share of shadows. But tonight, it was time to cast them aside.

"Are we really doing this?" I asked, my voice barely rising above the distant hum of the city. I could feel the weight of my words hanging in the air, a mix of hope and trepidation.

Jonah turned to me, his brown eyes reflecting the twilight like polished amber. "We can't keep hiding forever, Mia. It's time to step into the light."

His words echoed within me, a call to arms that sent shivers down my spine. With a half-smile that masked my fears, I nodded. The decision had been made; we would face whatever lay ahead together. Our journey had begun, and I could feel the anticipation coiling tightly in my stomach, a mix of exhilaration and dread.

We stepped off the balcony and into the soft embrace of our cluttered living room, filled with memories both sweet and bitter. The scent of burnt coffee lingered in the air—a remnant of my last failed attempt at normalcy—and I wrinkled my nose, but laughter bubbled forth. "Maybe we should start with a little less caffeine and a lot more courage?"

Jonah chuckled, a sound that always managed to smooth the jagged edges of my anxiety. "I'm all for courage, but I draw the line at decaf. That's just a betrayal to coffee drinkers everywhere."

"Fair point," I replied, my heart lighter. "So, what's first on our grand agenda?"

"Let's talk to Grace," he suggested, his expression serious. "We owe it to ourselves to confront the ghosts of our past, and she's a part of that."

Grace was a name that held a multitude of emotions for me—friendship, betrayal, and, ultimately, forgiveness. We had drifted apart after the incident, our shared laughter overshadowed by the weight of unspoken words. I had lost a piece of myself when she walked away, and I was hesitant to reach out, fearful of the hurt that might linger beneath the surface. But Jonah was right; it was time to reclaim that part of my life.

"Okay," I said, my voice steadying as I took a deep breath. "Let's do it. I'll call her."

As I picked up my phone, my fingers hesitated over the screen, hovering over her contact like it was a ticking bomb. But Jonah's presence steadied me, and I pressed call. The familiar ring echoed in my ear, a sound that felt like the heartbeat of our past.

When Grace picked up, her voice was hesitant, as if she too was standing on the precipice of our shared history. "Mia?"

"Hi, it's me," I said, the words spilling forth like a dam breaking. "Can we meet? I think we need to talk."

There was a pause, heavy and laden with everything left unsaid. "Of course. Where?"

"We could meet at that little café on Fifth?" I suggested, memories of laughter and warm pastries flooding my mind.

"Sure, I'll see you there." The call ended abruptly, and my heart raced in the silence that followed, a tumult of hope and anxiety crashing within me.

"Here we go," I said, trying to mask the tremor in my voice with a brave smile.

Jonah reached for my hand, squeezing it gently. "No matter what happens, we've got each other. Remember that."

The café was a quaint little place adorned with mismatched furniture and the rich aroma of freshly brewed coffee wafting through the air. It was filled with the chatter of patrons, but as I entered, all the sounds seemed to fade into a soft murmur. My gaze landed on Grace, seated at a table by the window, her auburn hair catching the fading light like autumn leaves.

She looked up, surprise flickering across her features as our eyes met. It was a gaze that spoke volumes, carrying both warmth and distance, a fragile bridge between our fractured past and the potential for healing. I took a step forward, Jonah by my side, and I felt the ground shift beneath us, the weight of years pressing heavily on my shoulders.

"Hey," I greeted softly, my heart pounding with uncertainty.

"Hey," she replied, her voice equally soft, but tinged with a hint of caution.

The silence that followed was thick, filled with unspoken words and unresolved feelings. It felt as though we were all standing on the edge of something monumental, a fragile thread connecting us in that bustling café. I could feel Jonah's presence grounding me, a reminder that whatever lay ahead, I wasn't alone.

"I'm glad you came," Grace finally said, her eyes flickering with something akin to relief.

"Me too," I breathed, and in that moment, I realized that this wasn't just about the past. It was about forging a path forward, together.

As we settled into our seats, the air around us crackled with unspoken tension and the possibility of forgiveness. The journey had begun, and as I looked into Grace's eyes, I felt a flicker of hope ignite within me—a spark that promised a new dawn, a future we could shape together.

The café hummed with life, the murmur of conversations blending seamlessly with the clinking of cups and the rich aroma of baked goods wafting through the air. As I settled into my seat, the warmth of nostalgia wrapped around me like a favorite blanket, tinged with a slight chill of apprehension. Grace, sitting across from me, looked both familiar and alien—her smile a ghost of our shared past, yet hesitant, as if unsure how to bridge the distance between us. I glanced at Jonah, who leaned back slightly, giving us the space we needed while maintaining an air of quiet support.

"Can you believe it's been almost a year since we last saw each other?" I broke the silence, my voice softer than I intended, but it felt necessary to shatter the fragile barrier that hung in the air.

"Yeah, a lot can happen in a year," she replied, her eyes darting away for a moment, as if she were gathering her thoughts from the shadows. "It feels like a lifetime."

"Tell me about it," I said, a half-laugh escaping my lips. "I thought I'd never find out how good a burnt soufflé could taste until I tried making one myself. Spoiler alert: it's terrible."

Grace chuckled, a sound that warmed my heart, but her laughter carried an undertone of something unspoken, a layer of sorrow woven through our shared humor. "I'm still trying to master pancakes without setting off the smoke alarm. You'd think I could manage by now."

"That's what takeout is for," I countered, the words tumbling out with more bravado than I felt. "You could always just call in a 'pancake emergency' and have them deliver."

Her smile widened, and for a brief moment, the years of tension dissolved, replaced by the comforting familiarity of our friendship. "You know, I could really use a good pancake emergency right about now."

As we both laughed, I felt a flicker of hope ignite between us—a fragile thread that could either unravel or strengthen our bond. But the lightness quickly faded, replaced by the weight of our past.

"Grace, I—" I began, but she cut me off with a wave of her hand, her expression shifting from light-heartedness to something more serious.

"Let's not pretend it's all fine and dandy. We both know it's complicated." Her voice was steady, yet I could sense the tremor beneath it, a churning current of unresolved feelings.

"I didn't mean for things to end the way they did," I said, my heart pounding. "You were my best friend, and then it all... fell apart. I miss you."

Her eyes softened, but a shadow crossed her features. "I miss you too. But it wasn't just that we drifted apart. There was so much hurt, Mia. I felt betrayed, and maybe it was easier to walk away than to confront the mess we were in."

"I get it," I replied, the words catching in my throat. "I was scared too. Scared of what we'd become, and scared of losing you. But avoiding each other... it just made everything worse."

Silence settled between us, heavy and laden with the weight of our shared history. Jonah's presence was a steady comfort beside me, and I stole a glance at him. His expression was attentive, a silent reminder that I wasn't alone in this moment.

"You know," he interjected, his voice warm yet firm, "sometimes facing the truth can be more liberating than running away from it. What happened between you two was painful, but it doesn't have to define your friendship."

Grace looked at him, her brow furrowing slightly. "Who appointed you the relationship expert?"

Jonah smirked, his charm evident. "Well, I'm not. But I've had my fair share of messes to clean up. Just ask Mia about my cooking."

She laughed, a genuine sound that warmed the air around us. "Fair enough. But it still doesn't make it easy to just move on."

"I know," I said, my heart aching for the bridge we needed to build. "But maybe we can take small steps. Talk about the good times? Remember what brought us together in the first place?"

Grace's expression shifted, uncertainty mingling with curiosity. "Like our epic movie marathons?"

"Exactly! The one where we ate enough popcorn to sink a ship and debated whether the villain was misunderstood?" I leaned in, my voice animated, and Jonah grinned at our shared history.

"Okay, I could go for that," Grace replied, a hint of a smile tugging at her lips. "But only if you promise not to bring those awful romantic comedies. I have standards."

"Ah, but standards are subjective! Besides, we both know you secretly loved every second of those movies," I teased, my heart racing at the prospect of reestablishing our connection.

"Fine, I'll concede to one movie night," she said, her resolve softening. "But no more than that. I'm still cautious."

"Cautious is good," Jonah chimed in. "It means you're thinking ahead. But maybe you should also allow yourselves to be a little reckless in reconnecting."

His words hung in the air like a challenge, sparking a newfound sense of bravery within me. Grace and I exchanged glances, a silent agreement forming between us.

"Let's be reckless then," I said, my voice steady. "Let's remember what it felt like to be best friends before everything got complicated."

"Okay, but I'll only agree if I get to pick the first movie," Grace said, a playful smirk gracing her lips.

"Deal," I laughed, the sound more genuine than it had been in months. "But you better come prepared with a list of acceptable genres."

"Fine, but if you make me watch one more cheesy romance, I'm staging a mutiny."

Just then, the café door swung open, a gust of cool air rushing in, followed by the sound of laughter. A group of people spilled in, their energy contagious, and I turned to see who had arrived.

At the forefront was a familiar face—Lila, my co-worker and friend, her exuberance lighting up the room like a burst of sunshine. "Mia! Is that you?" she called out, her bright smile radiating warmth.

"Yes! Over here!" I waved, the joy of seeing her weaving seamlessly into the bittersweet moment with Grace.

"Mind if I join?" Lila asked, sliding into the empty seat next to Grace without waiting for an answer. "I could use some girl talk, and what better place than this haven of pastries?"

"Just be warned, we were delving into the abyss of past friendships," Grace replied, her tone lightening as she welcomed the interruption.

"Perfect! My favorite topic!" Lila grinned, her presence an invigorating force that lightened the atmosphere further. "I'm ready to hear all the juicy details."

As the conversation flowed, Lila's infectious spirit drew us closer, weaving threads of laughter and shared experiences that mended the frayed edges of our friendship. It was in that moment I realized the past didn't have to be a weight we carried but a tapestry of lessons, laughter, and love. I glanced at Grace, her eyes sparkling with renewed hope, and felt the delicate threads of our friendship beginning to stitch back together, stronger than before.

Lila's arrival transformed the atmosphere, injecting a refreshing vitality that rolled through the café like a cool breeze on a hot day. With her bright floral dress and exuberant personality, she was the human equivalent of a double shot of espresso, capable of waking even the sleepiest of souls. Her laughter was contagious, wrapping around us like a warm embrace. I felt my earlier apprehensions slip away, making space for a renewed sense of camaraderie.

"So, what's the story here?" Lila asked, leaning forward with the kind of enthusiasm that made it clear she was about to dig into something delicious. "I hope it's more scandalous than your usual Friday night rom-com marathons."

Grace shot me a teasing glance, her eyes sparkling with mischief. "Oh, it definitely is! We're diving into the thrilling world of long-lost friendships and the dramatic fallout of poorly timed misunderstandings."

I nudged Grace lightly under the table, pretending to be offended. "Excuse me, I think my very exciting life counts as an action-adventure movie in its own right."

Lila raised an eyebrow, clearly enjoying the banter. "Action-adventure, you say? Were there explosions involved? Maybe a daring escape from a particularly aggressive email chain?"

"More like a daring escape from the weight of my own indecision," I admitted, a hint of seriousness creeping back into my voice. "But thankfully, we're trying to fix that."

"Ah, the emotional arc! Classic," Lila declared, nodding sagely. "And what about you, Grace? Any villainous characters to contend with?"

Grace took a deep breath, her expression shifting momentarily as she gathered her thoughts. "Well, I guess you could say the real villain was miscommunication. But I'd like to think I've made my peace with it."

"Good for you! Growth is essential," Lila chirped, her enthusiasm unwavering. "But that doesn't mean we can't indulge in some juicy gossip while we're at it. Just remember, I've got the world's best ear for drama."

"Actually, it's the world's worst," I shot back, and we all laughed, the sound bright and light. The simple act of sharing laughter began to weave the strands of our friendship tighter together, and I couldn't help but feel optimistic about our path forward.

As the conversation continued to flow, I marveled at how seamlessly we fell back into our rhythm. The memories we shared were like a secret language, a tapestry woven from laughter, late-night confessions, and dreams exchanged over cups of steaming coffee. It was then that I noticed a subtle shift in the air, a quiet tension lingering at the edges of our playful banter.

"By the way, Mia," Lila began, her tone shifting slightly as she leaned in conspiratorially, "I heard a little something about your potential promotion at work. Spill the tea!"

I felt my heart race at the mention of my job. The promotion loomed over me like a storm cloud, heavy with expectations. "Well, there's nothing official yet," I said cautiously, "but my boss hinted that a position is opening up, and I'd be in the running. But it's all very... tentative."

"Ah, tentativeness, the realm of all that is nerve-wracking and exciting," Lila mused dramatically, placing a hand over her heart as if she were about to faint. "But seriously, if you're offered it, you'd be amazing!"

"Thanks, but it's not that simple," I replied, the weight of uncertainty settling on my shoulders. "What if I'm not ready? What if I screw it up?"

"Hey," Jonah interjected, his gaze steady. "You've worked hard for this, and you deserve to seize the opportunity. Just remember, it's not about being perfect. It's about making your mark."

"Yeah, well, my mark often looks more like a doodle than a masterpiece," I said, trying to lighten the mood, but the truth was that the self-doubt churned within me like a tempest.

"Trust me, every masterpiece starts with a doodle," Grace added, her encouragement genuine. "You can do this, Mia. We're all rooting for you."

Their support was a balm, soothing the nagging insecurities that clung to me like a persistent shadow. Just as I was about to respond, the café door swung open again, the bell chiming merrily. A sudden rush of cold air swept through, causing us to shiver and pull our jackets a little tighter around us.

A man entered, his presence instantly commanding attention. He was tall, with tousled dark hair that fell over his forehead, a slightly crooked smile that felt both inviting and dangerous. As he moved further inside, my stomach flipped uncomfortably, an inexplicable sense of familiarity washing over me.

"Is that...?" Grace began, her voice trailing off as she squinted toward the newcomer.

Lila followed her gaze, her mouth forming a little "O" of surprise. "No way! Is that Kyle? The one from college?"

My heart raced at the name. Kyle had been part of a whirlwind of memories, some sweet and others laced with confusion. Our paths had diverged so dramatically that it felt surreal to see him here, of all places. "It can't be," I murmured, not quite believing my own eyes.

He scanned the café, and for a split second, our eyes locked. The world around us faded into the background, the chatter of customers dissolving into an echo. Memories flooded back—late-night study sessions, shared laughter, and the unfulfilled tension that had lingered between us like a half-remembered dream.

"Mia?" he called, a smile spreading across his face, and I felt my breath hitch. I hadn't seen him in years, not since everything had spiraled into chaos, but here he was, stepping into my life once more, unannounced and completely unexpected.

"Hey," I managed, my voice barely above a whisper, as a wave of warmth and confusion crashed over me. "What are you doing here?"

"I just moved back to the city," he replied, his tone casual, but I could sense the underlying current of something more profound. "Thought I'd drop by this little café everyone raves about. Didn't expect to see you here."

"Well, here I am," I said, forcing a smile that felt slightly fragile.

As he approached our table, the air grew thick with unspoken words and possibilities, each second stretching out like a rubber band about to snap. Jonah's protective demeanor shifted subtly, his expression curious yet wary, while Grace and Lila exchanged glances, a silent conversation passing between them.

"Still loving those awful romantic comedies?" Kyle asked with a teasing lilt, his eyes sparkling with mischief, just as I remembered.

"Only the ones with questionable plot twists," I retorted, laughter escaping me, though it felt somewhat strained. "I've been known to dabble in the art of binge-watching."

"I'll have to join you for a marathon sometime," he said, a suggestion that sent my heart racing. "Maybe we could catch up?"

"Uh, yeah, sure," I replied, my mind swirling with the implications. The easy camaraderie we once shared now tinged with the weight of history, expectations, and unresolved feelings.

"Great!" He leaned against the table, his smile infectious. "How about we make it a double feature? You, me, and some popcorn that may or may not catch fire?"

"Only if you promise to help extinguish the flames," I shot back, the playful banter a welcome distraction from the undercurrents swirling around us.

The laughter that erupted around the table was genuine, but beneath it lay an electric tension, the kind that comes before a storm. I felt the eyes of my friends on me, watching, waiting. I knew this moment could shift everything—our past, my future, the choices that lay ahead.

"Can I get in on this?" Jonah asked, feigning indifference but unable to hide the sharp edge of protectiveness in his tone.

"Of course!" Kyle replied, his gaze unwavering as he looked at Jonah. "The more, the merrier. The three of us could rekindle the magic of our group—minus the drama, of course."

Jonah's expression darkened slightly, and I sensed an unspoken challenge in the air, like the calm before a tempest. I felt caught in a web of emotions, teetering between the comfort of familiarity and the thrill of the unknown.

Just as I was about to respond, the café door swung open once more, a flurry of cold air rushing in. A hooded figure stepped inside, their features obscured in shadow. An uneasy tension crackled in the room, a sudden chill sweeping over us. My pulse quickened as I tried to shake off the feeling of dread that settled in the pit of my stomach.

The figure paused at the entrance, scanning the room with an intensity that sent a shiver down my spine. I exchanged a glance with Grace, who looked as startled as I felt. Kyle seemed to notice the shift in atmosphere, and Jonah's protective stance tightened beside me.

The figure took a step forward, and I held my breath, every instinct screaming that something was about to change irrevocably. And just when I thought I might recognize who stood there, the figure lifted their head, revealing a face that sent my heart racing for entirely different reasons.

"Hello, Mia," the stranger said, their voice smooth yet laced with an edge of something darker, sending ripples of unease through the air.

I felt my pulse quicken, and suddenly the warmth of the café felt like a distant memory, swallowed by an impending storm.